# "Fine," Sheldon said. "Maybe I didn't do the right thing."

"Maybe?"

"I was afraid, Tyanna. I had no clue what the right thing was."

"You cared about yourself."

For a full five seconds, neither of them spoke. Their hot breaths mingled, and Sheldon was aware of the rise and fall of Tyanna's chest. He looked into her eyes, at the surprise in their depth, and he damn near forgot what the hell he'd been talking about.

"I cared about you, Tyanna," he managed on a ragged breath. "Yes, I was afraid for myself. But if anything had happened to you, something because I'd been too stupid to keep my emotions in check . . ."

"Seems like that's all you ever did."

Ouch. The words hurt more than he'd expected. Despite the fact that they were true.

Tyanna continued to stare up at him, her eyes challenging him to deny what she'd just said. He remembered the fire, the passion of their relationship. His gaze lowered, settling on those full lips of hers. They were moist and slightly parted, almost like she was silently begging him to kiss her.

So, God help him, he did.

## Also by Kayla Perrin

IF YOU WANT ME
SAY YOU NEED ME

# KAYLA PERRIN

# Tell Me You Love Me

HarperTorch
*An Imprint of* HarperCollins*Publishers*

This is a work of fiction. Names, characters, places, and incidents are products of the author's imagination or are used fictitiously and are not to be construed as real. Any resemblance to actual events, locales, organizations, or persons, living or dead, is entirely coincidental.

HARPERTORCH
*An Imprint of* HarperCollins*Publishers*
10 East 53rd Street
New York, New York 10022-5299

Copyright © 2003 by Kayla Perrin
ISBN: 0-06-050350-5

First HarperTorch paperback printing: February 2003

HarperCollins ®, HarperTorch™, and ◆™ are trademarks of HarperCollins Publishers Inc.

Printed in the United States of America

Visit HarperTorch on the World Wide Web at www.harpercollins.com

10  9  8  7  6  5  4  3  2  1

For the world's best agent,
Helen Breitwieser.
Thanks for your continued belief in me.

# Chapter 1

"Lord have mercy, it's hot," Tyanna Calhoun uttered as she stepped out of the air-conditioned gym and into the muggy Miami night. It didn't matter that the sun had gone down hours earlier; it was still as hot and sticky as it had been during the day.

The city was going through one of those summer heat waves where the nights were as hot as the days. As always, it was the humidity that was the killer. It was barely June. What would July and August be like?

Tyanna frowned. She shouldn't have bothered to shower in the gym. She would only have to take another one when she got home.

Not that Tyanna was complaining—entirely. She'd lived in upstate New York when she went to college, and it was then that she learned how lucky she was to have been raised in South Florida. For four years of her life, she had complained to anyone who would listen about how much she hated the cold, how she couldn't stand the North after October. She became less active, not wanting to do anything if it meant trudging through one of the winter's many large snowfalls. Her four-season friends had gotten a chuckle out of her misery, telling her that her blood was too thin from having been raised in a warm climate. Well, whatever the reason, Tyanna knew she wouldn't endure another winter up there if her life depended on it.

Whenever the heat got to her, Tyanna remembered her days in the North—days when she'd wanted some freedom from her family—and she kept her mouth shut.

Her body adjusting to the temperature, she strolled through the parking lot, making her way to her car. She'd parked near the back, as the gym's manager preferred the staff do, in order to leave the front spaces open for clients.

Man, was she ever looking forward to going home and jumping into bed. Maybe she'd have a glass of wine first to help take the edge off. It had been one of those days. She'd had to go into work early to fill in for another personal trainer who'd gotten sick on the job. It wouldn't have been so bad if she hadn't had to spend two of her sessions dealing with men who clearly had complexes when it came to women. Sure, she was filling in for Morton, but just because she had a pair of breasts didn't mean she was incapable of doing the job.

And then there was the one pervert who'd been so fascinated by her that all he'd been able to do was ogle her body during his supervised workout.

Tyanna was used to dealing with creeps and idiots, whiners and chauvinists, but she much preferred not to if she didn't have to. She was happy with her own clientele, some men and mostly women she'd been working with for the past few months. They knew she was good at her job and respected her for it.

All in all, she enjoyed her job at the gym. Every day brought something new, which not many people could say about their line of work. The one snag she'd had in the past months was Jay, one of her clients who had developed a crush on her. He was no longer using a personal trainer, but he still frequented the gym. He was harmless—just annoying—though on occasion his ridiculous come-on lines did make her smile.

Now nearing her car, Tyanna dug into her purse for her keys. And dug a little farther. Where were they? She'd gotten rid of her bigger purse, thinking it would be easier to find items in a smaller one. But no. Murphy's Law had to have a hand even in purse issues.

Damn that Murphy anyway.

Just as she was resting her purse on her car so that she could get a better look, she heard the sound of shuffling feet nearing her. Before she could turn to see who it was, a hand closed around her upper arm.

Her heart pounding, she instantly sprang into action. While turning her whole body, she swung a fist. The punch landed under the stranger's chin, knocking his head back. Tyanna followed the punch with a quick kick to the man's abdomen.

The man cried out and toppled backward. With him down, Tyanna reached into her purse and was relieved to feel her keys. Clutching them in her sore fist, she scrambled to the driver's-side door. She tried to get her key in the lock, but her throbbing fingers let go and the keys dropped to the ground.

She quickly stooped to retrieve them. The man groaned again, and as her hand settled on the keys, something made her pause.

That groan. There was something familiar about it. . . .

Her heart pounded even harder. And while her brain told her to get in the car and drive away, something else made her slowly turn and look.

The man was back on his feet, although still hunched over in pain.

And suddenly Tyanna felt like she was the one who'd just had the wind knocked out of her.

It couldn't be him.

She stared at the man in the dim light, certain her eyes had to be playing some kind of trick on her. It looked like him. But could it be?

"Sheldon?"

"Yeah," he replied, then coughed. "It's me."

He sounded horrible, like she'd really done some damage. She couldn't help asking, "Are you okay?"

"I'll live," he retorted testily. Then, "What were you trying to do? Kill me?"

Her defenses went up. "Ever hear that it's not polite to sneak up on a lady?"

Sheldon clutched his side as he stared at her. "I didn't sneak up on you."

"Oh, really? Then what would you call it?"

He hesitated. "You could have at least tried to see who it was before you became Rambo."

"At this time of night?" Her voice was full of skepticism. "Aren't you the one who always told me that wasting a moment could mean losing your life?"

In the illumination from the streetlight above, Tyanna saw Sheldon smile.

"Very good," he said. "In fact, I'd applaud you, but I'm trying to hold my liver in place."

Tyanna couldn't resist a chuckle. "I'm sorry, Sheldon. I didn't know it was you. If I had, I wouldn't have hurt you." *Even though you deserved it.*

"Yeah, well. I guess I should be happy you took those self-defense classes I encouraged you to take. But you made one mistake."

"Oh?"

"You weren't looking up as you approached your car. I told you before, that puts you at risk of someone sneaking up behind you. Take your keys out earlier, and look around as you approach your car to make sure you're safe."

"I still got you. And good."

"Don't I know it."

Silence fell between them, and it suddenly hit Tyanna that Sheldon Ford was really here, really talking to her as if no time had passed since she'd last seen him. Her stomach bottomed out as a million questions flooded her mind.

She knew she shouldn't ask why he was here, why he'd been waiting for her in the shadows; it didn't matter. But she was curious as hell, and he wasn't talking.

"What?" she began sarcastically. "You show up after a year to give me a test in self-defense? To see if I've taken all your advice?"

"Very funny."

Sheldon straightened, and Tyanna couldn't help giving him a sweeping glance from head to toe. He was dressed in black—not exactly a good thing for a man who didn't want to appear suspicious after dark. But black definitely suited him. He wore a tank top and knit shorts, the kind of outfit someone might wear to the gym or to go jogging.

Despite the dim light, Tyanna's eyes didn't fail her as they perused Sheldon's body. His golden brown skin looked smooth and flawless. His hair was more closely cropped to his oval-shaped face than the last time she had seen him, and it took Tyanna only an instant to decide that she preferred this look. His shoulders were still as broad as she remembered, his biceps still perfectly sculpted. And there was no way she could miss the shape of his strong pecs, even in the darkness.

Sheldon's black tank top hung over his shorts, but that didn't obscure the outline of his flat stomach and his narrow waist.

Tyanna's gaze went lower, and she was almost embarrassed at her reaction to his thighs. Her breath actually caught in her throat, as if she'd never seen the man's strong thighs before.

Of course she had. She'd seen every beautiful inch of him. . . .

And goodness, the man was still fine. Too fine for his own good.

When she lifted her gaze to his face, she saw him smiling. She quickly looked away.

His smile irked her. There was nothing remotely funny about this situation! For the last year, she had remained in love with Sheldon Ford. She'd fallen for him hard and fast, and she still wasn't sure why. Everything she hadn't previously imagined for herself—like 2.5 children and baking cookies on a Sunday afternoon—she'd allowed herself to dream about when he came into her life.

Four years ago, Tyanna had seriously dated a guy named Chad who worked at the same restaurant where she had—it was her first love relationship. She'd been smitten with the dark-skinned brother, but he had never inspired the kinds of domestic feelings that Sheldon had brought out in her. Besides Chad, there had been two other men with whom she'd been fairly seriously involved, but again, neither of those men had made her feel anything close to what she'd felt with Sheldon.

Tyanna's own family members had called her a wild child. And she had been as surprised as everyone else at her domestic fantasies when Sheldon had come into her life.

But he had left her life as suddenly as he had entered it, and he hadn't even had the decency to face her when he'd broken off their relationship. She still remembered the pathetic letter he'd sent her—how she had eagerly ripped it open because she was so worried about him. Instead of an explanation for his disappearance, he had simply stated that things "weren't working out" for them and he was moving on.

If they hadn't spent the last night they were together making wild, explosive love at her place, she might not have been so confused by his sudden absence. But they had—their lovemaking was always earth-shattering—and she'd been even more devastated by his easy dismissal of her.

She swallowed uneasily as she pushed those thoughts aside. The last thing she needed was to remember how she and Sheldon had connected between the sheets.

"Well, we can stand here all night and play twenty questions," Tyanna said flippantly. "But

I'd rather not. Why don't you tell me what you're doing here."

"I came here to find you."

*Why?* was the next question on her tongue, but she held it in check. Instead, she glared at him for a good few seconds, and then said, "Go to hell."

She turned back to her car, wishing the door was already open so that she could slip inside and quickly disappear. But it wasn't, and as she was turning the key in the lock, she felt a hand on her shoulder.

She shook it off. "Leave me alone, Sheldon. I've had a very long day, and I just need to—"

"Tyanna."

The rest of her protest died on her lips. Damn. Why did he have to say her name all soft and whispery? Her knees actually went a little weak, and she didn't need weak right now. She needed the strength she'd built over the last year after he'd abandoned her for no rhyme or reason.

Yet her hand stilled on the key.

"Listen, I know this is a shock—"

"Shock? You call this a shock?"

"All right. Maybe that's an understatement. The point is, I want to explain a few things."

"You're a year too late."

"I kind of figured you'd say that. And I don't blame you. But I'm also sure you have questions, and what I have to tell you will explain the last year, why I did what I did."

*I don't know what possessed him, child.* Tyanna

could still hear his mother's voice, on one of the occasions she'd visited her after Sheldon had disappeared. *He said this woman's the one for him, and that I need to be happy for him.*

She steeled her jaw and faced him. "Things didn't work out with the new lady, I guess? If you even think you can begin to explain that away—"

"What other woman?" he asked. Then, "Oh, that."

"Yeah," Tyanna mocked, "that." Her blood started to boil, and she knew she was close to giving him another one of her self-defense moves—one that would leave him writhing on the ground. "I don't have time for this."

Once again, she turned the key in the lock. But again Sheldon reached for her, wrapping his fingers around her arm.

"Let me go, Sheldon, before I top what I did to you a few minutes ago. And if you think I'm joking, go ahead and test me."

"Tyanna, please," Sheldon said. Tyanna met his gaze. He was looking at her with a serious yet vulnerable expression.

"I don't want to let you go yet," he went on. "Like I told you, I have a lot of things to explain. And even if you get in your car and I never see you again afterward, please, just give me a few minutes." He paused, as he continued to stare at her. "Okay?"

Groaning, Tyanna rolled her eyes. "Somehow I

don't think you're going to take no for an answer."

"Smart girl."

"Fine," she said mockingly. "I'll give you three minutes. That's all."

# Chapter 2

Sheldon stared at Tyanna a moment before continuing. Her beautiful wide eyes flashed fire, and he knew she had agreed to his plea with total reluctance.

He swallowed, regret passing over him. Regret for a wasted year of time without her.

She was so damn beautiful, even with her full lips curled in a frown. Every time he looked at her, something pulled at his gut. He wanted to pull her ebony hair from its ponytail and tangle his fingers in the silky strands. He wanted to stroke her honey-colored skin the way he had so many times before. He wanted to pull her into his arms and kiss her senseless.

"I'm waiting," she said.

Right. It took Sheldon a moment to get started. "About that other woman." He cleared his throat. "I didn't mean that the way it sounded. Let me set this straight. There was no other woman. I had to make you believe certain things—my mother too."

"Maybe you shouldn't have come back to Miami. Maybe you should have moved to Hollywood."

Sheldon flashed her a mock scowl. "I thought you said you'd listen."

Tyanna blew out a weary breath. Although she wished she wasn't, she was intrigued. "I don't see what difference it will make."

"Just . . . listen."

His eyes met hers, and she saw almost a desperate quality in them. "You're down to two and a half minutes."

Sheldon finally released her arm. "You remember Dino Benedetto from Ultimate Fitness?"

Of course she remembered Dino. She had worked at Ultimate Fitness for nine months, and Dino had been the juice bar's owner. "Yes."

"You may not have known, but Dino was into shady business. Illegal steroids . . . everything you can imagine. Sustanon, HGH, Winstrol . . . He used to deal all kinds of stuff right from the club."

"That's absurd," Tyanna blurted out. "Dino worked out, drank those protein shakes . . ."

"And that's how you think he built all his muscle?"

"Don't patronize me. I know people use steroids. Mostly when competing. Dino's just a guy who likes to work out. He has no reason to use them."

"Really?"

"Yes, really."

"Well, sorry to disappoint you, but he was using them. The big issue, however, is that he was dealing them."

Tyanna shrugged, a look of doubt on her face.

"Why would I lie about that?" Sheldon asked.

"I don't know. Why would you send me some stupid letter to break up with me?"

"That's what I'm trying to explain."

"Really? It sounds to me like all you're doing is smearing Dino's name. He sold health products, for goodness sakes. Nutrition bars and fruit smoothies—"

"And Testrivol and HGH."

"Human growth hormone?"

"Yes."

Tyanna gave Sheldon a sour look. "How could he deal steroids and growth hormone at the gym—do that every day—without anyone knowing? People talk. I would have heard something."

"He was doing it for years. He was smart."

Tyanna shook her head slowly. The attractive, dark-haired man she had always considered a big teddy bear? The one who was always cracking jokes? She couldn't imagine it. "Surely there's some mistake."

"There is no mistake." Sheldon had known Tyanna would be upset with his sudden reappearance, but he hadn't figured she'd defend Dino so fiercely. He knew Dino had been a smooth talker—it was something he had learned while working with the man, but he didn't think

Tyanna had known him well enough to vouch for his character. "Are you going to listen, or what?"

Tyanna gave Sheldon a plastic grin and rested her butt against her car. "Fine."

"You're a fitness trainer. I'm sure I don't have to tell you that dealing anabolic steroids is just as bad as dealing heroin or cocaine in the eyes of the law."

"No."

"Well, the juice bar was merely a cover for Dino's truly profitable activities. My brother—"

"Wait a second," Tyanna interrupted. "Your brother? What brother?"

"I'm getting to that. I had a brother. You never knew him, because he died before you started working at the gym. Before I started working there. Anyway, he used to work at the juice bar, and he helped Dino out, selling his *products*. I didn't find out what he was up to until it was too late. My brother was one of those guys who was basically good, but he was always running with the wrong crowd. He needed to please, and people took advantage of him. He got stopped one night with Dino's latest shipment, was arrested, and the steroids were confiscated. Dino was pissed because the goods were worth over two hundred thousand, and a short time later my brother was murdered. To this day, the murder remains unsolved.

"I started working at the gym—then hanging at the juice bar—to try and get evidence on Dino. I needed to gain his trust so he would open up to me about what he was selling. And everything was going smoothly—until one day, he found me going through his personal files. He'd made me, and I knew I had to get out of town, Tyanna. Fast. Because Dino was going to kill me. I couldn't even head back to my apartment. Dino knew where I lived; he'd been to my place a few times as we were getting to know each other. Going back there would have been suicide. All I could do was take off." Sheldon inhaled deeply. "And now I'm back."

"Figured a year would do it?" Tyanna's tone said she was doubtful.

"No. I found out that Dino was killed by police in a shootout. That's how I knew it was safe to return."

Sheldon stopped talking and stared at Tyanna. She stared back in disbelief.

After a moment, she said, "That's it?"

"The important parts."

"Aren't you forgetting a part of the story?" When Sheldon merely stared at her, Tyanna said, "The part where you tell me that Dino was connected to the mob?"

"Actually . . . he was."

Tyanna burst out laughing.

"What's so funny?" he asked.

"Oh, Sheldon." She covered her mouth while she got her laughter under control. "Forget Hollywood. You really should be a writer. The mob? Come on. Just because the guy's Italian—"

"Wait a second. You think I'm lying?"

"I have to admit, I give you an A for effort with that one." She chuckled again, but the laughter stopped abruptly, moments later. She gave him a cold stare. "Do you think I was born yesterday?"

"Hold up," Sheldon said. He'd known this wasn't going to be easy, but he was surprised at her reaction. Actually, he was a tad miffed. "I spill my guts to you about this, and you don't believe me?"

"Bingo."

"You think I'd lie about this?"

"I'll admit to having zero clue what goes through your mind." She threw her hands up. "Not a year ago when you left, and not today."

"I'm telling the truth."

"Sheldon, I know Dino." She sounded exasperated. "Granted, we weren't best buddies, but I saw him at work practically every day. He's a sweetheart. There's no way he would ever sell anything illegal, much less kill anyone. And this brother—*if* you had one, I'm sure you would have mentioned him during the seven months we were together. This is all too convenient now."

"Tyanna—"

Tyanna yanked her car door open. "Don't bother, Sheldon. You may be able to sell this story to a publisher, but please, give me some credit. Your letter was pathetic enough. Save me the lame-ass stories." She paused, but not long enough for him to start speaking. "I have no clue why you left me, but you know what? You did me a favor. I'm stronger now, and I wouldn't change that for anything. Please stay away from me."

She slipped into her car and slammed the door shut. Though her hands were suddenly shaking, she managed to lock it before Sheldon could open it. A quick pause to pull herself together, then she stuck the key in the ignition and started the car.

Sheldon called her name, but she ignored him. Didn't even look at him.

Then, as though he hadn't shaken her world, Tyanna put the car into reverse and backed out of the parking spot, leaving Sheldon standing in the dust as she peeled out of the lot.

*Chapter 3*

Damn Sheldon Ford!

Tyanna drove like a madwoman along the Palmetto Expressway, heading to Miami Lakes from her home in Aventura. She knew she was going to get the third degree from her sisters. It didn't matter the occasion, she was always late.

But this time it wasn't her fault. She would have been up early if she'd been able to get a decent night's sleep. It was bad enough that she'd worked longer hours than normal, but Sheldon's reappearance in her life had pretty much guaranteed that she wouldn't sleep a wink. She'd been so wired that she hadn't drifted off until the sun had started to rise over the Atlantic. She was now a good hour late heading to Charlene's place, where her sisters were waiting on her to help make the plans for their parents' anniversary party.

Peach- and tan-colored houses were visible behind the high walls that bordered the expressway, as were beautiful palm trees. Normally Tyanna enjoyed driving. A drive never failed to clear her mind. She loved the always-lush scenery in South Florida, from the numerous palm trees to the vibrant green bushes with hibiscus flowers and the perfectly landscaped lawns. Everything was always so pretty. But today the scenic view didn't help soothe her troubled mind.

After she'd left Sheldon standing in the gym's parking lot, Tyanna had told herself to put him out of her mind. Oh, she had tried, but she hadn't been able to do it. Even now she couldn't help wondering why the hell he had decided to accost her outside her car. If he had wanted to let her know he was okay, he could have called her at the gym.

Or better still, he could have written her another pathetic letter.

Tyanna was bored with the Maxwell CD playing in her car, and she turned on the radio instead. She needed something upbeat and funky, something she could play at top volume and sing along to.

She heard Ja Rule's throaty voice as she scanned the radio stations, and she stopped there. "Oh, yeah," she said, turning up the volume. This was exactly what she needed: the kind of song that wouldn't make her think about love.

About Sheldon.

For the next twenty minutes, Tyanna let the music take her mind from her troubles. She didn't even remember when she'd hit the curve on the Palmetto that took the expressway south, but as she glanced up, she saw that she was almost at her exit.

Tyanna took the exit and headed west. Office complexes lined the street for the first couple miles, but she was soon past that and into the residential area.

There were a lot of gorgeous new properties in Miami Lakes. Many of South Florida's middle and upper-middle class enjoyed living here, and the low-rise apartment complexes boasted everything from saunas to tennis courts.

Tyanna slowed as she reached Charlene's complex. A colorful array of flowers graced both sides of the entrance, behind which were rows of mature palm trees. At night, lights lit up the trees, and the view was inviting.

Charlene's apartment was on the far right side of the lake—another attractive feature of the property. The lake divided the property in half, allowing many of the tenants a view of the water and the beautiful fountain in its middle. The tennis courts were on the left side of the property, and each half had a pool and saunas. It was resort living, right in her own home.

As Tyanna whipped into a parking space near her sister's building, she glanced at the clock radio and cringed. An hour and fifteen minutes late. Oh, well. What could she do?

She turned down the radio before shutting the

car off, then scrambled out of the car. Practically doing a hundred-meter dash, she was at Charlene's door seconds later.

Tyanna tried the door first before knocking. Finding it open, she made her way inside the apartment.

"Finally," Lecia said. Though her tone was light, she gave Tyanna a reproving look.

Charlene looked at the nearby clock, flicking her long braids over her shoulder as she did.

"Hello to you, too." Tyanna approached the dining-room table, where her sisters sat. She dropped her purse onto the table, then bent to kiss her young niece on the forehead.

"Hi, Michelle," she cooed. Six-and-a-half-month-old Michelle rewarded her with a big smile and waving arms.

Tyanna looked at her sisters. "I'm sorry I'm late. I didn't sleep well last night." Which wasn't a lie, though she didn't expect Lecia or Charlene to believe her.

"Oh, when are you ever on time?" Charlene asked, smiling. With wide eyes and a round face, Charlene was the sister whom Tyanna most resembled. They were both the same height, five foot six. But Tyanna had cute dimples, like their mother, and Charlene did not.

"I had a long day at work yesterday. I don't know. I guess I was too wound up to sleep."

"At least you didn't keep us waiting three hours like that one time," Lecia said.

"There were circumstances beyond my control that time," Tyanna reminded Lecia, remembering the overturned truck on the highway that had kept her in traffic for hours.

"I guess everyone's entitled to sleep in on Saturday morning," Charlene said.

"And some people are lucky to have the day off. I still have to work this afternoon." Tyanna slipped into a chair. There was no point in defending herself. Since her sisters weren't going to believe a word she said, she may as well change the subject. "What have you and Lecia come up with so far?"

"Other than bellies full of frozen yogurt?" Lecia leaned back and patted her stomach. It didn't matter what day of the week it was, Lecia always dressed like she was heading into the office. Today, she wore black slacks and a white silk blouse. She was tall and graceful, with a slender face and short, relaxed hair. On rare occasions, Lecia curled her short coif in tiny curls, but for the most part, she wore it straight.

"I don't know where she puts all that food she eats," Charlene said, rolling her eyes playfully at Lecia. Then she looked at Tyanna. "We haven't made any decisions. We were waiting on you. But we were thinking that with all the people we're planning to invite, it seems like we might have to rent a hall."

Tyanna was the youngest of three children. But while she was the baby, she'd done more living than either of her sisters had. She'd worked at almost every job out there—much to the dismay of her parents. Somewhere along the line she'd realized that, as much as she enjoyed fitness, she may as well try to work in that field. That's when she'd started work as a personal trainer, a job she loved. It was the one job where her clients didn't yell at her; they actually thanked her once they started to see the payoff from months of hard work.

The only reason she had quit her job at Ultimate Fitness was because she had needed to get away after Sheldon had ended their relationship. It had been way too difficult to go in there every day, hoping to see Sheldon but knowing she wouldn't. Even driving by the nearby restaurants where they'd often dined had been difficult.

But the worst part had been her own apartment. After all the passionate times she and Sheldon had spent there, it was almost unbearable to stay there once he was gone. It hadn't taken her long to realize that she needed a break from Miami, a break from all that reminded her of the man who had broken her heart.

The solution had come in the form of a job on a cruise ship. For six months, she had traveled the Caribbean, working as a bartender. It was a fun job, certainly different, but after a while, she had tired of it and was glad to return home. Tyanna had now been home for four months.

Her family hadn't understood her impromptu decision to give up her job at the gym to work on a ship. But then, they hadn't understood many of the decisions she'd made during her adult years, starting with her decision to move north to go to college.

In the end, it didn't matter. She knew she'd done the best thing for her. She didn't regret the six months away. Once that job was over, she had returned to Miami with a fresh perspective, and with memories of Sheldon firmly behind her. Finally she was on the road to rebuilding her life, one she now knew wouldn't include happily ever after with any man.

It wasn't only her experience with Sheldon that had turned her off of love. Chad, her first love, had turned out to be a pathological liar. While she had trusted him completely, he had been creeping out on her with God only knew how many other women. Her heart hadn't been completely on the line with Steven, whom she had dated after Chad, so when she had learned of his violent past with women, she had been able to dump him easily. But years earlier, there had been Ian, her first fairly serious relationship after high school. While he had seemed sweet and charming in the beginning, it soon became clear that he was only interested in her for her family's money. "Can you just lend me five hundred?" Ian had asked her once. "As soon as I get a job, I'll pay you back." She had believed him—the first time. Foolishly, she had lent him the money. Then there had been more requests for "loans," and on those occasions when Tyanna told him she didn't have it, Ian had gotten irate. "You can always go to your parents for money," he had told her snidely. "Why do you have to be so cheap?"

Of course, he hadn't paid her back the five hundred dollars. Instead, he had stopped returning her calls.

After Sheldon, Tyanna had done some serious thinking. For whatever reason, she had horrible judgment when it came to men. Either that, or the worst luck. She had come to accept that fact while working on the cruise ship.

Her sisters' heartbreaks had only solidified her decision to remain alone. Lecia, her oldest sister, had married a doctor, someone her parents had approved of wholeheartedly, and after two years their fairy-tale marriage had ended with her husband's blatant infidelity. And Charlene, the middle sister, had experienced her own devastating heartbreak. Nine months ago, her husband of four years had been killed in a traffic accident on I-95. Charlene had been seven months pregnant with their first child at the time.

Tyanna had seen how long it had taken for her sisters to get over their broken hearts. It became quite clear to her that falling in love with someone wasn't worth the pain of having your heart broken.

Tyanna brought her thoughts back to the situation at hand. She glanced down at the potential guest list lying on the table. It had grown since the last time she and her sisters had talked.

"I called around," Tyanna announced. "If we're going to rent a hall, we'll probably be better off having the event on a Sunday. With so many weddings each week, Saturdays are pretty much booked from now until next year."

"That's a good point," Lecia admitted. "I hadn't considered that."

The anniversary celebration was to be a surprise for their parents, who, come October, would be married for thirty-five years. It was a wonderful milestone, and they wanted to do something extra special.

Little Michelle reached for the scattered papers on the table. She gripped one in her tiny fist. Charlene gently unfolded her fingers and freed the paper.

A smile touched Tyanna's lips as she looked at her sister and niece with adoration. So many days, she'd wondered how Charlene had gotten through the heartbreak of losing David.

Tyanna reached for Michelle, and her niece leaned toward her. Charlene slipped her child into Tyanna's arms.

"Hey, there," Tyanna said to Michelle. "Whatcha doin'? Whatcha doin', huh?" Michelle giggled happily as she reached for Tyanna's face with her tiny fingers. She was such a happy baby, and—all bias aside—one of the cutest little girls she had ever seen.

Michelle gave Tyanna a big open-mouthed grin, and Tyanna's heart melted. It was time spent with her niece that made her feel the strongest pull to have a family. Made her long to have her own children. Made her miss out on the dream she'd lost with Sheldon.

Before, she'd never even considered having children. In many ways she was still a child herself. She enjoyed her life's spontaneity, traveling from place to place when she felt like it, keeping the hours she wanted. Having a child would change all that.

It's not like her biological clock was about to sound an alarm. She was still young, only twenty-six. She had plenty of time to think of children.

But there was something about looking into little Michelle's eyes that tugged at her heart. . . .

Damn Sheldon. It was his sudden reappearance that had her mind wandering to the dream she'd once had.

But she had to forget those dreams, move on with the other plans in her life. Who knew? Maybe one day she would meet a man she could trust, but with her track record, she wasn't banking on it. Besides, in her heart, she knew she would be a better aunt than mother anyway.

"Tyanna?"

Tyanna jerked her head up. "Huh?"

"What's the matter?" Charlene asked.

"Nothing."

"You sure? You zoned out there for a minute."

For several seconds, Tyanna debated telling her sisters about Sheldon's appearance at her car last night. But she thought better of it. No one in her family had been particularly fond of Sheldon. Charlene had been nice to him, while Lecia had barely tolerated him. Her parents hadn't even done that. He didn't have a college degree, and was beneath Tyanna's standards in their opinion.

But in addition to his lack of education, everyone in her family had wondered about his quiet nature, how he and Tyanna would truly get along. Tyanna was vivacious and outgoing. Sheldon was often as quiet as a wall. On more than one occasion her mother had hinted at the fact that Sheldon must be hiding some deep, dark secret because he didn't have much to say.

Clearly, her mother had been right.

No one in her family—not even Charlene—had been surprised when Sheldon had ended their relationship without any warning. Tyanna hadn't been able to stand all the I-told-you-sos.

No, she decided. Telling Lecia and Charlene about Sheldon would only make them concerned, and there was no reason to make them worry about a situation that wasn't going to go anywhere.

So she said, "I'm just thinking . . . wondering . . . Do you guys want to go all out with a big shindig? Or have something smaller? Maybe at their place? Close family and friends."

Charlene answered, "I say we go big. Thirty-five years is a huge milestone. We could wait for fifty, but there's no guarantee of anything in life. I say we don't wait."

Charlene's eyes ventured to her daughter at her words, and Tyanna knew she was thinking of David. Tyanna reached across the table and squeezed Charlene's hand.

A moment passed before Tyanna said, "This is going to be like a wedding."

"Sounds like it," Lecia said. "But at least we have four months to plan it."

Charlene smiled. "Maybe they'll even renew their vows."

"That would be nice." Tyanna agreed. "Hey, Lecia," she said, changing the subject. "How's it going with Martin?" Martin was the new man in Lecia's life. She'd been seeing him for a month, but she didn't say much about him.

Lecia waved a hand dismissively. "I'm not seeing him anymore."

"Oh, no." Charlene frowned. "What happened?"

"Nothing." Lecia smiled. "That was the problem. There really wasn't a spark. I think I'm just not supposed to date another doctor."

Or maybe it was just the issue of trust that Lecia couldn't get around, Tyanna thought. She'd discovered that her ex-husband, Alan Parker—a respected obstetrician like her—had had numerous affairs with patients and staff. Considering they had only been married for two years, Lecia had not only been shocked, she'd been devastated. It was her parents who had introduced her to Alan, and everyone had been surprised at his betrayal.

"I'm too busy to be dating anyway," Lecia added. "He still calls me from time to time, but the most we really say is hi and bye."

"You know what I say about all work and no play," Tyanna joked.

"Yes, I do. And for that reason, I'm planning a cruise for the end of the year."

Both Charlene and Tyanna looked at Lecia in surprise. "You're kidding," Charlene said. "I thought you would never take a break."

"Martin and I had tossed around the idea," Lecia explained. "In case we were still together at Christmas. But now that it's over, I figure there's no reason I can't go by myself. I haven't taken a vacation in, what . . ."

"Since your high-school trip to Jacksonville," Tyanna supplied.

"Probably," Lecia agreed, then chuckled.

"It's about time," Charlene said.

Tyanna smirked. "I'll believe it when I see it."

# Chapter 4

Tyanna was driving home when her cell-phone rang. It was shortly after one P.M., and she had to be at the gym by three.

"Hello?"

"Girl, I have got the best news for you."

Tyanna smiled when she heard her good friend's voice. "Hey, Wendy. What's up?"

"Take a guess."

"I don't know." Tyanna wanted to keep her mind focused on the road. "Tell me."

"All right. I heard from Ronnie Vaughn's office last night."

"Ronnie Vaughn!" Tyanna exclaimed.

"Uh-huh."

"And you only just called me now?"

"I called you last night, but I didn't want to leave a message. I called this morning too."

"I got home late from work last night. And this morning, I was at Charlene's place. Making plans for my parents' thirty-fifth anniversary party."

"Well, listen to this."

Tyanna's heart accelerated as her free hand clenched the steering wheel. "What did they say?" she asked anxiously.

"I swear, those Hollywood people must keep the weirdest hours. The call came after eleven P.M."

"Oh, you're going to drag this out, are you?"

Wendy chuckled softly. "Okay. I won't torture you. The guy who called me said that Ronnie was intrigued by our business proposal. He wants more from us." Wendy paused. "He'd like a demo tape!"

"Oh, my goodness. You're kidding?"

"Nope. A demo tape, Tyanna. Can you believe this?"

"Oh, my God." Tyanna was so excited, she veered into the lane to her left. Thank God, no car was there. She recovered, then said, "He really wants to see one?"

"Yep."

A million thoughts were swirling through Tyanna's mind. "When?"

"As soon as possible. I told him we already have one, but we're just editing it."

"Wendy!"

"I didn't want to tell him we haven't put one together. All that means is, we'll have to get to work right away."

Tyanna felt a moment of panic. "What are we going to do?"

"Don't worry. I'm going to call Phil. He's

directing a lot of music videos these days. I'm sure he can help us."

"Oh, that's right. That'd be great. He could get us a camera—"

"And even add music to the video once we've shot it. It doesn't have to be the best quality, but I think we should make it as professional-looking as possible."

"I agree. Then we send Ronnie Vaughn a video that really shows him what we can do."

"We could actually go to Los Angeles with the video, show him how serious we are." Wendy paused. "I'm so excited, Tyanna. This could really be a great break for us."

"I know." Tyanna was both excited and nervous as hell. This was a great opportunity. A step in the direction of a mutual dream. They couldn't blow it.

"So anything new with you?" Wendy asked. "Anything exciting happen at the gym last night?"

For a moment, Tyanna wondered if Wendy knew. Sometimes the two were so in tune, it scared her.

Wendy had been her best friend since fourth grade, and over the years they'd developed a kind of telepathy. Not always, but Tyanna and Wendy could often finish each other's sentences, and one often knew what the other was thinking before she mentioned it.

When Tyanna hadn't been able to tell her sisters all that was in her heart about Sheldon, she'd been able to tell Wendy. And Wendy, bless her heart, didn't judge her.

Tyanna made her way into the right lane, heading for her exit off the highway. "Why do you ask, Wendy?"

"I don't know. Conversation." Wendy paused. "Did it?"

Tyanna sighed. She'd now committed herself to telling Wendy the story. "Actually, something did happen. You're not going to believe this—I *still* can't believe it—but guess who surprised me outside the gym last night?"

"Jay," Wendy said. "What did he do this time, show up with flowers?"

"No, not Jay." A few weeks ago, he had surprised Tyanna with chocolate. She'd had to sit him down and tell him that while she was flattered by his attention, she wasn't interested in dating anyone. Since that time, he had pretty much left her alone.

"If not Jay, then who? You have another admirer?"

Tyanna paused a moment before answering. She may as well just say it. "Sheldon."

"What? Speak up, girl."

Tyanna raised her voice. "Sheldon."

Wendy squealed. "Oh, my goodness. Sheldon! The same Sheldon—?"

"Yes, the same Sheldon."

"He just showed up at the gym?"

"Uh-huh."

"To surprise you." Tyanna heard Wendy sigh happily. "What did he say?"

Tyanna couldn't help rolling her eyes, somewhat annoyed. Now on a city street, she quickly pulled the car into a gas station so she wouldn't continue driving and talking. As she placed the car in park, she said, "Sorry to disappoint you, Wendy, but it wasn't a joyous reunion. He surprised me outside the gym, with some ridiculous story as to where he'd been for a year."

"Aww."

"Wendy!" Good grief, her friend was too much of a romantic. Even though she was still looking for her Mr. Right, she hadn't been jaded by the negative experiences she'd had.

"I'm sorry. It's just that—you and Sheldon. You were such a great couple."

"And he obviously forgot that. Or just didn't feel the same to begin with."

"What did he say?"

To Tyanna's dismay, her stomach actually fluttered as she remembered the vision of him by her car. Still as strong and handsome as she'd remembered him. "Well, he didn't say much at first. I . . . I hit him."

"Tyanna."

"I didn't know it was him," Tyanna said in her defense. "I thought it was some psycho following me."

"How badly did you hurt him?"

"Not that bad. He was okay after a few minutes."

Wendy groaned, and Tyanna could picture her shaking her head. "All right. What did he say once he caught his breath?"

"He said he needed to talk to me," Tyanna explained. "I had no idea why."

"Hmm. Maybe we should hire a rocket scientist to figure this one out."

"Ha ha. Aren't you just too funny."

"Fine. I'll keep my opinions to myself—for now. You said he told you some kind of story?"

"Yeah. Some far-fetched bit about doing some undercover work to catch the guy who killed his brother."

"Brother?"

"Exactly. He's never had a brother before. I'm supposed to believe he has one now? *Had* one?"

"That's definitely weird. How did he explain that?"

"Girl, this story had enough murder, mayhem, and drugs to make a *New York Times* best-seller. I gave him an A for effort."

"Oooh."

"It was too incredible. I don't even know what to think."

"Well, whatever his reasons," Wendy said, "he obviously wanted to see you. That took a lot of guts after so long."

It was just like Wendy to look on the bright side. "The effort is too little, too late," Tyanna said pointedly. "I don't even know why he thinks it would matter now. I'm over him."

"I know you are." But Wendy didn't sound convinced. "Which is really too bad—since no one has ever gotten to your heart the way Sheldon did."

"And thank God I'm over that. Do you remember how pathetic I was? Canceling dates to be with him. Never going out; just hanging with him watching a movie. Like some boring housewife or something. I totally lost all my spunk. I mean, since when am I a homebody?"

"Hey, with the right guy . . ." Wendy let her statement hang in the air. "And the way you told it, you two barely came up for air."

Oh, Wendy did not have to go there. Tyanna did not want to be reminded of her sex life with Sheldon.

"The truth is," Tyanna said, feigning nonchalance, "sex isn't everything." But just the mention of it had Tyanna remembering how great it had been with Sheldon, which had her suddenly missing what she'd gone without for a year.

*Forget the sex*, she told herself. *Please, forget the sex.* The sex with Sheldon was her weakness. For months she had spent restless nights reliving their most intimate times together. Thankfully, she'd gotten past that stage, although she did have some nights on occasion where she would remember their lovemaking.

"Tyanna?"

Wendy's voice pulled her from memory lane. Damn, she hoped her friend didn't realize where her thoughts had ventured. "I needed more than sex, Wendy. I needed honesty. I needed him to let me into his world. No matter how we connected in bed, I always felt he was holding back. It wasn't a pleasant feeling."

"You did mention that before."

"I brushed a lot aside then," Tyanna went on. "For the sake of great sex." And because in her heart, she had felt that all Sheldon needed was a little extra nurturing before he would open up completely. "But I've grown up."

"It sounds like you miss the sex."

"Of course I don't miss the sex!" Tyanna protested.

"It's only natural," Wendy continued, as if she were deaf. "I mean, after the way you described it. Even I was jealous."

"All right. So I miss the sex. *Sometimes.* It's not like I think about it every night." Pause. "Anymore."

Wendy burst into laughter, then so did Tyanna.

"Girl, you are too silly," Wendy said.

"Yeah, yeah, whatever." Tyanna shook her head with chagrin. "Look Wendy, you know we can chat all day, but I've got to get ready for work."

"All right. I'll let you go."

"Let me know what Phil says about using his video equipment."

"Sure. I'll call him now. I doubt it will be a problem, but we'll have to figure out a time."

"And music, and location. All that stuff." Tyanna inhaled deeply, trying to quell her excitement. "So much to plan."

"Definitely. I'll be in touch."

"Talk to you later, hon."

"Later."

Tyanna disconnected the call and got back on the road. Between Sheldon and Ronnie Vaughn, she was a ball of nervous energy.

She was looking forward to heading to work. A good workout was what she needed to get her mind off everything.

Especially Sheldon.

And if Jay was at the gym and he flirted with her, maybe today she would flirt right back.

*Chapter 5*

Sheldon pulled his Explorer along the edge of the gravelly road and killed the engine. For a long while, he stayed seated in his vehicle, looking out at the row of headstones.

He finally pushed the door open and hopped out of the car. His brother's plot was a little off to the right, and Sheldon slowly made his way there.

FORD. His hands perched on his hips, Sheldon looked at the headstone that marked his brother's life and death.

FORD
Dwight Brendan
April 17, 1980–October 26, 2001
*Gone too soon, but always in our hearts*

Sheldon stared at the words etched into the granite rectangle where his brother had been placed in the ground. Grass had long grown over what was once a mound of dirt.

It was still so hard to believe that his brother's body was forever interred in this spot. That this represented a life that had once been vivacious and full of curiosity. It didn't seem possible, much less real.

Digging into his jeans pocket, Sheldon pulled out the charm he had brought with him. He sunk to the ground, resting his butt on his heels beside the headstone.

"Hey, little brother. I brought you something." Sheldon always carried some type of gift for his brother. He left the flowers to others; Dwight had never been a flowers-type guy, so Sheldon didn't bother with that.

"Nothing much. It's just a charm." Sheldon fingered the angel wings. "No matter what anyone else says, I know you were a good kid. You had a good heart. You just got mixed up in some crazy stuff."

Sheldon took the charm in two fingers and slipped it between the granite and grass, pushing it down so that no one else could see it. "That's an angel to watch over you. The way I couldn't in life."

A painful lump lodged in his throat, and Sheldon found himself brushing away a sudden tear. "I failed you, bro. And I'm sorry about that. I should have been able to get you out of this mess." He swallowed, but the lump remained. "But at least Dino is dead. No ifs, ands or buts. I know that won't bring you back, but at least he got the punishment he deserved."

A drop of rain splattered against Sheldon's nose, and he looked up at the sky. Between the time he had arrived at the cemetery and now, the sky had grown dark and Sheldon hadn't even noticed. He knew how hard the rain came down in South Florida, so he quickly got to his feet.

"I'll come back and visit you, bro."

Sheldon took a step backward. His glance moved to the left, beyond Dwight's grave to his father's.

Despite his objections, his mother had buried Dwight beside his father. Years ago, his parents had bought plots at this cemetery, planning for all of them to be buried here when the time came. Sheldon knew it made sense that his mother had gone ahead and buried Dwight here, but a sour taste coated his tongue every time he came here and saw his father's headstone.

The man hadn't been a father. He'd been a brute. An alcoholic, a philanderer, a wife beater—yet through it all, his mother had always forgiven him. Made excuses for him.

She later told Sheldon that she had stayed with their father because she had wanted desperately to keep the family together. It was the kind of mistake many women make. Kids always knew when things weren't right, and they grew up with emotional scars.

That's exactly what had happened with Dwight, Sheldon was sure. Though a good kid, there had always been a void in his life. Sheldon could see this, but he had no clue what to do to make it better. In the end, his brother had looked to the wrong type of people for approval.

Their father had died six years earlier from liver failure. He had finally drunk himself to death. When he died, Sheldon had felt a sense of loss more than sadness. Loss for what could have and should have been. But he knew his mother would finally have some peace.

Sheldon had been living on his own at the time, something else he felt guilty about. He had been so tired of dealing with a drunk and abusive father, day in and day out, that he'd left home shy of his eighteenth birthday. Maybe if he hadn't taken off, he would have been there for Dwight when he really needed a man. But if he hadn't left, he had no clue what he might have done to protect his mother.

"You have to let go of the anger," his mother once told him. "The anger will kill you."

The sprinkling of raindrops turned to sheets within minutes, and Sheldon quickly hurried back to his Explorer. He got inside and locked the door.

He blew out a ragged sigh. He didn't see himself as particularly angry, but he knew he had his issues. Sometimes, though he was nothing like his father, he wondered if he was capable of that kind of cruelty. If he could be with a woman, claim to love her, raise a family with her, then turn into a monster overnight.

His father had had a streak of bad luck in life,

losing a job he loved due to an injury. He'd never been quite the same after that. Sheldon couldn't forgive him for what he'd become—but he did wonder if every human being had that fine line that, once crossed, turned him into something else.

He knew that whatever issues he hadn't worked out regarding his father had affected his relationship with Tyanna. Hopefully, one of these days he'd figure it all out.

Sheldon parked his car alongside a pay phone at a gas station. He got out and dashed through the pouring rain into the dry cubicle.

Inside, he emitted a frustrated groan, then tried to brush the water off his arms. Damn all this rain. He had to get used to it again, being back in South Florida in the summer.

He reached into the pocket of his jeans and withdrew the scrap of paper on which he'd written Maria's number. Maria had been Dino's girlfriend for four months, and when she decided to leave him, Dino had wanted her killed. Maria had had to go into hiding. Though he'd never met her, Sheldon had been able to locate her without tipping off Dino to that fact, and had established phone contact. His interest in Maria had to do with her knowledge of Dino's illegal operation.

Leaning on the metal shelf in the booth, he reached for the receiver. He gave it a quick check to see if it was decent or gross. It looked pretty clean, but still he rubbed the ear and mouthpieces on his jeans just to be sure. He took the calling card out of his other pocket and dialed the access number, followed by Maria's number.

A couple rings later, she answered. "Hello?"

"Hey, Maria."

There was a pause, then, "Is that Sheldon?"

"Yep." Sheldon turned around in the phone booth, leaning his back against one of the walls. "It's me."

"How are you?" she asked cheerfully.

"I'm all right," he told her. "Just a little wet. But happy to be back in town." And he was. He'd been tired of watching his back at every turn, not knowing if Dino had tracked him down. It was through Maria that Sheldon had learned of Dino's death. Maria was still in touch with someone from Ultimate Fitness who had given her information the few times she called.

"I know you are. I was praying for you. For both of us."

"I'm grateful for that. The prayers were definitely answered."

"Mmm hmmm. As tragic as the situation is, I feel happy that I no longer have to watch every step I take. It's all worked out for the best."

Maria had stayed in Florida, but moved farther north. She was still relatively close to her family, so she didn't mind. Plus, she had met another man and was happily involved with him.

"Were you able to find out if Dino's body was actually taken up north?" Sheldon asked.

"Yeah. It was. He was buried in New York, next to his mother and some other relatives. So that's the end of that."

"All right." Sheldon had hoped to pay a visit to the grave if it was in the area, almost as if he needed to see for himself that Dino was really dead, but it was probably best this way. With Dino dead and buried, he could put this whole issue to rest once and for all and get on with his life. "At least that's finally finished. A miserable chapter in our lives that we can close the book on."

"Yes. Thank God."

Sheldon suddenly realized that he didn't have to call Maria from pay phones, for safety reasons, anymore. He could really get back to living his life the way he once had. Have a cellphone in his name, a job in the area. No more running around and watching his back.

"You know what's weird?" Maria asked. "I feel like I know you so well, yet I've never met you."

"I know what you mean." They had talked often enough on the phone, and the situation had made good friends of them.

"I hope we can meet one of these days. I bet you're as cute as your brother was."

"Cuter, of course," Sheldon joked, but his chest tightened at the words. He supposed it always would when he thought of Dwight and how he'd died so tragically.

Maria chuckled softly. "Well, if you ever get up to West Palm Beach, call me. And you should give me your number. I'll be heading down to Miami much more often now."

"That's a great idea. I'd love to meet you."

"We can go for coffee or something. Or a health shake. Whatever you want."

"I'm staying with my mother for now. I haven't gotten a cellphone yet, but I will soon. And maybe a place of my own. I'll see what happens for me." Sheldon gave her his mother's number.

"And what about joining the police force?"

Sheldon ran a hand over the back of his neck. His entire life, he had hoped to have a career playing basketball. But a shoulder injury in college had killed those dreams. Ultimately, Sheldon had started working as a fitness trainer, because it was the one area he loved. But after Dwight's death and his year in Kansas, he had felt compelled to get a job that would make a difference in people's lives.

In Kansas, he had started mentoring a neighbor's teenage son. Soon after that, he began working at a youth center. The kids looked up to him, and he'd had some serious talks with a few of them who had displayed behavioral problems. But it was thirteen-year-old James's arrest that affected him most. The cops had gone to his house and dragged him out screaming and crying.

Sheldon had tried to intercede, pleading with the cops to treat James like the kid he was, but it had been to no avail. It was a memory that still haunted him.

After witnessing that, and after hearing a few other horror stories from the teens he mentored, Sheldon had come to realize that this country could use some sympathetic cops who related to teens—especially in the black community.

To Maria, he replied, "That's something I still want to do."

"You didn't get around to it yet?"

"Not yet. I'm basically getting settled. And I want to make sure my mother's okay. She had a heart attack while I was gone."

"Oh, no."

"She's fine now, but taking it easy. Doctor's orders." Sheldon had always planned to get his own place when he moved back to Miami, but he was worried about his mother.

"Well, I hope everything works out for you soon. I'm sure you'd make a great cop."

"I hope so." Later this year, he would turn thirty. He planned to apply to the academy by then.

"And what about your old girlfriend?"

Sheldon groaned. "Ah, I don't know. She won't even see me right now. I don't think she believes what happened at all. And I can't say I blame her."

"It *does* sound crazy. I prob'ly wouldn't believe you if I was her."

"I guess."

"You want me to talk to her? 'Cause I will, if you think it will help."

Sheldon pondered the idea for a moment. Tyanna already believed that he had left her for some other woman, which had been a lie, of course. But if he let Maria talk to her, Tyanna might wonder if there had been someone else.

"I'm not sure. If I need you, I'll let you know."

"Okay."

"She'll come around," Sheldon said, though he had no clue if she truly would. "I think once she's had time to mull things over, she'll understand why I did what I did."

"Well, good luck. Give her time, but let her know you're still interested."

Thinking about it now, Sheldon realized that there was so much he had told Maria that he hadn't told Tyanna. The situation had warranted it; given the fact that he'd found her when she hadn't wanted to be found, and that he had been affiliated with Dino, he'd had to share his pain with Maria so she would know he wasn't one of Dino's goons. Still, he thought of the expression on Tyanna's face when he told her that he'd had a brother. One not only of utter disbelief, but of hurt. Despite her efforts to make wisecracks.

Sheldon gritted his teeth, wondering how he was ever going to work through this issue with Tyanna. He'd lied to her because he had to. But everything had changed with Dino's death.

"Thanks," Sheldon said in response to Maria's comment. "Sounds like a plan."

"That's the only way she's gonna know you still care."

"No doubt, no doubt."

Maria sighed softly. "All right, Sheldon. Thanks for calling. I'm so glad this is finally over."

"Me too."

"Talk to you later."

"Yep. Later."

"God bless."

# Chapter 6

"Paging Tyanna Calhoun to the front desk. Tyanna Calhoun to the front desk."

*Brother*, Tyanna thought sourly. Everyone knew she was on a much-deserved break. She had barely started her salad.

She closed the top of the plastic container over the salad, then pushed her chair back and stood. She hoped there wasn't some type of emergency. It was tough enough trying to fit lunch into her hectic schedule at the gym, and she appreciated the few moments she had to herself.

A minute later, she was at the front desk. "What's up, Shirley?"

"Someone's here to see you."

Tyanna rolled her eyes. "Didn't you tell them I was on my break?"

"Of course, but he was pretty adamant. Said he's looking for a personal trainer and heard you were the best."

Tyanna bit her scowl. "Where is he?"

"He's sitting back there, in your office."

"Why's he in my office?"

"He said he'd prefer to wait for you there."

Fine. Tyanna wasn't going to make a big stink about it. "Shirley, please make sure that next time, anyone who wants to see me waits out here?"

"Sure," Shirley said.

Tyanna turned and headed in the direction of the club's offices. Except for the manager, no one had an official office. There were simply a series of desks partitioned off from one another.

Tyanna was all set to tell this man that he would have to wait a few more minutes for her, but her mouth dried the moment she saw Sheldon sitting in front of her desk.

He looked up at her and smiled.

"Oh, no."

Tyanna whirled on her heel, prepared to tell Shirley that there was no way in hell she was going to work with this man. But Sheldon softly called her name and she froze.

Damn, she wished he didn't have the power to do that to her.

"Come on, babe," he said. "There's no need to run from me."

She marched back into her office and sat down behind her desk. "Let's get a couple things straight. First of all, I'm not your baby. Not anymore."

"And second?"

There was a hint of a smirk on his mouth, and

that irritated her. "And second, do not come to my workplace pretending to be a potential client."

"But I *am* a potential client," he protested. "And I want to work with the best."

Tyanna stared at Sheldon for a good five seconds, wondering what on earth was going through that mind of his. Finally she asked, "*You* need a personal trainer?"

"Sure."

"Oh, come on." Realizing that she had raised her voice, Tyanna made a concerted effort to speak in a lowered tone. "Look at you. You're in fabulous shape." Her eyes ventured to his wide shoulders and well-muscled arms. Today he wore a white tank top—as equally flattering on him as black. As she did a quick scan of his body, *definition* was the only word that came to mind.

Oh, Lord help her.

She quickly averted her gaze and cleared her throat. "No one in their right mind could think you need a personal trainer."

"I want one."

"What—did you lose your memory in the year you were away?" Tyanna asked. "You *are* a personal trainer."

He merely grinned. "You know that it's hard to motivate yourself. You accomplish much more when you work with someone else."

*What is your game?* Tyanna wanted to ask, but didn't. She was sure she wouldn't like his answer.

"You never had a problem when it came to being motivated."

"Maybe I made it seem that way, but it wasn't so. Besides, this past year on the road, I haven't been able to work out the way I wanted to. My body's starting to suffer."

*Could have fooled me.* He was still in amazing shape. Hard and defined the way most men aspired to be.

Tyanna shuffled some papers on her desk. "If you're serious about this, I'd suggest Mike Cooper. He's one of the best. He's competed in Mr. Olympia and placed in the top three. Besides, he's a man, and I'm sure you'd be much more comf—"

"Look at me."

Reluctantly, she did. "What?"

"There. That didn't kill you, did it?"

"What's that supposed to mean?" she asked, annoyed.

"Nothing. Listen, you can save the spiel about Mike. I'm not interested. Besides," Sheldon went on, "you know my body better than this Mike character."

Tyanna steeled herself against the feelings Sheldon's comment elicited, against the image it brought to mind. "I don't see what that has to do with personal training."

Sheldon instantly raised an eyebrow, and Tyanna could have kicked herself for what she'd said. She'd made it sound like her only interest in his body was sexual. "What I mean is—"

"I know exactly what you mean."

"No, I don't think you do."

"You know my body, Tyanna. You're the best one to check it out and see if there are any areas that need improvement."

Tyanna chuckled, but the sound had no mirth. The man had to be out of his mind. "I don't think so."

Sheldon sat forward in his chair. "What are you afraid of, sweetness?"

The sound of the old endearment he used to call her caught her off guard. She had to take a moment to remember the question he'd asked her. "I—I'm not afraid of anything. It just isn't a good idea." When his eyes narrowed questioningly, she wondered what had gotten into Sheldon. This man was different. Sure, he'd had his moments when he was very playful and flirtatious, but it had taken a while for him to feel comfortable being that way with her. Even then, he had done so only when the two were in her apartment. Now, he hadn't seen her for a year, yet he was calling her sweetness? In a gym, no less?

Things had certainly changed since he'd been gone.

Tyanna met his gaze head-on—gave him the kind of look that said she wasn't afraid of anything. "Why don't you tell me what this is really about. I don't buy it that you want me to help you build up your pecs."

His face went serious. "You really don't believe me, do you? About why I was gone for a year."

Tyanna sighed. "Come on, Sheldon. A brother? Dino dealing steroids?"

"Why would I make something like that up?"

"That's exactly what I'd like to know. Clearly, it's important for you to feel I believe you when you say you had a good reason for abandoning me. But the truth is, I can't imagine why, at this point."

Sheldon was distracted by the movement of her mouth as she talked. He remembered how that mouth had felt against his. Wet and pliant.

"During this past year—"

She went on with her protests, and God, he was tempted to shut her up with a kiss. He knew what could happen when their mouths met—the same thing that had happened every other time. All words vanished, leaving in their wake hot and heavy breaths and simmering desire.

"—as if I'm just supposed to forget all that—"

Damn, he literally ached to kiss her. It had been a whole year since he'd been with a woman, a year since he'd touched one. Just being this close to her had given him a painful erection.

But he couldn't lean across the desk and kiss her senseless. They were in a public place, after all—her workplace, and he knew she wouldn't appreciate it. Hell, she'd probably belt him again.

So instead, he let her talk until she ran out of steam. As for making sense of a thing she was saying, he didn't, partly because she was rambling and partly because he was mesmerized by the way she put her whole body into her words.

She finally finished with, "Okay?"

"I'm sorry, I didn't catch everything you said."

She glared at him. "You're impossible."

"*I'm* impossible?"

The corners of his mouth curled, and Tyanna wished she could wipe that smirk right off his face. She didn't get this. Didn't get *him*. And she certainly didn't want to be around him.

"You know what, Sheldon? I want you to leave. This bull has gone on long enough. And I certainly don't want to sit here and mince words with you about *anything*. It's pointless." Despite her anger, she kept herself under control.

"Sweetness, you won't even listen to the truth. Which makes me think there's something else you're afraid to face."

"Like what? That you've got me all hot and bothered because you've shown up in my life again?" But her face and body grew hot as she said the words, and she hoped to hell he couldn't tell.

"Your words, not mine."

She forced a laugh. "Men. I almost forgot how juvenile they can be. Unfortunately, as much as I'd love to stay and have you continue to entertain me, I have to get back to work."

"Wait," he said. Tyanna met his gaze before rising. "Maybe we can meet later? Go somewhere to talk? There's a lot more to what happened, and I'm hoping you'll listen to it."

"It doesn't matter, Sheldon."

"Yes, it does."

"Why?"

"Because . . ." But Sheldon didn't finish his sentence.

Tyanna stared at him, waiting. Her heart pounded, but she'd be damned if she'd let him see that he was getting to her in any way.

And she'd be damned if she started to believe that he had come back into her life for the silly reason that kept floating through her mind.

"It just matters," he said.

Tyanna pushed her chair back, frustrated.

"Tyanna." Sheldon shot to his feet.

"I'm not going to work with you, Sheldon. And I'm not going to hang with you later. This is . . . this is silly."

Sheldon blew out a loud breath. "I haven't been with anyone in the time we were apart. I don't know. I guess it's been a long time—"

Tyanna's jaw nearly hit the floor. "Oh, no. I can't believe that just came from your mouth. You're here because you want a booty call?"

"You make it sound . . . illegal."

"My God, that *is* why you're here!"

"Are you telling me you don't miss it?"

No "*I'm sorry for hurting you; I was a fool.*" No "*I missed you like crazy when I was gone.*" No "*I know I never said the actual words before, but I love you.*"

*Just a basic, "I'm horny and I hope you are too, so we can hit the sack."*

Anger and disappointment fought for control of her emotions, with anger having an edge. "You—I don't believe you, Sheldon! You're so friggin' shallow!" But her own body was throbbing, remembering the explosive nights she'd tried so hard to forget. "Just because we were once great in bed doesn't mean we need to go there again."

"So you've been seeing someone else."

"That's none of your business."

Pause. "I guess it isn't."

A weird expression crossed Sheldon's face, and Tyanna actually felt a tug of guilt at her heart for making him believe she had been involved with someone else when it wasn't true. But why should she feel bad? In the year since Sheldon had left, she could have easily become seriously involved with someone else. And if she had, that would have been his loss.

It wasn't up to her to make him feel any better by letting him know that she hadn't been able to share her body with another man since him, much less give her heart to one.

And she certainly didn't want him to think that just because she hadn't been with anyone else, she'd gladly jump into bed with him again.

"Sheldon." Tyanna spoke softly. "I . . . I'm glad to see you again. I'm glad to know you're okay. For a while I wondered. Worried. Anyway, I realize that's all that matters. That you're okay. But as far as resuming any type of relationship with you, I'm just not interested."

"Because I hurt you too much."

"Are you going to feel better if I say yes?" she asked, a tad perturbed. "Fine. Yes, you hurt me. Obviously. But while you were gone, so much clicked. I'd changed so much when I was with you, Sheldon. I was no longer me. I mean, I never went out anymore. Just stayed in with you and watched movies, had quiet dinners. I barely hung out with my friends and family . . . I'm not saying you did anything to change me." He certainly hadn't told her not to see her friends and family. She had just been so enamored of him that she hadn't been able to get enough of him. "I guess I just wanted different things back then."

Sheldon didn't say anything, and right now, Tyanna desperately wished he would. Instead, he was just standing there, making her feel extremely uncomfortable.

Tyanna glanced down at her wristwatch. "I really have to get back to work. I have an appointment."

"All right."

"And please, don't show up here again. I hope you can respect that."

She started off, but he called her name, making her pause. Swallowing, she once again faced him.

"For what it's worth," he said softly, "I'm sorry."

His apology actually shocked her. She hadn't expected it—not after she'd told him to stay out of her life.

But she replied, "Too little, too late, Sheldon."

Then she turned and walked away, not giving Sheldon a chance to say anything. She only hoped she had pulled off a calm demeanor, because inside, she was a complete mess.

She'd spent a whole year getting over Sheldon Ford. The last thing she needed was a constant physical reminder of her greatest failed relationship.

*Chapter 7*

The next day, Tyanna still couldn't get Sheldon out of her mind. It wasn't so much that she was thinking about him, but she was thinking about what he'd told her about Dino.

The story was really crazy, but for some reason she couldn't completely dismiss it. Maybe because it *was* so crazy. If Sheldon had simply wanted to lie to get back into her good graces, he could have told her something less outrageous.

And there was something that had eluded her until last night. After Sheldon had disappeared, Tyanna had been frantic. She had asked everyone at the gym if they had seen Sheldon or heard from him. Pete, the gym's manager, had been furious with Sheldon. Clearly, Sheldon hadn't bothered to give notice before quitting. Other people expressed shock. But Dino . . . Dino had ended up questioning *her*. At the time Tyanna had thought nothing of it, but now his questions about the nature of her relationship with Sheldon and how close she was to his family seemed odd, especially in light of Sheldon's story. In fact, for at least four weeks Dino had continued to ask her whether or not she'd heard from Sheldon.

As much as Tyanna didn't want to believe him, the Sheldon she'd known would never lie about anything like that. She couldn't ignore how adamant he was in trying to get her to believe him—and he seemed completely truthful.

After thinking about it all night, Tyanna suddenly realized it would be fairly easy to check up on his story. See if it was true or not. A quick trip to her old gym in Coral Gables would answer her questions.

So that's what she did. Got up, had a quick bite to eat, and then headed to Ultimate Fitness.

She felt weird as she walked toward the door of her old place of work, because she hadn't been here since the day she'd quit, and she hadn't kept in touch with anyone she'd known here.

Like Jaguar Fitness, this gym was normally very busy, but the parking lot wasn't full this Sunday afternoon. A quick glimpse inside the front door told Tyanna the gym was only half full.

It was the weekend, and a beautiful day at that. Perhaps people were spending time at the beach or doing some other outdoor activity.

Tyanna made her way to the juice bar, a few steps to the immediate left.

Bar stools could accommodate ten people at the

curved bar area. Two women sat in the center, chatting. Tyanna walked to the far end and took a seat there.

She didn't see Dino. In fact, no one was behind the counter. But the door to the back storage and office area was open, so Tyanna figured Dino had to be there.

Moments later, a woman came from the back room. It was Leona, who had worked at the reception desk when Tyanna was here.

Leona came to the bar, all business. "Hi, what can I—" she began. Then she stopped, recognition flashing in her eyes. "Tyanna?"

Tyanna smiled widely. "Hey, Leona."

"It really *is* you!" She reached for Tyanna's hands on the counter and gave them a squeeze. "Girlfriend, you look so good."

"Thanks. So do you." Petite Leona didn't have an ounce of unwanted fat on her body. Her strawberry blond hair was cut in a cute above-the-shoulder style, unlike the much-longer style she used to wear. Leona was one of those women who looked like the classic girl next door.

"What are you doing at the juice bar? Weren't you working reception?"

"I was. Things change." Leona grinned brightly at her. "Didn't you go away for a while?"

"Yep," Tyanna replied. "Sailing the high seas."

"That's right. How was that?"

"Fun while it lasted."

"When did you get back into town?"

"I've been back for a little while."

"And you're only now coming to visit?"

"I know. But I've been busy. I'm working at another gym now. And that's even busier than this place."

Leona leaned forward on the counter. "I thought you would come back and work here. What happened? You were tired of us?"

"No, I'm actually a little closer to home," Tyanna explained. "At Jaguar Fitness."

"Ah. The competition."

Tyanna smirked. "Well, their juice bar is nowhere near as good as this one. Speaking of which, you know what I'd love? One of those vanilla protein shakes with pineapple and strawberries."

"You got it."

Leona walked the short distance to the blender, filled it with shake powder and water, then added morsels of frozen strawberries and pineapples.

As the blender whirred, Tyanna looked around. A guy she didn't recognize had entered the juice bar from the back room while she and Leona had been talking. Normally only two people worked the juice bar. So the fact that Leona and this other guy were here meant that Dino likely wasn't around.

Dino had worked every day—it was almost as if he didn't trust the running of the operation to anyone else. But maybe he had finally taken everyone's advice and hired more help.

Yeah, he was probably out somewhere enjoying this Sunday afternoon. She allowed her eyes to roam over the young man's profile while she thought. He did look a lot like Dino, in fact. Except for the glasses . . .

Leona returned with a large Styrofoam cup filled with the protein shake. She placed it on the counter in front of Tyanna. "There you go."

Tyanna reached into her purse. "How much?"

"For you, nothing."

"You sure?"

"Absolutely."

"Thanks." Tyanna took a sip of the shake through the fat straw. "Mmm. This is excellent, Leona. Just like the ones Dino always made me." She met Leona's gaze and asked, "Where is Dino, by the way? I never knew that guy to take a day off."

The pleasant expression on Leona's face morphed into one of pain. "I guess you never heard."

Tyanna felt a sudden chill. "Heard what?"

Leona closed her eyes, then slowly opened them. "Dino was killed. A couple months back."

"Oh, my God."

Leona gave a jerky nod. "Yeah. He was shot." Leona inhaled.

"Shot?" *So it was true.*

"Yeah."

Leona seemed badly shaken over the news, and Tyanna reached across the bar for her hand. She squeezed it tightly. "You two were close?"

Leona paused before answering. "Mmm hmm."

"This must be very hard for you. To lose a friend this way." Though Leona's reaction made Tyanna wonder if their relationship had been strictly platonic. She and Leona hadn't been more than casual friends, so Tyanna hadn't been concerned with Leona's love life. However, when she thought back, she remembered seeing Leona hanging out at the juice bar a lot. Tyanna had figured that was because Leona was chatty, and it was easy to talk to Dino while he worked. But maybe she had been wrong.

"Since his death, I've been running the juice bar," Leona explained. "But I'm sure his father will want to sell it soon."

"Good Lord," Tyanna muttered, mostly to herself. "Sheldon was right."

"Pardon me?"

"Oh. Sheldon. Sheldon Ford. I don't know if you knew him. He used to work here too. We were dating." Leona shook her head. "I'm not surprised. He was pretty quiet. Private. He didn't really want anyone at the gym knowing that we were a couple. Anyway, I ran into him a couple days ago, and he told me he'd heard that Dino was dead. . . . I was sure he was mistaken."

Leona gave her a curious look. "Really? How did he hear?"

"I'm guessing on the news. Or maybe someone who used to work here told him. I was praying it wasn't true."

"Unfortunately, it is."

"Oh, Leona. I can't believe this."

"Neither can I."

"This place just isn't the same without Dino. His smiling face. His jokes . . ."

"That's for sure." She sighed sadly, then looked past Tyanna. "Oh, give me a second."

A young man and woman approached the bar and sat one seat over from Tyanna. She was glad for the interruption, because Leona moved over to them, leaving Tyanna to her thoughts.

And the thoughts that were running through her head! They were almost overwhelming. She had come here today hoping to see Dino alive and well, joking and smiling like he usually was.

But Sheldon was right. Dino was dead. Leona had said that he'd been killed—not that he'd died in an accident or from a surprise heart attack, but that he'd been killed. And if Sheldon's account of Dino's having been shot by police was true, then it wasn't surprising that Leona was resistant to talk about the details of his death.

Oh, man.

Tyanna had to face it—Sheldon was telling her the truth. He couldn't have guessed that Dino was killed. Of course, he could have learned about Dino's fate on the news. . . .

But if he hadn't . . . the whole crazy story he'd told her was true.

Which would mean he had left town because his life was truly in danger.

Tyanna finished the last of her shake and climbed off the stool. "Leona, I'm gonna have to run."

"Oh. Already?"

"Yeah. I was just in the neighborhood and figured I'd drop in to say hi."

"Okay."

"Once again, I am so sorry about Dino."

"Thanks." Leona paused, then added, "Don't be a stranger."

Tyanna forced a smile. "I won't."

*Chapter 8*

Dino Benedetto truly was dead!

That reality kept playing over and over in Tyanna's mind long after she returned home. She had felt so optimistic when she walked through the doors of Ultimate Fitness, expecting to see Dino working behind the juice bar.

But Leona telling her that Dino was dead—somehow she had kept it together in front of her old colleague. But now that she was home, she couldn't shake the sick feeling that had settled in the pit of her stomach.

As much as she'd wanted to believe that Sheldon was lying to her about Dino, she now knew he wasn't. It wasn't a coincidence that he knew of Dino's death, and Tyanna was willing to believe that if she checked out old newspapers, she would find information about it. Clearly, Sheldon hadn't come back to town with some far-fetched story meant as a lame excuse to justify why he'd left her.

She inhaled a choppy breath and let it out in a rush.

She wasn't thinking so much of Sheldon now as she was trying to deal with the truth about Dino. Dealing illegal steroids? Mob connections? He'd seemed so . . . nice.

So had Ted Bundy, apparently.

Tyanna's eyes wandered to the phone. She lay stretched out on the sofa and the television was on, but she wasn't registering a word or image from the TV. All she could think about was what Leona's words had confirmed.

She needed to know more. Sheldon had given her a skeleton of the events because she hadn't let him tell her everything.

Tyanna bit down on her bottom lip, wondering what to do. Should she try and track Sheldon down? She still spoke to his mother from time to time, and knew her phone number. If Sheldon wasn't staying with her, surely his mother would know where he was. The more Tyanna thought about it, the more she realized that calling wouldn't be a bad idea. Goodness, how could she not? There were so many missing pieces, including why Mrs. Ford had never mentioned Dwight either.

She sat up and edged across the sofa, moving closer to the phone. If she called, it would just be to get the whole story. If nothing else, Sheldon owed her that. But she would make it clear to him that hearing it would not change things between them.

Whatever he would tell her now, he should have told her a year ago.

Tyanna stared at the phone for a long time, almost as if she expected the receiver to jump into her hands. Of course that wasn't going to happen. *Just do it. It's not going to kill you.*

Before she lost her nerve, she grabbed the receiver and dialed Mrs. Ford's number. After three rings, a familiar voice instantly brought a smile to her face.

"Good evening."

"Mrs. Ford. Hello."

There was a pause, then, "My goodness. Is that Tyanna?"

"Yes, ma'am. It's me."

"Oh, sweetheart. It is so good to hear from you. Where have you been?"

"You know me. Here, there and everywhere. I'm sorry I haven't been in touch lately. I've been pretty busy with the new job. I'm lucky if I get two days off a week."

"Yes, I know how that can be. With some jobs, it's always go, go, go. Like mine. I'm so glad it's the summer and I have a break."

Mrs. Ford was a teacher, and Tyanna didn't doubt she was one of the best out there.

"Did Sheldon go to see you?" Mrs. Ford asked.

"Uh, yeah," Tyanna replied, a tad surprised. "How did you . . ." Things were starting to make sense now. "Did you tell him where to find me?"

"I hope you're not upset. I remembered the

name of that new gym you said you were working at, and he asked if I'd heard from you. . . ."

"No, no. That's okay." There was no way she could ever be upset with Mrs. Ford. In many ways, Tyanna felt closer to her than to her own mother. "Actually, I was calling for Sheldon. Is he there?"

"He's around here somewhere. I think outside, working on his car. One minute."

Mrs. Ford put the receiver down and Tyanna heard some shuffling sounds. A little over a minute later, Sheldon came on the line.

"Hey, Tyanna."

His voice held warmth, and Tyanna felt a small smile creep onto her face. "Hi, Sheldon."

"I didn't think I'd hear from you."

"Yeah, well. Life is full of surprises, isn't it?"

"Touché."

"Listen, I need to talk to you. About Dino. That whole story that I didn't let you tell me."

"Oh?"

"Yeah. I'm ready to listen, if you still want to tell me about it."

"All right. But I'd rather not talk about this over the phone."

"Sure, that makes sense."

"I can head to your place."

"My place?" Tyanna's heart spasmed. The thought of being alone with Sheldon in her apartment again . . .

She had wanted to move from her apartment

after returning from working on the cruise ship—get rid of the place that held so much history for her and Sheldon—but moving was such a big job. Ultimately, she had decided against it, certain that her six months away had helped her get over Sheldon once and for all.

"You still live at the same apartment?"

"Yeah—"

"All right. It won't take me long to get there."

Tyanna hesitated. She wanted to tell him to meet her somewhere else, but that would make it seem like she was afraid to have him come over. And if she was afraid, he'd wonder why. He might think that she still had feelings for him.

Which was exactly what she didn't want him thinking. If it was the last thing she did, Tyanna would play it cool with Sheldon.

"Okay," she finally said. "I'll be home."

"Great. See you soon."

Sheldon couldn't keep a silly smile from spreading across his face as he drove the short distance from his mother's house to Tyanna's apartment. Her call had shocked him. He truly hadn't expected to hear from her. But the fact that she *had* called him proved that she'd been thinking about him.

And that was a good sign.

The year they'd been apart seemed like forever and yet only yesterday. He'd missed her. Seeing her again had driven home just how much.

She wanted to hear the whole story. A definite plus. He could only hope that she had come around to forgiving him for how he'd disappeared, or at least would soon. He regretted how everything had gone down, but he wouldn't change how he'd done things if given the chance. His life had been in danger the moment Dino had figured out his relation to Dwight, something he hadn't been able to do before because Sheldon had given him a false surname. From what he'd learned, Dino's connection to organized crime had been extensive, and if he'd gotten wind of Sheldon's relationship with Tyanna, he would have hurt her for sure.

There was no way Sheldon would have allowed that to happen. He'd done the only thing he could do, even if it was the hardest thing he'd had to do.

Sheldon exited I-95 at Aventura Boulevard and drove east. It took another several minutes for him to reach the water. Tyanna lived in a nice apartment on the beach. It wasn't quite as far south as South Beach, so while she still had a great view of the ocean, she had it at a better price.

Moments later, Sheldon signaled his turn and drove into the apartment's lot. He automatically headed to the section reserved for visitors' parking. He found an open spot and maneuvered his Explorer into it.

His stomach did a few flip-flops as he turned

off the ignition. He wanted to see Tyanna—couldn't wait to see her—yet he was suddenly afraid to get out of his vehicle. Earlier, he had been convinced that this visit could only mean something positive—that she was ready to forgive him—but what if he was wrong?

He leaned his head back against the headrest. Hell, that wasn't what he was afraid of. He knew she was ready to listen to his story. Maybe it wasn't so much that he was afraid, but that he felt a mix of nervous anticipation.

He remembered vividly what had happened the last time he'd stepped into Tyanna's apartment. It hadn't taken more than thirty seconds for them to end up hot and heavy on her sofa, doing what came so naturally for them.

Going into her apartment now . . . he couldn't help that his thoughts had turned to sex. He couldn't help but want her. Hell, he'd never stopped wanting her, no matter how many times he told himself to forget her and move on. No matter how many other beautiful women had offered themselves to him in the past year. He hadn't been able to do it, because when it came to sex, the only person he wanted to be with was Tyanna.

So the way he saw it, he was now walking into dangerous territory—especially since she'd pretty much laughed in his face when he'd hinted at the idea that they could become sexually reacquainted.

He didn't know what had come over him in her office, except that Tyanna had been so passionate as she'd spoken, and watching that full mouth of hers—his body had simply reacted. A man couldn't help it sometimes.

"Get a grip, Ford," he muttered. "This time you're gonna have to help it." He didn't know what the future held for him and Tyanna, but it'd be a grim one if he couldn't get his mind off sex right now.

"I don't even know why you're thinking this crap about a future," he said to himself. "Her family doesn't like you. . . ." That had been the one thing that bothered him the most during their relationship. He wasn't ashamed of not having a degree—he'd fallen short by a year, after dropping out in hopes of healing his shoulder—but he knew that the Calhouns thought Tyanna could do better. He'd never felt comfortable around them, simply because he felt they'd never truly let him into their inner circle. Like they thought he was responsible for everything their daughter had done that they didn't approve of.

Despite that, he and Tyanna had had a passionate relationship, and she hadn't cared about her family's opinions. But a person had to think about the long term. Somewhere along the line he had started to realize that he and Tyanna couldn't have a future. Sure, her family considered her the wild child, but one of these days, she would prob-

ably give in and please them by marrying someone they thought was suitable.

Sheldon had pushed those thoughts from his
mind while they'd been involved, but now he
couldn't help thinking of that reality.

He had to remind himself that right now, all
he really wanted was for Tyanna to forgive him,
and hopefully be willing to resume a friendship
with him.

*Damn it all to hell.* He gripped the door handle
and opened it. If he continued to sit here and
think, he would talk himself right out of going
upstairs to see her.

Sheldon hopped out of his Ford Explorer and
started for Tyanna's low-rise apartment building.
In the lobby, he hit the code for her unit. Tyanna
buzzed him up without speaking into the intercom.

Sheldon took the stairs two at a time to her
third-level apartment, but paused before opening
the door to the hallway. He blew out a quick
breath, then swung open the door and stood in
front of Tyanna's end unit. He was about to knock
when the door opened.

Tyanna smiled up at him. "Hey."

His shoulders drooped, the fight going out of
him. Damn, if she was going to look at him like
that, it was going to be near impossible to keep
his mind off sex.

"Hi." Suddenly nervous, he rubbed a hand
over the back of his neck. "See, I told you I'd be
quick."

"Guess you didn't run into any traffic."

"Not at this time on a Sunday evening."

"Well." Tyanna stepped backward. "Come in."

Sheldon stepped slowly into the apartment. He glanced around, looking for signs of change. It was pretty much the way he remembered it. A variety of shoes were scattered near the doorway, and looking further into the living room, Sheldon could see a pile of clothes in one corner that no doubt needed to be laundered.

Some things never changed. Tyanna was a sweetheart, but she wasn't the tidiest person around. Whenever he teased her about that, she always told him that in Florida, an apartment was just a place to shower and sleep. There was so much to do outdoors that she couldn't be bothered with beautifying the inside of her place.

Not that it was a complete mess, but . . . well, she wouldn't win any Martha Stewart awards.

"That's new," Sheldon said, pointing to a painting on a nearby wall. It was a watercolor of a beach, with palm trees and seashells and a lone sailboat in the distance.

"Yeah." A smile touched Tyanna's lips. "I painted it when I was on the cruise ship."

Sheldon's eyes bulged as he stared at her. "*You?*"

She placed both hands on her hips and replied, "Yes, me. You don't have to act so shocked."

Shaking his head, he chuckled softly. "Guess that shouldn't surprise me. What job haven't you done?" She'd worked a stint as a chef, as a fundraiser for a local charity foundation, a waitress, a personal trainer. "Wait a second—did you say a cruise ship?"

"Yep."

"Business or pleasure?"

"I was working."

"You don't slow down, do you?"

"Why? So much to do, so little time." She paused, then said, "After you left, I got a job as a bartender on a cruise ship. I figured I should see more of the world. I did that for six months."

She didn't have to say that she'd needed to get away because of the heartbreak he'd caused her. "Where did you travel?"

"All over the Caribbean. It was fun for a while, but one day I woke up and realized that I needed to move on."

"And you just felt inclined to start painting one day?"

"One of the other bartenders on the ship was an artist. He taught me some of the basics."

"He?"

"Uh-huh."

Sheldon could just imagine the kind of basics this guy tried to teach her, and it wasn't a thought that sat well with him. He stared at Tyanna, waiting for more. But she remained tight-lipped. Shit, she wasn't going to offer him any more details. But what did he expect?

"Basically," Tyanna continued, "I was just fooling around. Something to pass the time. Believe it or not, it can get boring when you're staring out at water."

"With all the excitement cruise ships are known for?"

"Mmm hmm."

What else had she done to pass the time on that ship? he wondered. And did it include painter-boy? He almost asked her, but as the words were on his tongue he realized how pathetic he would sound prying. Instead, he said, "Well, your painting is pretty amazing."

"It's the only one I ever did. Who knows— maybe one day when I'm long gone someone will discover me, and the painting will be worth a lot of money."

"Maybe," Sheldon agreed.

Tyanna flashed Sheldon a wry smile and rolled her eyes. "Yeah, right. Well, one can always dream." She strolled into the living room. "You want anything to drink? Water? Soda?"

"Naw," Sheldon said, following her. "I'm fine." He gave the entire room a quick perusal, then sat on the sofa.

"All right." Tyanna casually walked to the arm-chair, where she took a seat.

He didn't blame her for putting some distance between them. Even as he'd looked at the sofa, he had remembered her naked there. Which wasn't hard, because she had often walked around naked. Who needed clothes when they'd spent the better part of their time indoors making the kind of love that made their toes curl?

Tyanna crossed one leg over the other, and the first thing Sheldon noticed was the toe ring on her extended foot. He had never thought of himself as the kind of guy who'd have a foot fetish, but Tyanna had the most beautiful feet. Aside from her sparkly toe ring, her toenails were painted a bright red. It was a hot combination.

He had loved the feel of those feet stroking his thighs, or wrapped tightly around his back as he'd thrust deep inside her.

Sheldon's eyes went higher. He allowed himself a good, long look at her sexy body. She was in amazing shape, even better than he remembered. She had long, lean legs that were beautifully sculpted. Her arms were slim, yet the muscles defined. With all the working out she had done, she was firm but had remained feminine. Her mocha-colored skin was smooth and flawless on every inch of her perfect body.

But what got to him most were those sexy dimples. She had the kind of smile that made him think warm, cozy thoughts *and* get hard. Which was a deadly combination.

He remembered the New Year's Eve they'd spent together, how she'd drawn her slinky black dress over her head to reveal a sparkly bra-and-panty set. He'd had a hard-on so bad, he hadn't bothered to take the extra time to slip the items off her body. He had simply pushed her panties aside and entered her warmth. . . .

"Sheldon?" Tyanna was looking at him with a weird expression.

Aw, shit. So much for not thinking about sex. He was as hard as a flagstaff. He hoped she hadn't been able to read his thoughts.

"Um . . . I think I'll take that drink," he said.

"Oh." Tyanna stood, and her navel ring twinkled at him. Oh, yeah. He remembered the navel ring.

"What would you like?" she asked.

"Water," he answered quickly, darting his eyes to her face. "With ice."

That was the closest he could get to a cold shower, and he hoped to hell it would work.

# Chapter 9

Wendy pulled her convertible LeBaron into a parking spot on Washington Avenue, then killed the engine. It was late and not even a weekday to boot, but considering Phil was at the office this Sunday evening once again working overtime, she figured she'd hazard a chance at seeing him.

Wendy got out of the car and put money in the parking meter. She walked the short distance to Phil's office. Peering through the window, she couldn't see him. He must have been in the back part of the office, which made sense, as the front area was a reception and waiting area.

Stepping back, Wendy used the glass as a mirror. Her stomach began to contract painfully as she saw her reflection.

Good Lord, she looked like one of the tramps who frequented the South Beach strip.

She stared at herself a moment longer and realized that she was being hard on herself. She didn't look low-class. In fact, the outfit she wore flattered her well-toned body. But she was suddenly self-conscious, not sure if her outfit was too much.

Well, "too little" might be a more accurate description.

It wasn't like she wasn't used to dressing in slinky outfits; she routinely wore HotSkins, a popular choice among many fitness buffs. Popular and sexy. But she couldn't help wondering if this black skirt was too short, her form-fitting white cut-off T-shirt too revealing. It was the kind of outfit many trainers wore when they wanted to be sexy, but was it appropriate now?

She tugged at the hem of her tight skirt, but it didn't move much lower on her thighs. She did the same with her shirt, but her breasts nearly popped out of the low-neck number—and wouldn't that have been a wonderful scene!

She huffed out a breath and realized that she was either going to have to head into the office or head home. And she'd come here this evening with a plan. Sexy was part of the plan, right from her tight T-shirt down to her high-heeled sandals.

Normally, she wasn't shy about what she wore. Working at the gym required form-fitting clothing. So why was she so nervous now?

Because she was trying to impress Phil.

And she wasn't used to going to see him in an outfit she deliberately hoped would turn him on.

She couldn't help wondering if he would see

through her motives. But then, maybe that's exactly what she needed. One of them had to make the first move.

Wendy had known Phil for nearly four years, ever since they were neighbors at her last apartment complex. From day one, she had found him attractive. Attractive and nice. Attractive and living with his girlfriend.

They had quickly become friends, which had been fine with Wendy. She hadn't pictured him as anything more than that back then.

Over the years, they had both dated other people, and even though Wendy had since moved from that apartment, she and Phil had stayed friends. They got together every once in a while. In the past few months, though, Wendy had felt her attraction to him grow. Ever since his relationship with Laura—his most recent girlfriend—had ended.

Phil had talked to her a lot about Laura, about all the games she used to play with him, and Wendy had known that his heart was going to break in a big way. For some reason, he had really been attracted to Laura, more so than some of the others in the past, but Wendy had known from the beginning that the buxom model was as flaky as a piecrust.

It was during his relationship with Laura that Wendy had realized she was interested in Phil—not simply because of her extreme disapproval of Laura, but because she felt a stab of jealousy whenever he talked about her. Somewhere along the line, Wendy's attraction had snuck up and bit her in the butt, and, quite selfishly, she had been relieved when Phil's relationship with Laura had ended. As far as she knew, he wasn't dating anyone at this point.

Wendy had given him her shoulder to cry on after Laura, as she had done in the past—as he had done for her as well. And after that, any time she got together with Phil for dinner or a drink, she was overly friendly with him. She had tried, subtly, to get him to notice her in a way he hadn't before. Being somewhat old-fashioned, Wendy wanted Phil to make the first official move. Until that point, it was clear she was going to have to use all her feminine wiles to gently push him in that direction.

The problem was, Phil had never looked at her with even so much as a hint of interest, and didn't seem to get the idea that she was interested. The way Wendy figured it, that was because they'd always been "good buddies."

Tonight, she hoped to change that.

Her stomach tickled with nerves as she opened the door to the offices of The Right Touch Production Company. She had called Phil earlier and told him she would stop by to discuss the plans for the video shoot. He was a workaholic, not letting the weekends stop him. And because it was Sunday, she knew he would be alone.

She stepped into the office. "Hello?"

"Back here," Phil replied.

Wendy slowly walked toward the back. Seeing Phil standing over a desk full of pictures, she smiled.

"Hey, you," she said.

Phil looked up, greeting her with a grin. "Wendy."

They walked toward each other, meeting for a hug. Wendy savored it, inhaling his distinct masculine scent mixed with a light hint of cologne. Man, did it ever feel good to be in his strong arms.

Just as she closed her eyes, Phil pulled away. It was as jarring as a douse of cold water. She popped her eyes open with lightning speed, hoping he hadn't noticed that she was enjoying the hug just a little too much.

Flustered, she looked up at him. "It's so good to see you again, Phil. You've been keeping way too busy with work."

"I know. But business is booming."

"That's always positive."

He nodded. Then, he gave her a quick once-over. "You're looking good."

"Thanks." But Wendy felt a tickle of disappointment in her stomach. He'd said the words in much the same way one would say, "Nice weather we're having." Like it was mandatory conversation, but not necessarily true.

"Let's sit down."

Phil walked back to the desk and Wendy followed him. He pulled a chair up beside his and patted the seat.

Sitting down next to him, Wendy glanced at the array of headshots on his desk. "What're all these for?"

"We're shooting a music video for a local rap group. They want women—hot women—and these are the headshots we've gotten from agents."

Wendy nodded her understanding. "They're pretty."

As Wendy watched him, Phil lifted one picture for closer examination. His eyes narrowed; he was suddenly in work mode. "Ginelle's a definite yes." He placed her picture to one side. "She's gorgeous."

"Hmm," Wendy replied. For some reason, she felt a twinge of jealousy. Not in a possessive way, but she suddenly wondered if Phil saw her as pretty.

Considering the way he had looked at her—or rather, the way he hadn't—Wendy couldn't help wondering if he thought of her as pretty in a sisterly-type way.

Which would suck.

"Anyway," Phil said. He slapped a palm on the table and turned his attention back to her. "I know you didn't come over to discuss headshots."

"No." Wendy chuckled softly, then leaned back

in the chair. She crossed one leg over the other, giving Phil an ample view of her thigh.

If he noticed, he didn't show it. "Give me the details of the project."

"Like I told you, Tyanna and I need to shoot a fitness video. We hadn't thought we would be doing one so quickly, but we heard back from Ronnie Vaughn's office sooner than expected. Anyway, we're hoping to shoot this video as quickly as possible. It's not going to be the best, we know, but hopefully good enough to get him interested. I know we have to work around your schedule, so we'll have to be as flexible as possible. If need be, Tyanna and I can reschedule our shifts at the gym. But if you can work it for a Sunday, that would be best, since Tyanna and I are both off on Sundays."

Phil pursed his lips, deep in thought. "And how soon is 'as quickly as possible'?"

"Hopefully in the next couple weeks. I still need time to figure out what our routine will be."

Phil nodded, still thinking.

"But if that isn't doable—"

"No," Phil said, cutting her off. "I'll figure something out. You know I'll always be there for you, any way I can." He gave her a soft smile. "Let me see what my schedule looks like for late next week. I should be able to do Sunday for sure. Even if it means bribing my guys with a few incentives."

Wendy leaned forward in the chair. She reached out and placed a hand on Phil's leg. "I will love you forever if you can work this out for us."

"Yeah, that's what they all say."

*But they don't all mean it*, Wendy thought.

Silence fell between them, and Wendy pulled back her hand. Had Phil even checked out her cleavage? She wasn't sure.

Phil turned back to his desk and scribbled some notes on a paper. Wendy bit her inner cheek, nervous. Should she take this moment to come on to him and make it real clear what her intentions were?

Before she got the chance, Phil pushed his chair back. "All right. I've got the info. I'll try to get next Sunday nailed down for you." He stood. "I hate to cut this short, Wendy, but I'm finally going to head home. It's been a long day. A long week."

Wendy stood as well. "I'm sure it has. You need to take a break."

"Hopefully one day soon."

He walked the few steps toward her and gave her an impromptu hug. "As always, it's a pleasure to see you." Then he kissed her on the cheek.

The kiss was . . . sweet. Not electric. Not exciting. Just . . . sweet.

But it was *something*. She had to cling to that.

And as Wendy made her way back to her car, she analyzed the possible meanings of the peck Phil had given her. Maybe it wasn't quite as chaste as it had seemed. . . .

"Oh, who are you kidding?" she asked herself as she got behind the wheel of the car. Her grandmother had given her more exciting kisses.

But she wasn't going to give up on Phil. At least not yet.

It was simply time for Plan B.

# Chapter 10

The glass of cold water helped somewhat, though what Sheldon had really wanted to do was dump the entire contents right on his crotch. Since this was out of the question, what he did was get down to the business of why he'd come over to Tyanna's place—and that was to discuss Dino.

He placed the empty glass on the coffee table, then cleared his throat. "So, Tyanna. Exactly what did you want to know?"

"I know you were surprised to hear from me, but I've been doing a lot of thinking," she began. "About what you told me. And—" She blew out a harried breath, suddenly nervous. Just the mere idea that Dino was some corrupt character had her feeling like she was living out a *Miami Vice* episode. "Anyway, I was thinking—the Sheldon I knew would never lie to me. Keep things from me, maybe, but not outright lie. Certainly not something so outrageous. So I'm figuring your story about

Dino is true." She didn't want to tell him she had talked to Leona. Telling him that would make her sudden interest in his story seem less genuine, like she couldn't believe him without proof.

And she truly was interested in hearing what he had to say. By keeping her chat with Leona out of this, she would avoid offending him.

"I'd like to hear the complete story," she continued. "If you don't mind sharing it."

"I don't mind."

"All right. Can I ask you something first?" Sheldon nodded, and she went on. "When you started working at the gym, did you know Dino Benedetto was a . . . a criminal?"

*Criminal* was an understatement. The man was a low-life S.O.B., but Dino had covered all that with a charming smile. *Like coating dog turd with honey.* "Yeah, I knew he was a criminal. When I first started working at the gym, my brother had already been murdered."

Tyanna shivered visibly.

"I know it's not a nice word, Tyanna, but that's exactly what happened." Sheldon swallowed painfully, remembering. He wondered if it would ever get easier. "He was found in an alley with two bullets in the back of his head."

Tyanna gasped, throwing a hand to her mouth. "Oh my God."

Sheldon's face twisted as the image of his brother, alone and dying in that alley, flooded his brain. "Yeah, it was tough."

"And you're sure it was Dino?"

"I can't be sure if Dino was the one who actually pulled the trigger, but if not him personally, then it was one of his henchmen. When I told you that Dino is connected to organized crime, I wasn't kidding. He grew up in New York, and apparently is affiliated with some mob family. I know—it sounds too incredible to be true. And at first I thought he was talking a big game, trying to sound like some tough guy no one could mess with. But I learned other things that made me believe his connection to the mob was fact."

"I know a lot of them love Florida for the weather," Tyanna commented. "At least that's what I've seen on some of A & E's crime shows."

"I think Dino would have stayed in New York, but it sounds like he pissed some people off there and his father sent him to Florida. Gambling debts or something, which his father had to pay for him. I know that even though he ran the juice bar, wore a Rolex and drove fancy cars, he claimed poverty when it came to his taxes."

"What?"

"Everything was in his father's name."

Tyanna rolled her eyes. "Brother."

"Tell me about it. His father had a lot of money, and so did he. He had a legitimate business with the juice bar, but it wasn't enough for him. It was like he couldn't be happy unless he was doing something underhanded. I'll never understand that mentality."

"Neither will I." Though Tyanna had parents who were well off, she had taken care of herself since college. And while there were times when she'd had to do some penny-pinching, she had never even considered anything illegal. Why would someone with money even bother to take the risk that came with committing crimes? She supposed they must get some sort of high out of it.

She asked, "What did the police say about the murder?"

"Not much. They investigated, of course, but there wasn't enough evidence to lock Dino up and throw away the key. I'm not sure Dino actually pulled the trigger. Actually, I'm sure he didn't. The police said he had an ironclad alibi. But I know he ordered the hit."

As much as Tyanna wanted to believe that the bad guys always got what was coming to them, she knew that wasn't true. Criminals often got away with murder, simply because they were smart and took the time to carefully plan their crimes. "I don't know what to say, Sheldon. If anything ever happened to any of my sisters— especially something senseless like that—I have no clue what I'd do."

"The first few months were unbearable. The police couldn't act without evidence, and each day that went by—watching my mother go through hell—I knew I had to do something. Because I was working in fitness, it was easy enough for me to get a job at the gym. And from there, I started hanging around the juice bar, getting close to Dino."

Tyanna looked at Sheldon, watched the pained expression on his face. She wished there was something she could do to take away his agony, but knew there wasn't.

After a moment, she said, "You know, that's one thing I'm confused about. Not that I talked to your mother every day, but she never mentioned Dwight."

Sheldon shrugged. "I guess it brings her down. It was pretty hard for both of us to even talk about it together. I just knew I needed to take action."

It was a plausible explanation. Tyanna could understand the subject being too painful even to mention. "So you got a job at the gym," she prompted, reminding Sheldon where he had left off.

"Mmm hmm. About a month before you did."

"Help me understand this, Sheldon. Why didn't you tell me about Dwight before now?" She thought of all the nights they had lain in her bed, how she'd shared her dreams and heartbreaks with him. How could he not tell her about something so important in his life? He had left before her brother-in-law's tragic accident, but if he had been around she would have leaned on him for support. Why hadn't he felt he could do the same with her?

He didn't have to tell her the circumstances of Dwight's death if it was too hard to talk about, but he could have at least shared with her that he had had a brother.

"When I started working at the gym," Sheldon began in reply, "I had one purpose. To get enough evidence to put Dino away. When you started working there—you weren't part of the plan. You were actually a snag. And when I say that, I mean that I'd hoped I could work at the gym and see Dino put in jail without forming any attachments with anyone."

Tyanna remembered how they'd met. How she had been more intrigued by his quiet nature than put off. What had started off as "hi" and "how are you" had progressed to slightly longer conversations, then longer still. Eventually, she had been the one to ask him out for a drink, and was almost surprised when he accepted.

Sheldon was hard to read, but there was something about him that drew her to him. Her parents would say that she was attracted to trouble, but that wasn't it. There was a vulnerability in Sheldon's eyes, even when he tried to hide it, and that had intrigued her.

Like her, Sheldon was a personal trainer at Ultimate Fitness, working with clients on a day-to-day basis. But after a couple months, she noticed that he was spending more and more time with Dino behind the juice bar. Helping out if he didn't have a client at the time. Staying after his scheduled shift was over to work with Dino. She hadn't thought anything of it, other than that Sheldon and Dino were forming a close friendship.

"You and Dino seemed pretty tight," Tyanna pointed out.

"And that's exactly the way I wanted it. I had to get to the point where he would trust me. Let me into his inner circle. It wasn't like I had applied for a job at the juice bar. But that was where I needed to be. To get the information I needed." He paused. "Surprisingly enough, Dino trusted me after a while. I'd drop a hint here and there that I'd had a violent past, as if I was testing him, and he slowly started to open up. If he had someone else from New York down here, he probably wouldn't have taken me into his confidence, but he really needed help with his operation. He had mentioned having a cousin who had lived in Florida for a while, who worked with him at the juice bar, so I assume that's who was doing his dirty work. Apparently, that cousin had moved back to New York.

"Anyway, I didn't want Dino to know that I cared about anyone at the gym, which is why I kept my personal life totally secret. Because if he did know, that could have been dangerous for anyone I was involved with. These guys stop at nothing when they want to get back at someone. He could smile with you one day, and dump you along Alligator Alley the next—just to make sure he hurt me."

"Gosh, that's the stuff of all those crime movies."

"Exactly. As it turned out—since I got caught going through his stuff—it was a good thing that Dino didn't know we were involved. He would've gone to you immediately after he made me. And if I had told you about Dwight, you could have mentioned it in passing to someone else, and it could have gotten back to Dino." Sheldon paused. "Why are you looking at me like that?"

"I don't know. You almost seem like a different person. I guess you never spoke so . . . freely to me before." Which was true. Even when she thought about it now, she wondered what had attracted her so fiercely to him. In the seven months they'd been together, he had never showed her any affection at work. Well, nothing special anyway. He pretty much kept her at arm's length in the gym, which was difficult because she loved being romantic.

And for her, romantic meant being touchy feely. It meant giving impromptu kisses and hugs, and handholding if she felt like it. Which had surprised Tyanna as much as anyone. She couldn't remember having felt that way about someone before—wanting to be so openly demonstrative. Not even in eighth grade when she'd had her first crush, on Stan Carlton. So in a way, it had hurt her when Sheldon had not returned her affections.

Of course, he had more than made up for his lack of public attention in the privacy of her apartment.

"I had to be a different person then," Sheldon said simply.

Tyanna brought the conversation back to Dino. "You said Dino was selling steroids? Tell me about that."

"Hell—where do I start? I knew about that right from the beginning, because of my brother, but it took Dino nearly five months to trust me enough to let me know he was selling steroids at the gym. Like I said, I figure he needed someone, and he thought I was a badass because of some of the stories I'd told him. Willing to do anything.

"As for the steroids, he had his hand into all kinds of stuff. Anabolic and anti-catabolic steroids, fertility drugs for testosterone production. Growth hormones. There was a ton of money in it. Some of the serious bodybuilders spend over a hundred grand a year on all this stuff."

Wow. That was a lot of "stuff." Sheldon made it seem like the juice bar must have been a steroid junkie bar. "I never saw anything," said Tyanna.

"Some people did. They suspected what he was up to. Proving it was another matter. Even for me, proving it was tough. And I think he was giving the gym's manager a cut to keep his mouth shut."

"Stranger things have happened."

"My brother had told me about Dino's ex-girlfriend—and this is where Dwight really got into trouble. Apparently, when Maria broke up with Dino after dating him for four months, he wanted her killed." When Tyanna's eyes widened, Sheldon said, "I'm serious. I know. This all seems too strange to be true."

"Wait a minute," Tyanna said. "Back up. What ex-girlfriend?"

"Before I started to work at the gym, Dino had been dating a girl named Maria. It sounds like they moved in together after only a month. She apparently knew everything about his business operations. The guy wasn't particularly bright, sharing that kind of information with a lover so quickly. But it was all part of the New York mobster image that he was so desperate to convey."

"I never saw it. But then, I didn't really hang out with him."

"Anyway," Sheldon continued, "Dino apparently had a real temper, and when he and Maria fought, he scared her. She had grown tired of the relationship and wanted to get away from him. Plus, she found God, and after that, she didn't want to support his illegal business operation any longer."

Tyanna chuckled sarcastically. "She found God?"

"So my brother said. She used to talk to Dwight about Dino, about how he scared her when he got angry. She wanted to get away from him, but wanted to leave so he wouldn't find her. Dwight helped her do that. Told her how to hide. According to Dwight, when Maria up and moved out one day when Dino was at the gym, Dino questioned him about it. Several times. He knew that Maria and Dwight had become friends and he suspected Dwight had helped her. Even though he didn't have any proof, my brother noticed a difference in Dino's attitude toward him."

"Good Lord."

"One of the things Dino wanted me to do when he started to trust me was find Maria. And I knew why—because he still wanted her dead." Sheldon held up both hands at Tyanna's startled gaze. "This has the makings of a TV movie, absolutely. I know that. But it's true. The guy was so obsessed with her, so pissed, he wasn't thinking rationally. So I told him how I had an ex-girlfriend who did me wrong, and how I hoped she would die a painful death."

"Sheldon!"

"Because of what Dwight had told me, I knew that Dino had it bad for Maria. So, I played like I had an ex I really hated. And it worked. I made this ex out to be a total tramp, someone who'd cheated on me, taken money from me. But as for Maria—I couldn't figure out why Dino was so angry with her, except for the fact that she'd left him. I guess no one was allowed to leave him and get away with it."

"Brother."

"Anyway, after looking for Maria for a couple

months, Dino suddenly puts it on the table that he wants to see her dead for a price. I know this was Dino's way of testing me, considering I'd made myself out to be a guy with a temper and a dislike for certain members of the opposite sex. So I had to act as if I would be down with that."

"How did you play along with such a horrific plan?"

"I kept thinking of my brother. I wanted Dino put away."

"Did you find her?"

"He gave me all her old cellphone records, her family's information. Every lead turned up a dead end. About another three weeks after he'd put the death request on the table, I got lucky and was able to track her down through an old friend."

"My God. What happened?"

"I wasn't about to have her blood on my hands, that's for sure. I never let Dino know that I'd tracked her down. But I did get ahold of her for my purposes. I asked her about the steroids and what she knew about Dino's operation."

Frowning, Tyanna shook her head. "I still can't believe that Dino could be capable of any of this. Murder plots. Illegal steroids. Honestly, I feel as though you've zapped me into the twilight zone."

"But you believe me?" There was almost a desperate quality to his tone.

She didn't want to, simply because she didn't

want to believe that the Dino she'd cared about as a colleague could be so coldhearted and evil. But she knew he was dead. And if he'd been killed by the police, then that meant that the rest of Sheldon's story had to be true. "Yes. I believe you."

"That really means a lot, Tyanna."

She saw something stir in Sheldon's eyes, something that disturbed her. And she felt a pull in her own stomach.

This couldn't be happening. They couldn't be talking about murder and mayhem and actually be feeling the stirrings of desire.

Or could they?

# Chapter 11

Tyanna swallowed, uncomfortable with the sudden direction of her thoughts. She didn't like them—not one bit. They were completely inappropriate.

The last thing she wanted was for this conversation to steer off course, so she gave him only a slight nod in recognition of his comment. Then she went on. "So your brother was helping Dino sell the steroids?"

"Unfortunately. He had started off working as an assistant in the juice bar. The next thing, he's involved in this shit? I don't know how the hell he got caught up in that, but Dwight was always the type of guy to follow, not lead. I'm sure Dino offered him a lot of money to do the pickups, to make sure that if anything ever happened—like someone getting caught—Dino wouldn't be the one caught with his hands dirty."

"I'm sure your brother wasn't the only one involved. An illegal operation like that—it's got to take a whole crew."

Sheldon's lips curled in a small smile. He appreciated that she was trying to make him feel better through all of this. It was a quality that had attracted him to her in the beginning, her caring nature.

"I'm sure of that too," Sheldon told her. "Not to put down my brother, but he didn't have the initiative to start this kind of illegal operation. But he could drive a car, pick up some packages for some cash. Keep an eye out at the gym while Dino administered steroid shots to his various clients in the back. Still, I wish to hell I'd known what he had gotten himself into at a time when I could have done something to stop it."

"Do you know who else was involved—the other members of Dino's operation?"

"I know Dino got his stuff via a connection in New York, and that person got the steroids from Mexico. I was trying to find out who his connections were so I could give the police a flawless trail. But Dino was very tight-lipped about that. You know the saying that there's no honor among thieves?"

"Yeah."

"Well, I figured that Dino didn't tell me about his contacts because he didn't want me to steal any business from him. I didn't press the issue. I just tried to snoop around as much as I could. And then when I finally got close—"

"Something went wrong," Tyanna supplied.

"Yes. Like I said before, Dino caught me in the back of the juice bar one day going through his personal files. Stuff I had no business touching. I tried to come up with some lame excuse, but he wasn't hearing it. And the expression on his face—it was like he was looking at me for the first time."

"Dwight," Tyanna said softly.

"Yeah. I guess he finally saw the slight resemblance. Anyway, I knew I was in trouble. Serious trouble. All I could do was get in my car and take off."

"You mean you left right then?"

"Yeah. I didn't even go home, because Dino knew where I lived, and I was certain he would send someone there to take me out. I had been so careful—then I screwed everything up."

"If you didn't go home, where did you go?"

"First, I went to the bank and took out every penny I had. I couldn't chance using credit cards. I called my mother from a pay phone and told her that if anyone called asking about me to deny she knew me. I had given Dino a false surname, and because I didn't officially work for him, he never knew me by anything else. But he knew Dwight's last name, which meant that once he made me, he would no doubt start looking for anyone named Ford. After that, I just drove. For days. I headed north, to get as far away as possible. I finally ended up in Kansas City. I have some relatives there."

"Not a girlfriend?" Tyanna asked, though she was pretty sure of his answer.

"No. I didn't have some other girlfriend. I eventually told my mother that so she would tell you that story. She told me you'd been asking about me. And . . . I wanted you to forget me."

Even though she had heard his entire story, those words stung. When Mrs. Ford had told her that Sheldon had a new girlfriend and a new life two months after he'd taken off, Tyanna had been devastated. Before that, she had hoped he would come back to her and give her the kind of story he'd given her now—something to explain his out-of-character behavior.

But when she'd learned that he had a new girlfriend . . . So many nights she had been tortured by the image of Sheldon and someone else. Kissing some other woman the way he'd once kissed her. Touching her the same way.

Making love to her with the same kind of passion.

Tyanna steeled herself against the hurt the memories brought. She said, "Like it was supposed to be that easy to forget you."

"Nothing about this was easy," he countered. "But I had to keep you safe. If you were angry with me, disillusioned by what I'd done, you were less likely to look for me. And if Dino by any chance found out about our relationship—then subsequently learned how pissed you were with me after I'd taken off—he would have been less likely to bother with you. At least that's what I hoped."

Tyanna drew in an uneasy breath. His story, his reasoning—it made sense. But still it hurt. "I wish you would have told me."

"I couldn't risk it."

"You didn't trust me."

"This wasn't about trust."

"Wasn't it?"

"I did the best thing I could."

"Really?" She gave him a hard look, but he didn't say anything. "What exactly do you think I would have done if you'd told me the truth about Dino? Gone to the gym all emotional and confronted him?"

"Maybe not intentionally."

"At least I would have understood. I wouldn't have gone half out of my mind with worry." Her eyes narrowed. "And what do you mean 'not intentionally'?"

"Tyanna, if you knew what Dino was truly about, you might have acted differently around him. I wouldn't have blamed you; it's only natural. Maybe you wouldn't have." He shrugged. "It was a chance I couldn't take."

"You should have told me," Tyanna insisted. "Given me more credit," she added pointedly. "I could have quit. Gotten a job somewhere else." *Gone with you.* "At least I would have understood what was going on. I wouldn't have gone crazy worrying."

"Wouldn't you? If you knew that Dino had connections to organized crime around half the country, you're going to tell me you wouldn't worry about me, no matter where I was?"

Tyanna opened her mouth to speak, but promptly shut it. He'd caught her with that one.

"Exactly."

Tyanna shot to her feet. "Don't give me that. Like you made the right decision. And so easily." She could hardly believe her ears. At least at this point, she hoped he would have understood the gravity of the decision he had made, how hard it had been for her. Show some regret over that. "Do you have any idea what I went through, Sheldon? Wondering what the hell had happened to you? Wondering if you were dead or alive? Maybe I didn't know about Dino, but with the way you just disappeared . . . I worried about you anyway. I was terrified that you were dead. I watched the news for stories of any unidentified bodies turning up, car accidents. I was afraid to call your mother initially, because I dreaded hearing bad news. I know it doesn't make sense, because I wanted to know, but then I wondered if I could really handle knowing something awful had happened to you.

"I waited a good few days before calling your mother. I was relieved to learn that you were okay, but she didn't know why you'd left or where you were, and once again, I thought that maybe you had an accident wherever you'd been driving to. Sure, the doubts had started in my mind, but I pushed them aside, even while my family kept telling me they were sure you'd dumped me but didn't have the courage to say so. But I couldn't—"

Tyanna stopped abruptly when she felt the sting of tears. Even now, the memory of that time hurt. She had never known she could care for a man the way she had cared for Sheldon, and his disappearing had almost been her undoing. But she'd be damned if she'd let her emotions get the better of her.

"Then when I got that *lame* letter from you in the mail—all I heard was 'I told you so' from my relatives. Do you know how that made me feel? I looked like a fool. I called your mother to find out what was really going on, and that's when she told me—reluctantly—that you had apparently moved away to be with another woman."

"Fine," Sheldon said. "Maybe I didn't do the right thing."

"Maybe?"

"I was afraid, Tyanna. I had no clue what the right thing was."

"You cared about yourself."

Sheldon was on his feet in a flash. Before Tyanna knew what was happening, he had gripped her upper arms and drawn her toward him.

For a full five seconds, neither of them spoke. Their hot breaths mingled, and Sheldon was aware of the rise and fall of Tyanna's chest. He looked into her eyes, at the surprise in their depth, and he damn near forgot what the hell he'd been talking about.

"I cared about you, Tyanna," he managed on a ragged breath. "Yes, I was afraid for myself. But if anything had happened to you, something because I'd been too stupid to keep my emotions in check . . ."

"Seems like that's all you ever did."

Ouch. The words hurt more than he'd expected. Despite the fact that they were true.

Tyanna continued to stare up at him, her eyes challenging him to deny what she'd just said. He remembered the fire, the passion of their relationship. And soon his thoughts were venturing beyond the parameters of their current conversation. His gaze lowered, settling on those full lips of hers. They were moist and slightly parted, almost like she was silently begging him to kiss her.

So, God help him, he did. A deep moan rumbled in his chest as his mouth covered hers, anticipation and desire spilling forth in a mind-numbing combination. Sweet Jesus, it had been so long.

At first she was stiff, but her body soon relaxed in his arms. Her lips opened wider, accepting more of him, and his tongue delved hungrily into her hot mouth. His hands were tangled in her shoulder-length ebony hair. He could no longer think. Only feel. And what he felt was hot and wet and turning him on more than he'd ever imagined possible.

Damn, he'd lived without this too long.

He was aware of her body leaning into his, of her soft breasts pressing against his hard chest, her arms slipping around his neck. Her soft mewling.

His rock-hard erection.

A year had passed, but it was just the way it had always been between them. Once they touched, it was all fire and need.

Sheldon's hands urgently roamed Tyanna's body. He pressed his palms into her back, then dragged them lower, cupping her buttocks. Christ, he wanted to rip off these damn athletic shorts she was wearing with one hard pull. He wanted to feel her naked body against his.

He wanted himself inside her warm softness.

"Tyanna . . ." He growled. "Ah, baby. It still feels so good."

His hands moved for the waist of her shorts, and there they paused. He waited for some reaction from Tyanna, a gentle movement that would let him know he should continue.

There was something different about what he was feeling with her today. . . . Intense was the only word that would come close to describing it. He'd wanted her before with every fiber of his being, but this feeling was different. It was the kind of feeling that consumed him completely, in a way that frightened him.

Tyanna moaned softly and pulled away. As she looked at him, she brought the back of her hand to her mouth. "Sheldon . . ."

Sheldon was suddenly disturbed, and he didn't know why. He turned away, needing to gulp in air. This was, as he'd known it would be, dangerous territory.

"Sheldon, I . . ."

She didn't finish her statement. Sheldon didn't say a word. He couldn't.

After a moment, she said, "I don't think you should be here."

He slowly turned back to look at her. Tyanna stood with her arms crossed over her chest, a confused expression on her face.

She was right, of course. Things had gotten out of hand. But damn, if he didn't want to pick up where they'd left off a year ago. "I know this all seems fast. Out of the blue, even."

"When you left, I had to go on."

"I understand."

"Then what do you want from me?"

Sheldon simply stared at her, unsure of what to say. What did he want?

"I'm still attracted to you," he finally said.

"And you want to sleep with me?"

"Is that so wrong? I mean, your body still reacts to mine. . . ."

Tyanna chuckled mirthlessly.

"Tyanna—"

"No, Sheldon." Her eyes met his, her expression unreadable. "Sex. I know, I shouldn't be surprised. And sure, it would be so easy to fall into bed with you again. But my heart's not there." And even if it was to some degree, it sure as hell shouldn't be. "I've moved on. You gave me no choice."

And while it had hurt, she was much better for his breaking off the relationship. She was back to her old self again, no longer deluded by this thing called love.

What had happened with Sheldon had proven to her that no matter when the end came, it always did, and it was bound to be painful. She needed to protect her heart, and the truth was that Sheldon was still a threat.

"I'm trying to figure out who I really am," Tyanna went on. "What I'm supposed to do with my life. I can't be a personal trainer forever."

"It suits you."

"For now. I know I'm not a nine-to-five–type girl—that much is a given. But it will be much easier to figure out what I'm supposed to do if I'm on my own." *And if your touch isn't distracting me.*

Sheldon nodded, though his eyes told a different story. "I didn't come here planning to do this. But I guess . . . Well, I guess sex was always easy for us."

"Maybe too easy."

Sheldon's eyebrows shot up. "And that's a bad thing?"

"I'm not saying that. But I think we probably

concentrated more on sex than on the relationship. Sex won't keep a relationship alive. When I look back, there's a lot that was missing."

The question "Like what?" was on the tip of Sheldon's tongue, but he held it in check. A man had to have a bit of pride, didn't he?

So instead, he said, "Yeah, I guess you're right."

"Good. That means you understand why . . . why this would be a bad idea. I know you were in a tough situation, but the fact that you could just walk away . . . That says something. It says a lot. Maybe I didn't give you something you needed, or maybe the relationship was strictly about sex. I don't know." Tyanna shrugged. "All I know is that looking back, it certainly wasn't about love."

Aw, shit. Not that. And she even said it with a straight face.

If this was a test, he knew he'd just failed. He cared about Tyanna, yes. But love?

There were many days when Sheldon had lain in bed, wondering just what love was. He knew he felt strongly for Tyanna. But the word *love* got stuck in his throat the few times he even thought of saying it to her.

And he knew it was a bone of contention with her.

His old man had used the word all the time, threw it around so often it became meaningless. Maybe he wouldn't have felt that way if his father hadn't beat the crap out of his mother all the time.

How could he hurt her so often, reduce her to tears, yet turn around and say "I love you," like that made everything all right?

"Our relationship wasn't as superficial as you make it out to be," Sheldon finally said.

Tyanna hesitated just a moment, and that moment said everything. She didn't think he loved her. And maybe he didn't, if he couldn't say the words.

But to say the words now—that would be like applying a Band-Aid—exactly what his father had done time and time again.

"Regardless, it's over. Look, I'm sorry about what you went through. But I'm glad you're okay. I'm glad that Dino got what he deserved, considering everything."

"But can we be friends?" Sheldon asked, cutting her off before she could deal the final blow. "No matter what you think, I'll always care about you. I never lied when I told you that. I want to be able to call you from time to time, see if you're okay. Maybe even hang out now and again."

He had long ago realized that it didn't matter what he felt for her, because her family would never approve of him. Therefore, they could never have a future. So he'd been content to live in the moment until things came to an end. But there was a part of him that knew he would always care about her, always want to know she was happy, and always want her in his life on some level.

"I think . . . I think we can work toward that," Tyanna told him. "That's the best I can offer you."

"All right."

"Thanks for coming by. I appreciate it."

So she was kicking him out. "No problem."

She walked to the door, and he followed her. "I'll talk to you later, okay?"

Sheldon nodded as she opened the door. He stepped over the threshold into the hallway. "Call me whenever you feel like it," he said.

She smiled at him, but Sheldon wasn't sure it was sincere. "Sure."

Then she closed the door, leaving him standing there wondering if he would ever hear from her again.

## Chapter 12

*Not the phone*, Tyanna thought when it rang the next day around noon. She was still lying in bed, preoccupied with her thoughts, and didn't feel like talking to anyone now.

But when it stopped ringing and then promptly began ringing again, she grabbed the receiver from her night table.

"What?" she practically shouted into it.

"Whoa. What the hell kind of greeting is that?"

A slow breath oozed out of Tyanna. "I'm sorry, Wendy. I've got a lot on my mind."

"Anything you want to talk about?"

"Not really." She didn't want to tell Wendy about Sheldon's visit, and how she hadn't been able to get him out of her mind since the previous evening. How she was hot and bothered and didn't know when she'd stop feeling this way. "But," she added, "I'm sure you'll keep asking me questions until I tell you." She smiled, hoping the lightheartedness came through.

"Hey, where would you be without me?" Wendy chuckled.

Tyanna sat up, suddenly ready to talk. Wendy was the one person she felt comfortable sharing everything with.

"It's Sheldon. I never got to tell you, but I went to my old gym and talked to a woman who worked there when I did. And you'll never believe this. Sheldon was telling the truth when he said that Dino was dead." Tyanna filled Wendy in on all the details. "After that, I figured I should let him tell me the whole story. So I called him and he came by last night."

"Hold up. He was in your apartment."

"Yes, and nothing happened."

"Wow. That's some kind of miracle."

Tyanna guffawed. "Wendy, it would hardly be appropriate." But the truth was, she was still wondering how she had had the ability to push Sheldon away, considering how much her body had wanted him. "We're no longer a couple."

"Mmm hmm," Wendy replied in that I-hear-you-but-I-don't-believe-you tone. "You're telling me nothing happened?"

"I—well, not exactly."

Wendy squealed her delight. "I knew it!"

"He kissed me," Tyanna went on. For some reason, it felt good to get this off her chest. She'd needed to share it with someone. "We kissed each other. But I pulled away."

"I can understand that," Wendy said, surprising Tyanna. "You're in a tough situation. It's not like you can realistically pick up where you left off."

"Exactly. Besides, I'm not sure if he even wants to pick anything up. Or if I want to. The problem is, when it comes to sex, we've always been on the same page. But I don't want to go there just for the sake of my body's desires."

"So what's gonna happen? You two gonna be friends?"

Tyanna twirled the phone cord in her hand. That was something she had thought about all last night. "I really don't know," she admitted. "I'm not against talking to him from time to time, knowing that he is okay. But at this point in my life, my career is my number-one priority."

"I hear you. Anything you do, you'll have to take it slow."

"Exactly."

"But you know, I hope it works out. Sheldon was always a sweetie."

Tyanna shook her head, a small smile lifting her lips. Wendy, Miss Romantic. "What about you, Wendy? Anything new and exciting in your life?"

"I saw Phil last night." Wendy debated telling Tyanna about how she'd gotten all spiffed up in an attempt to get Phil's attention, but decided against it. There was nothing to tell. Besides, she was merely on a break at the gym, and going into her feelings for Phil would probably take a while.

"Great," Tyanna said. "What did he say about using the video equipment?"

"He's such a sweetheart. Totally willing to help us. You think we can pull this off two weeks from now?"

"Omigosh! Two weeks!" Butterflies tickled Tyanna's stomach. "Uh, I guess so, but that means we have a ton of work to do."

"I know. We have to start the planning right now. I was trying to figure out some of the routine this morning. One of my clients didn't show."

"Any luck?"

"A little. I know we can pull this off. Besides, failure is not an option."

"That's right," Tyanna said, psyching herself up. "We have to do this. And the sooner the better."

"I know it sounds cheesy," Wendy went on, "but I was thinking we could do the video on the beach. With the ocean as the backdrop. It would be a lot nicer than some closed-in studio."

"No, I don't think that's cheesy. It sounds like a good idea. When are we going to get together?" Though they worked at the same gym, they worked different hours. When Wendy was leaving work, Tyanna was just getting there.

"I've got two days off this week. Tuesday and Sunday. If you want, we can meet around noon at the gym on Tuesday and see about using a room to practice our routine. I'd rather we get together before Sunday."

"Yeah, of course. That sounds like a plan."

"All right, hon. I have to get off the phone. My next client should be here any minute."

"Okay, sweetie. If I don't talk to you before then, I'll see you tomorrow at the gym."

"Later."

Tyanna disconnected and dragged herself out of bed. She opened the blinds, letting the sunlight spill into her room.

The view of the ocean took her breath away. It always did. She would never tire of its beauty.

And that was the jolt she needed to get up and stop moping over Sheldon. It was too beautiful a day, and she was wasting it.

She would head to the beach for a swim, then shower before she went to work.


"One . . . two . . . nice and easy . . . three. Slow it down so you can really feel your muscles working . . . four . . . that's it . . . five . . . six . . . seven." Tyanna finished off the count to ten as Mandy continued to push down on the Nautilus machine for abs. With her last repetition, Mandy came up a little too quickly, and the weights slammed against each other.

Mandy flashed her a sheepish grin. "Sorry about that."

"No, that's fine. You were excellent, Mandy," Tyanna told her with enthusiasm. "You did real well today." She'd been working with Mandy for a couple months, and in that time she had greatly increased her weight levels on the various machines.

"It doesn't always feel that way." Mandy released a long breath as she stood.

"A good workout is always tough. But at least you're seeing results."

"Yes," Mandy replied, smiling widely. "Twenty-one pounds. And I finally have hope that my belly will truly disappear. Little Ashley was worth it, but man, it's about time I get my body back."

Tyanna smiled. This was the rewarding thing about her job. Seeing how happy people were once they began to achieve the results they wanted. "You should be proud of yourself, Mandy." Tyanna gently patted her shoulder in support. "See you Wednesday, same time, for your lower body workout."

"Ugh," Mandy said, but the happy expression on her face belied her tone.

"Am I that bad?" Tyanna asked, her tone playful.

"No, you're great."

"All right. I'll see you Wednesday."

"See you then."

While Mandy went to the water fountain to hydrate herself, Tyanna headed toward her office. She stopped abruptly when she saw Wendy standing approximately five feet in front of her.

Wendy wiggled her fingers at her. "Hey, Tyanna."

"What are you doing here? I thought you worked this morning."

"I did. But while I was here, I checked the aerobics schedule and it looks like they've started another step-aerobics class for the time we wanted to use the room tomorrow."

"Oh, no."

"Mmm hmm. You know how they're always changing things here. Can't make any plans. Anyway, I was wondering if you had any free time this afternoon. We could maybe go over the basic routine, figure some things out on paper."

"Yeah, sure."

"Then tomorrow, we'll have to find somewhere else to do some actual practicing. I was thinking even the beach—if you don't mind the looks we're gonna get."

There were enough freaks in South Florida that Tyanna didn't think they'd garner any more attention than the average person out there. "It doesn't sound like we have much choice. Unless we get Max to allow us to use the club after hours. Which we probably could, but you work so early . . ."

"We'll play it by ear."

"All right." Tyanna started walking, and Wendy fell into step beside her. "For now, let's talk in my office. I've got fifteen minutes before my next appointment."

Jaguar Fitness had a great reputation and was one of the area's busiest fitness facilities. For that reason, both Wendy and Tyanna were pretty much completely booked during their respective shifts. Sometimes their clients didn't show, but they couldn't plan a practice schedule around that.

They both sat in Tyanna's office. Wendy said, "When I talked to Phil yesterday, I didn't give him any specifics. Of course, I don't have any. So I'm hoping we can narrow some things down as soon as possible. The better prepared we are the smoother things will go."

"Makes sense."

"We tossed around the idea of shooting this at the beach, and I really love that. What about you?"

"Sure. Let's go with it."

"Given that, I think it makes even more sense to rehearse at the beach. But I don't think the beach is going to be conducive to step aerobics unless we set up some kind of platform."

"We don't have to do step aerobics," Tyanna said. Wendy had a background in that area, so it would be easy for her to design such a program.

"Not necessarily, but I think we'd still have to put up some kind of platform in any case. A few mats on the sand isn't going to cut it."

Tyanna sat back, considering Wendy's words. "We could, but that's going to be more work. Lugging it there and back. Not impossible, just tedious."

"That's what I was thinking."

"Hmmm." Tyanna folded her arms over her

chest. "You know, it's possible we can use my parents' house. You should see their backyard. It's lush. Very pretty. It backs onto a canal. And they've got a great pool."

Wendy's eyes lit up. "That's an idea."

"I know the ocean is a great backdrop, but their place still looks very tropical."

"Well, it is."

"And it will come off that way on camera." Tyanna nodded, mostly to herself. "We won't have any interruptions. Sound won't be a problem."

"How big is the area around the pool?" Wendy asked. "Big enough for a camera crew and us to be working?"

"For sure. The backyard is huge. This is my parents' 'we moved on up' house. It's beautiful. There's even a hot tub and sauna."

"Nice."

"Not that we'll incorporate that into the video." Tyanna smiled. "I'll give them a call and ask their permission, but I'm sure it will be okay."

"Oh, good. That'll be a major relief to finalize that. Then we have to figure out when. . . ."

"And what we're going to do." Tyanna leaned her body across the desk. "Kickboxing is popular, but I think there are too many videos out there like that. I was thinking about something like jazzercise, but again, that's not an entirely original concept. I don't want to do anything that will come off as dated, or like we're wannabes. I think we need to put together a video that shows we know the business of fitness and are in this for the long haul."

Wendy grinned. "I love how you think."

"That's why we get along so well."

"All right. So we should think of a way to blend the classic with the contemporary?"

"Yeah. And we could incorporate a few different things. Like making step aerobics, kickboxing and dance part of the routine. Show our versatility. That way, Ronnie Vaughn will know we can branch out." Tyanna paused to bite her bottom lip. "Gosh, I can't believe we're really sitting here talking about this. That we actually have this opportunity."

"I know. I'm trying not to *think* about it too much. Just get down to business, so I don't feel overwhelmed."

Tyanna looked at her watch, then pushed her chair back. "Oh, shoot. I've got to go. My next appointment should be here."

They stood. "Okay," Wendy said. "I'll try to come up with a varied routine. In the meantime, think about music. It's got to be great."

"Ooh. Speaking of which, I wonder if we can use whatever we want in a sample video, or if we'd have to get permission from the artists."

"Good point." Wendy began walking as Tyanna did. "I know Phil says there are generic beats available on the computer. We can probably do something like that to avoid problems. We'll see."

Reaching the open area of the gym, Tyanna gave Wendy a hug. "I'll talk to you later."

"Ciao for now."

For the rest of the day, Tyanna's mind was on Ronnie Vaughn and the routine she and Wendy would perform on the video.

She spent the few moments she had to herself in the aerobics room, watching what those fitness instructors incorporated into their routines. From time to time during the afternoon she even participated, just to get herself back into the swing of things.

It was easy to obsess over the routine, something she didn't want to do. She would trust Wendy to come up with something appropriate. Besides, she had the feeling that it wasn't so much the routine they did as how they performed it that would sell Ronnie Vaughn on the project.

Tyanna didn't want to jump the gun, but she figured she and Wendy had two of three essential qualities. They had the look and the enthusiasm. Now all they needed was to prove that they had the drive to get the job done within a reasonable time frame.

That thought comforted her through the rest of the evening and into the next day, when she and Wendy met at her apartment to go over a preliminary routine.

The routine Wendy had choreographed was in

the rough stages, but still it was impressive. Tyanna hadn't expected her to accomplish so much in such a short time.

This was going to work. She was sure of it. Wendy would be the primary instructor, the one who gave the verbal instructions to the audience. And Tyanna would follow her lead.

On Friday, Wendy hung around after her shift to see Tyanna, hoping they could practice if she got a free moment. They did, because luckily Tyanna had a cancellation—and they were able to grab some time in the aerobics room between classes.

They got their routine of jazzercise, dance moves, step-aerobics and kickboxing pretty much down. They still had to come up with a warm-up and cool-down, but they would work on that later. In the meantime, Tyanna would consider possible musical selections so they could use them the next time they practiced.

After Wendy left, Tyanna didn't have a moment's rest until just after nine P.M., when she finally took her lunch. She left the gym, went to a nearby sub shop and ordered a turkey submarine and a root beer. She brought the sub and soda back to her office, where she wanted to go through some files as she ate.

"Tyanna Calhoun, pick up line three. Tyanna Calhoun, line three."

Tyanna quickly wrapped up the half of the sub she hadn't finished eating and reached for the receiver, depressing the button for line three.

"This is Tyanna." There was no answer. "Hello?"

She heard a soft click, indicating that there was no longer anyone on the line.

Frowning, she replaced the receiver. Once again she reached for her sub. But just as she was about to unwrap it, she sensed someone behind her and turned.

Her heart slammed against her ribcage when she saw Sheldon standing there.

"Sheldon." Tyanna spoke his name almost reverently, which irked her. She didn't want him to think he had any chance of worming his way back into her life.

His lips curled in a smile. "Hey."

"Are you the one who just called me?" she asked, but her tone was accusing.

"No. Why?"

"I was paged and told that someone was on the line for me, but when I picked up, no one was there." He looked at her blankly, and she said, "No big deal." She paused. "What are you doing here?"

"I needed to see you," he said simply.

"I saw you on Sunday," she pointed out.

"That was five days ago. And since I hadn't heard from you, I wanted to make sure you were okay."

"I'm fine. Why wouldn't I be?"

He shrugged. "I don't know."

She gave him an odd look. "There's nothing else going on, is there?"

"No, nothing." He walked around her desk and took a seat opposite her. "But I guess I'm always going to worry about you. I just figured I'd come by, for my own peace of mind."

His words unnerved her. She wasn't sure how much of this she could deal with. His sudden appearance made a lie of what she'd told herself over the past five days—that if she never saw him again, it wouldn't matter.

She frowned at him. "I'm not sure what I'm to make of you coming to see me like this. You telling me you'll always worry about me."

He shrugged again, as if that gave all the answers.

Disappointment tickled her stomach. But what had she truly expected him to say? That he was in love with her? "I appreciate your concern, but as you can see, I'm perfectly fine."

"I guess you are."

"And I don't mean to be rude, but I think you should really let me be the one to call you the next time. When I'm ready to take that friendship step. Right now, I'm just not sure I'm ready for it. I've got a ton of things going on in my life."

"And when you see me here, will you ignore me, or will you at least say hi?"

"Here? Haven't you heard a word I've said?"

"Don't get all bent out of shape," Sheldon told

her, smiling to soften the words. "I'm trying to tell you that I've joined this gym."

Her mouth fell open, but she couldn't find any words to say to him. Finally, what came out was, "Sheldon, what are you doing?"

Hell if he knew. He only knew that he wanted to be around her. See her. Today, after not hearing from her for the week, he had almost gone crazy with worry.

There was something in his gut that told him something bad could happen. It wasn't logical, and Tyanna would call him crazy, but he wanted to be around to keep an eye on her to make sure she was safe.

"I just got a job at a youth center not too far from here," he explained.

"You did?" Her voice was deadpan.

"Yeah. I'll be counseling teens, supervising their sports programs. Stuff like that. And you know I like to work out. This gym is close to where I'm now working, and of course, it's one of the best facilities in Miami."

Tyanna eyed him warily. "I'm trying to figure this out. You stay away for a year, now you come back and you *need* to be near me. To make sure I'm okay?"

"I explained that."

"I know what you told me. The point is, we ended a year ago. You made that choice, Sheldon. Whatever the circumstances, we can't turn back the clock and change things." She took a deep breath before continuing. "So am I going to be thrilled to see you here all the time? Not particularly."

"I'm not going to hound you."

"No?"

"Of course not. I'm not a stalker."

"Could have fooled me," she muttered.

"I heard that," Sheldon said. He wore a playful grin. "Don't go having a hissy fit. I'll see you here from time to time. We don't have to be buddies, but we certainly don't have to be enemies."

Her eyes bulged as she stared at him. "*Hissy* fit? When have you ever known me to have a hissy fit?"

"Good," Sheldon said. "So there won't be a problem."

Oh, he was too much. Entirely too smooth. But she sure as hell didn't want him to think that he was rattling her in any way. "I don't have a problem with seeing you around here. It's a free country."

"Good." Sheldon paused. "Maybe we can make this official. Have a drink later and toast our friendship. Hmm?"

"Tonight?"

"Why not?"

Tyanna actually chuckled. Lord, the man was hardheaded. "A drink?"

"Sure. You're over me. We're friends. No big deal, right?"

"You got that straight."

"Then why do you still feel awkward around me?"

Tyanna opened her mouth, about to lie to him, then decided against it. She leaned across her desk. "Okay, Sheldon. You want the truth? I *am* a bit uncomfortable around you."

Finally she was coming clean. Which meant she felt it too. The spark that still lived between them. He couldn't have been the only one going crazy since last Sunday, remembering how they had been when they were together.

Suddenly his stomach fluttered as he waited for her to say the words he now longed to hear. *There's still chemistry between us, Sheldon. I dream about you being in my bed. . . .*

"I wonder where you get your nerve."

The fantasy promptly died. "W—what?"

"You told me you'd give me space. This isn't space. And quite frankly, I'm not impressed. If you must know, the way you're acting now is making me inclined to think there's no way we can be friends. You are totally not respecting me and how I feel."

Sheldon felt a hole growing in his stomach. He had hoped to come across as jovial and non-pressuring, but it hadn't worked. She was threatened by him.

He stood. He pondered what to say for a long moment, then said the only thing that came to his heart. "You're right. And I'm sorry."

Then he turned and walked out of Tyanna's office.

She watched him go, a bit surprised. Then she sat back in her chair, her shoulders drooping.

She should be happy. This is what she was telling him she wanted—some space.

So why did she feel a weird sense of frustration?

# Chapter 13

"Hey, Shirley," Tyanna said, approaching the main desk. It was Saturday afternoon, and Jaguar Fitness was filled with people.

"Hi, Tyanna. How are you?"

"Pretty good today. You?"

"Oh, today's looking to be a pretty good day."

Tyanna followed Shirley's gaze to the gym's floor. There were half a dozen muscle men working out.

She smiled to herself. Everyone knew how much Shirley loved coming in to work so she could check out the men.

"Do you have the aerobics schedule on hand for the coming week?" Tyanna asked her. She was hoping there was a time when she and Wendy could use the room.

"Yep." Shirley lifted a clipboard and passed it to Tyanna.

Tyanna perused the schedule. Great. Sunday afternoon was available for a good hour. She and Wendy both had the day off, and they could come

in here before Tyanna headed off to her parents'
place for dinner.

Other than Sunday, late in the afternoon on the
following Tuesday or Thursday also looked good.
She would be here anyway, and could probably
squeeze in a half hour with Wendy after her first
personal training session.

Yeah, this was doable.

"Thanks, Shirley."

"Uh-huh."

Shirley didn't even look Tyanna's way as she
reached for the clipboard, and Tyanna chuckled
softly. "You're too much, Shirley. I don't know
how you keep up with who comes and goes when
your head is always facing the back of the gym."

"Oh, I keep up with those who are worthy of
being noticed. Mmm. Look at those thighs. Have
you ever seen anything so powerful?"

Tyanna gave in. "All right. I'll bite. Which stud
are you checking out today?"

"He's on the far side. Using the leg press. The
brother with the golden brown skin."

Tyanna looked in that direction, smirking at
Shirley's brazen ogling. But the smile instantly
went flat when she realized exactly who Shirley
had been checking out.

"Hey, Tyanna. Isn't that the guy who came here
asking for you a week or so ago?"

"Oh." Tyanna did her best to pretend she
hadn't realized that. "Maybe. Yeah, probably."

Shirley scowled at her. "You had that man up

close and personal and you don't remember him?"

Tyanna shrugged nonchalantly. "I see a lot of hard bodies. After a while, they're all the same."

"Whatever, girl. Not that one." Shirley's gaze wandered back to Sheldon. "That body definitely stands out above the rest."

"Yeah, he's cute." Tyanna tapped the desk lightly, then headed toward her office.

*God*, her mind screamed. *Sheldon's here!* And dressed in an outfit that showed off his magnificent body.

What was she going to do? Work the gym floor with her clients and pretend he didn't exist? Last night, she thought she was game for this, but now she wasn't so sure.

She didn't care about saving face at this point. She knew she'd just feel better if he wasn't constantly around.

Tyanna settled behind her desk and looked over her schedule for the evening. But she hardly saw the words. The image of Sheldon in his athletic shorts and tank top kept interrupting her thoughts.

A long breath oozed out of her. She had a feeling this was going to be a long night.

Tyanna left the office area, rounded the corner and stopped cold. Her heart felt as if it was suddenly struggling to pump blood—as if someone had taken it out of her chest and flattened it with a steamroller.

Sheldon was practically draped across the gym's check-in desk, smiling like some kind of idiot, while Shirley had both hands under her chin and was laughing.

Tyanna had always hated that laugh.

Shirley threw her head back, giggling like a schoolgirl—not the twenty-something woman she actually was. Goodness, would the gym's manager continue to put up with Shirley so blatantly slacking off? The woman was here to do a job, not entertain select members.

And when had Sheldon come back? It was now close to midnight, and Tyanna's shift was practically over. Sheldon had left hours earlier, so what was he doing here again?

Gritting her teeth, Tyanna forced herself to start walking. She wasn't going to let Sheldon get to her. Her plan had been to head to the eucalyptus steam room to work out some of the kinks in her body, and she was going to go ahead with it. She had worked hard today, and she deserved this. She rarely treated herself to the sauna or steam room, even though she could use the facilities whenever she wanted.

As she headed toward the changing room, she once again heard the high pitch of Shirley's laughter. It suddenly seemed like a cackle.

"Oh, stop it," Tyanna told herself. If Shirley wanted to hang on Sheldon's every word, good for her.

She had better things to do.

Inside the changing room, Tyanna dug a towel out of her bag and headed for the shower. She stood under the cool spray for a long while. Afterward, she dressed in the black bikini she'd brought with her. It was a sexy number she'd picked up on St. Thomas while working on the cruise ship. She liked that it was simple, yet shimmered beneath the light. She'd gotten many compliments on it the few times she'd worn it.

Her belongings secured in a locker, Tyanna took her towel and made her way out to the eucalyptus steam room. She would hit the dry sauna after that.

Let Sheldon stay out there and talk to Shirley. Tyanna was going to enjoy a good forty minutes of pure relaxation.

Tyanna sat with her back pressed against the ceramic-tile wall of the steam room, her eyes closed, her legs crossed in front of her. She inhaled and exhaled slow and easy breaths, which made it much easier to deal with the heat.

As she had hoped, she was completely relaxed, and it felt wonderful.

A drop of moisture fell from the ceiling and splashed on her thigh. A moment later, she felt another drop trickle down her other leg. It was light and feathery, almost like—

Tyanna's eyes flew open. A cold shiver of shock ran through her entire body, despite the heat.

"Sorry, sweetie." Sheldon's voice was as

smooth as melted chocolate. "I couldn't help touching."

"Sheldon!" In a flash, Tyanna uncrossed her legs and sat up straight. She automatically reached for her towel, but remembered that she'd left it hanging outside the steam room door. Suddenly, she felt very naked.

"No need to be modest with me, sweetheart."

Even in the dimly lit room, Tyanna could see the heat in Sheldon's eyes. She knew, just knew, that he was seeing right through her skimpy bikini to all the areas he'd once been so familiar with.

Unnerved, she quickly looked away.

Sheldon climbed onto the high bench, sitting beside her. "You don't mind if I join you?"

"Actually." Tyanna stood. "I was just about to head out. I've been in here a while."

"Pretty hot, huh."

She looked at him then. Yeah, she was hot—and it wasn't because of the temperature in here. The smug look on Sheldon's face said he knew that.

"Yeah, it's hot. Too hot for me."

Sheldon reached for her and snaked a hand around her wrist. "You don't want to rush off. It's pretty slippery in here. You don't want to fall."

"I'll be careful."

"You do that."

But he didn't release her wrist.

The heat at the level where she stood was getting to her head. Reluctantly, she sat back down.

"Is Shirley coming in to join you?" Tyanna asked. She regretted the words as soon as they left her mouth.

"Shirley. She's a doll."

"Oh, yeah. A real charmer."

"No, she's not joining me. Why would she?"

"Well, you two seemed to be hitting it off." She hated it that she sounded jealous, but she'd opened this can of worms.

"She's a funny girl."

"That she is. Pretty easy, too."

"Pardon me?"

"Nothing." Tyanna was suddenly aware that her heart was pounding. Definitely not good in this heat. "I—I should head out." And right into a cold shower . . .

"All right," Sheldon said, not fighting her decision. "I guess I'll see you here again sometime."

Tyanna carefully stepped down to the floor. "Maybe. But don't count on it."

Tyanna didn't bother with the sauna. She was too hot from the steam room, and what she needed was a quick cold shower.

Though she tried to tell herself he couldn't affect her anymore, that was clearly untrue. Her meeting with Sheldon in that hot and steamy room . . . it had left her frazzled. Like she'd suffered a small electric shock and her nerves were burnt at the ends.

It was simply that he'd scared her.

She thought of that first moment she'd opened her eyes and realized he was in the steam room with her. All six-foot-two inches of him covered in a sheen of sweat, a cloud of smoke partially obscuring his features. But those eyes. Lord, those eyes. His gaze had burned her with its intensity, despite the heat.

"Oh, great," Tyanna mumbled. Her body was actually starting to throb.

Tyanna pulled off her suit and stepped into the shower. She squeezed a liberal amount of liquid soap into her palm and lathered up her body. What was wrong with her? Her brain knew it, kept in perspective that Sheldon was the one man who had hurt her more than any other—all of his good intentions aside. If she were smart, she wouldn't forget that.

Yet there was still something about him. . . .

Tyanna let the cool spray hit her face, determined to make her body relax. The throbbing had stopped, thank God, but she'd had to force the image of a near-naked Sheldon from her mind.

Oh, hell. There it went again. Such a small part of her body, yet when it demanded attention, it took control of all of her.

In the past year, she hadn't met another man who made her libido come alive, yet her body was suddenly turned on by thoughts of her ex-boyfriend.

Either she was just plain crazy for thinking of Sheldon in any sexual capacity at all, or she had to admit that what she heard some people talk about was true. Maybe there really *was* something to all that scientific talk about body chemistry and how it made you want someone with an almost animal passion—that certain something that had women creeping out on husbands they loved to steal a few moments with a man they couldn't resist.

Yeah, that was it. Tyanna now felt a lot better. She turned off the shower and reached for her towel outside the stall. Whatever body-chemistry thing was happening between her and Sheldon was completely normal, even if she wished she could control it. For some reason, Sheldon's body still spoke to hers—regardless of what her brain had to say about the matter.

Maybe this was more support for the argument for separation of sex and love. Yes, she had loved Sheldon, and their intimacy had been heightened because of that love. But he had also been the first man to bring out such a high level of sexual desire in her, so while her head and heart were over him, her body had a hard time forgetting it.

It all seemed so simple—now that she'd put things in perspective.

Dried and dressed, Tyanna headed out of the changing room. Even at this late hour, the gym had a large number of people. This was South Florida, and people here wanted to look good— no matter the cost.

"See you tomorrow, Max." Tyanna gave a quick

wave to the gym's manager before she headed out the door.

Tonight was cooler than the last few. The ground looked wet. It must have rained. Those summer showers were a godsend in terms of cooling things down.

Tyanna started for the right, where she'd parked her car. But after a few steps, a weird feeling came over her.

She whirled around, Sheldon's name on the tip of her tongue.

She saw no one.

Slowly she turned and continued walking. The weird feeling was still there. Like she wasn't alone, even though she saw no one else out there with her.

She quickened her pace and was at her car in several seconds. Like Sheldon had told her, she looked all around before reaching for her keys. Satisfied that no one was there, she dug her keys out of her purse, then quickly got in the car. She locked her door immediately.

Then sat for a moment as she once again scanned the darkened parking lot.

She was being stupid, she realized.

Yet as she backed out of her space and started off, she couldn't shake the feeling that someone, somewhere, was watching her.

Maybe it wouldn't be a bad idea if she slept with him.

For the millionth time that night, Tyanna rolled onto her other side. The air-conditioning was working, but she was still hot.

Still restless.

The memory of her encounter with Sheldon in the steam room continued to haunt her. She had tried to play it cool, but she hadn't been able to keep her eyes off his strong legs. Shirley certainly had been right about his body.

The problem was, being so close to him in a hot, steamy room, with both of them nearly naked—Tyanna was back to remembering all the hot nights they'd spent together at her place.

Every time she'd drifted off to sleep, she had dreamed of him.

She could no longer deny it. Her body felt like it would spontaneously combust if she didn't get some relief. And soon.

She wanted a man in her bed with her.

And not just any man. She wanted Sheldon. At the very least, Sheldon was familiar, and Tyanna knew he would not disappoint her.

But it was way too late to call him. Especially since he was at his mother's. And even if it weren't too late, she wasn't sure she could bring herself to pick up the phone. What was she going to say? *Hi, I'm horny. Wanna come over?*

Considering she had practically laughed in his face when he'd suggested that they become sexually reacquainted, a call to him now would seem . . . crazy.

No, if it was going to happen, it would have to be at a time when they saw each other again. She would be friendlier next time, not push him away. Maybe they'd even go for that drink he had suggested.

And if after a drink, Sheldon made any hints at getting together, she wouldn't turn him down.

But in the meantime . . .

In the meantime, she would just have to dream.

*Chapter 14*

One Sunday every month, the Calhouns got together for a family dinner. Tyanna and her sisters gathered at their parents' place in Fort Lauderdale. It wasn't the home they'd grown up in, but rather a place that spoke of the success her parents had achieved over the years. Located in a gated community off ritzy Las Olas Boulevard, this new house boasted six bedrooms, four bathrooms, and an impressive backyard that bordered one of Fort Lauderdale's many canals. There was also a dock for a boat.

On these family occasions, her mother cooked, and if the weather was good, her father barbecued. Tyanna, Lecia and Charlene always brought side items like potato salad and collard greens and sweet-potato pie.

After meeting Wendy at the gym to rehearse their workout routine, Tyanna had gone by the grocery store and picked up containers of coleslaw and potato salad, as well as some wine.

Before each of these Sunday dinners, she told herself, she'd cook something. But when the time came, she either overcooked the potatoes or just couldn't be bothered. Lately, she just couldn't be bothered. And why stress herself when she could simply pay for it?

She was the first to admit that she knew she'd never win any *Good Housekeeping* prizes. Oh, well.

Tyanna arrived at the community's security gate. She knew George, the security guard who worked there—had known him for a few years now—but he could never simply let her through. Policy required that he always call her parents to get approval to give her entrance to the community.

She rolled down her window as George stuck his head out of the booth. "Hey, George."

"How are you today, Tyanna?"

"Hungry." She smiled. "That's why I'm here."

He returned the smile. "Give me a second to call your parents."

Tyanna watched him slip back into the booth and pick up the phone. He chatted briefly, then hung up. A moment later, he stuck his head out through the booth's window again. "Okay, Tyanna. Go ahead."

Tyanna edged her car forward as George opened the gate. She drove through the neighborhood, admiring the lushness of the various estates.

Minutes later, Tyanna arrived at her parents' sprawling house and pulled into the semicircular driveway. She parked her Acura behind Lecia's BMW. In front of Lecia's car was Charlene's Jeep.

Yep, the gang was all here. Again, she was the last one to arrive.

Oh, well.

Once out of her car, she retrieved the items she'd bought from the backseat, then made her way to the front door.

Like she always did, she tried the door first. It opened, and she walked inside.

Laughter filled the air. It sounded as though her family was in the dinette off the kitchen. She headed in that direction.

Seeing her mother, Tyanna smiled. "Hi, Mommy." Even though she was an adult, Tyanna still addressed her parents the way she had as a child.

"Hi, baby," her mother said, walking toward her and wrapping her in a hug.

"Hi, Lecia."

"Hey, Sis."

"Where's Charlene?" Tyanna asked.

"In the backyard with Michelle and your father."

Tyanna nodded. She began to place the items she'd brought on the table, but her mother said, "Bring the food on out to the back. Your father is barbecuing."

"Mmm. Smells like his famous ribs."

"Of course."

Lecia slid open the screen door so Tyanna could pass. Tyanna stepped onto the back patio.

"Hi, Daddy," she called. She placed the potato salad, coleslaw and wine on the large glass table. With her hands free, she gave her father a hug and a kiss.

"Hi, sweetheart."

"Smells delicious, Daddy. I can't wait to taste one." Tyanna turned around. She headed toward Charlene, who was carrying Michelle around the perimeter of the pool.

"Hi, Charlene."

Charlene smiled and wiggled her fingers at Tyanna, her other hand wrapped around her daughter's back. Tyanna saw that Michelle was sleeping.

"Shh," Charlene said. "I just got her down."

Tyanna gently ran a palm over Michelle's hair. "She's such a little angel."

"She wasn't a while ago." Charlene scowled playfully. "She was fussing a lot. I'm gonna bring her inside."

Tyanna couldn't help beaming at her niece as Charlene walked away with her. It was amazing how much Michelle was looking like her father more and more each day. As sad as it was, Michelle was helping to keep David's memory alive. What a tragedy that he hadn't lived to see his beautiful daughter's face.

As Charlene disappeared into the house, Tyanna's mother and Lecia came outside. Tyanna met them at the table, which was set up beneath a large awning.

"What do you need me to do?" Tyanna asked.

"Lecia is setting the table," her mother said. "Why don't you bring out the pitcher of lemonade from the fridge, as well as some glasses."

"Sure." Tyanna made two trips to the kitchen to retrieve both lemonade and glasses.

"Oh, Mommy," Tyanna said. "Remember that business proposal I told you Wendy and I had come up with?"

"The fitness video."

"Yes. Well, we heard back from Ronnie Vaughn's office, and he's interested in getting a demo tape from us."

"Oh, that's wonderful," her mother said.

"That's really great news," Lecia added.

"Thanks. I have a big favor to ask you and Daddy. Wendy and I are trying to get it together fairly quickly, and we were hoping we could use the house next Sunday for the video shoot."

"You know I'll do whatever I can to help. I'm sure your father won't mind. Right, Byron?"

Tyanna's father was approaching the table with a platter of ribs. "The backyard?"

"Mmm hmm," Tyanna replied. "It's pretty. We'll have privacy."

Byron nodded. "Sure."

"What's the event?" Charlene asked, stepping outside. She carried a tray of fried chicken.

"Wendy and I have the go-ahead to send Ronnie Vaughn a demo tape."

"Ooh, that's fabulous."

"Yeah. And we want to shoot the demo tape here, next week." Tyanna turned back to her father. "I don't anticipate we'll take more than a few hours. And there'll probably only be a handful of people here."

"Whatever you need," Byron said.

"Thanks, Daddy." Tyanna wrapped her arms around him and gave him a hug.

"No problem," he replied. "Besides, you know that if your mother says yes, I can't say no. Isn't that right, Roberta?"

She flashed him a saucy smile.

"All my girls like to gang up on me."

"That's because we're always right." Lecia grinned at him.

"You see what I mean?" He shook his head.

Lecia giggled, then kissed her father on the cheek. "Oh, you know we love you. And we especially love your ribs."

"Exactly," Charlene chimed in. She was already sitting at the table. "Can we eat already?"

There was a chorus of agreement as the rest of the family settled at the table. Tyanna volunteered to say grace, then everyone dug in.

\*    \*    \*

"Anyway," Lecia said. "I've been ignoring his calls. I don't understand the man. One minute, he wasn't paying me any attention, now he can't stop calling."

Charlene chuckled. "Isn't that the way it always is? Just when you're no longer interested . . ."

"I thought Martin was a very nice man," Roberta said.

"I'm not saying he isn't nice. He's just not my type. I'm not sure I'm ready to be dating, anyway," Lecia added.

Roberta looked at her with sympathy. "Oh, sweetheart. Don't let what happened with Alan turn you off to dating. We were all wrong about him, but there are other nice men out there. Other dedicated doctors—"

"I'm not sure I want another doctor in my life."

"Your father and I have been very happy."

"I know," Lecia said. "But as it is, I work so many hours. . . ." She shrugged.

"This is your last year of residency," Byron said. "You'll get through it."

Lecia had no doubt she would get through it. The question was whether or not she wanted to. She had gone into the medical field because her parents had encouraged her to do so. Strongly encouraged. She had done everything they thought was best for her, including marrying Alan. But there was something missing in her life. In her heart, she didn't believe medicine was her passion, no matter how good she was at it.

"I know," she said. "I'm just not sure it's the best thing to be paired up with a man in the same boat as I am. When I think about having a family . . . two people who work so many hours . . ."

"We managed," Roberta said. "You will too."

Tyanna watched the expression on Lecia's face and wondered if something was going on that the family didn't know about. She got the feeling that Lecia was unhappy about something, but she hadn't talked to her about it.

Was she no longer interested in becoming a doctor? Tyanna wouldn't be surprised. Growing up, Lecia had always been creative. She liked to paint, to write stories. So when she'd gone to medical school, no one had been more shocked than Tyanna.

But Lecia was the oldest, and Tyanna knew she'd felt the most pressure from her parents to succeed. Charlene was a respected teacher, yet their parents still felt she'd fallen short of her potential.

Tyanna knew that she herself had totally failed in their eyes. "You're not doing anything with your degree," her father used to complain. Tyanna had learned how to block out the criticism. The way she saw it, she had one life to live, and she may as well do what she liked.

"What about you, Charlene?" Roberta asked. "Did you get a chance to go on a date with Theo?"

Charlene shook her head. "Not yet. And quite

frankly, I'm not sure I'm ready for that. I'm happy with my family as it is—just me and Michelle. But I thank you for introducing me to him."

Roberta sipped her wine, then nodded her understanding. "Of course. You're still grieving."

Tyanna grabbed a napkin and wiped barbecue sauce from her fingers. It was then that she noticed the table had gotten quiet. Slowly looking up, she found everyone looking at her.

"What?" she asked.

"What about you, sweetheart?" her mother asked. "Have you met anyone nice?"

"Oh. No." Tyanna quickly looked away, once again concentrating on cleaning her fingers.

"You don't seem so sure," Roberta said.

"I'm sure."

"So something else is going on?" Roberta raised an eyebrow in curiosity. "You seem . . . preoccupied."

Tyanna had not planned to tell her parents about Sheldon's return, but now she found herself wondering what the big deal was. It's not like she and Sheldon were involved again. She had nothing to hide.

"Actually," Tyanna began slowly, "there is something I haven't told you. And the only reason is because I know how you all will react." She took a deep breath, then announced, "Sheldon's back in town."

Everyone stopped eating and looked at her.

"I knew you would react this way, all surprised. Concerned. But there's really no reason to be."

"You've seen him?" her mother asked.

Tyanna paused before saying, "Yes."

"Oh, no," Lecia said.

"I've seen him, but . . . that's all. He showed up at the gym and we talked." They didn't have to know he had been in her apartment.

"Why?" Charlene asked.

"He wanted me to know he was okay."

Her mother guffawed. "Oh, wasn't that sweet of him."

"He . . ." Tyanna wondered how much of the story she should tell her family. "He told me some stuff. The reason he left me so suddenly. It's a long, convoluted story, but apparently his brother was murdered and he was trying to catch the killer. That got him into trouble, and he had to get out of town. That's why he took off the way he did."

Her father finally spoke. "That's what he told you?"

"In a lot more detail, yes."

"And you believed him?" Lecia asked.

Tyanna faced her. "Not right away. I did some investigating, and I learned that what he'd told me was true. Believe me, I was as shocked as anyone."

"So what does this mean?" Her mother gave her a pointed look. "You're not planning to get back together with him, are you?"

"Oh, no." Tyanna chuckled lightheartedly to

put their minds at ease. "But we'll talk from time to time, I'm sure. I guess I just wanted to let you know."

The family was silent as they continued to eat, and Tyanna sensed their worried glances even though she kept her gaze steady on her plate. Sometimes she hated being the youngest one in the family. Everyone seemed to forget that she was no longer a baby—hadn't been for a long time. She could take care of herself.

And she resented the fact that they seemed to think she wasn't capable of making her own decisions. If she wanted to see Sheldon, that was her business.

"By the way," her mother began, as if on cue, "I met the nicest resident last week. He's very well-mannered, Tyanna. And very cute. I might invite him over for dinner one of these days."

*Brother*, Tyanna thought. "I don't think I'm well suited for a doctor."

"You never know."

Tyanna gave her mother a weak smile. She knew her mother had long given up on her getting a respectable career. The best she could hope now was to marry her off to a respectable man.

"I'll agree that life is unpredictable," Tyanna said.

"Ain't that the truth," Charlene agreed.

Once again, everyone fell into silence. The silence hung over them as they finished their dinner.

*        *        *

An hour later, Tyanna simply wanted to leave.

Maybe it was the fact that her family had continued to look at her with concern and ask questions about Sheldon, or maybe it was her rebellious streak. She knew she had one, and when challenged, she almost always did the opposite of what was expected. And right now, knowing that her family wouldn't want her to see Sheldon suddenly had her wanting to see him.

Not only that, but during the rest of dinner, there had been comments here and there aimed at Sheldon. Nothing explicitly demeaning, but that was the sense Tyanna got. The talk had ventured to people who didn't have a degree in this day and age, and while her father hadn't specifically mentioned Sheldon, Tyanna knew he was talking about him. It peeved her to have her family continue to talk down about him in that way, proving that they had never liked him to begin with. She took the criticism personally. They were giving her no credit for being able to choose a decent man to spend her life with.

Granted, Sheldon had been the wrong choice, but not for the reasons they might believe. Besides, wasn't she entitled to make her own mistakes?

Tyanna watched her mother's animated face as she spoke about little Michelle, how she knew her young grandchild was going to grow up to be a doctor or a scientist or a world-renowned surgeon.

Tyanna bit back the urge to smirk. Oh, her mother's panties would get all tangled in a knot if she knew what was going through Tyanna's mind right now. And maybe it was a little bit crazy. But she was determined to do it. Somewhere during the previous hour, she had decided that she wanted to see Sheldon.

And quench her thirst.

But after the last time she'd spoken to him, she didn't figure she was his favorite person. At the very least, she had given him a loud and clear message. She had pushed him away big time, told him over and over again that she wasn't interested in resuming a sexual relationship with him, yet that was exactly what she planned on doing now.

If she called him, she was sure she would fumble her words. She would sound like an idiot, which wouldn't work. So if she was going to do this—convince him to spend the night with her—she would have to convince him she was serious.

And she figured the best way to do that was to surprise him.

Tyanna had tuned out the current conversation, so she wasn't sure what had caused the outburst of laughter. And she didn't want to know.

She pushed her chair back and stood. "Um, I've got to get going."

Her mother looked at her, surprised. So did

everyone else. "I'm not feeling very well," she quickly added. "I think I'm coming down with something."

Her mother looked at her with concern. "Oh?"

"Yeah. I figure I should go home and lie down."

"You can always rest here," Roberta suggested.

"No, I'd rather not," Tyanna told her mother. She rounded the table and kissed her mother on the cheek. "Don't worry. I'll be fine." She waved as she started to step backward. "Bye, y'all."

"Take care of yourself," Charlene said.

"I will."

There was a round of good-byes, then Tyanna entered the house through the patio doors.

She had gotten all the way to the front door before she realized that if she was going to head to Sheldon's place, she needed a peace offering. Whirling around, she scurried to the kitchen as quietly as she could, looked for something—anything—and saw the sweet-potato pie her mother had made cooling on the counter. She grabbed it.

Tyanna threw a quick glance over her shoulder to make sure no one had seen her. Later, she would apologize for taking the dessert.

Her father was standing, refilling wine glasses, obscuring everyone's view.

Perfect. Tyanna hustled the pie out the front door.

She sure hoped Sheldon would like it.

Sheldon . . .

Her heart rate accelerated.

*It's just a need*, she told herself as she headed toward her car. *A physical need. Once you've satisfied it, you will feel a lot better.*

And hopefully get Sheldon out of her system.

# Chapter 15

 Sheldon opened the door and got the
shock of his life.

A slow smile spread across his lips as a feeling
of warmth spread through his body.

There was no doubt about it. Tyanna was absolutely beautiful. The sight of her before him,
wearing a cute floral dress that hung to just above
her knees, stole his breath.

He couldn't believe she was really here.

On his doorstep.

With a sweet-potato pie, no less. His favorite.

Wonders never ceased.

"Tyanna."

"Hi." She looked up at him with those incredible brown eyes of hers.

He couldn't wipe the smile off his lips for the
life of him. "What are you doing here?"

"Oh, um." She moved her weight from one foot
to the other. "Weren't you the one who suggested
we get together from time to time?"

"Yeah."

"And I wasn't against that. So you don't have to look at me as if you think my spaceship is parked outside."

"Actually, you gave me the impression I was smothering you."

She flashed him a sheepish grin. "I did say I'd get in touch with you when I was ready."

"That you did. Guess I'm one of those guys who has to see something to believe it. I just didn't expect you, and you haven't called."

"I was in the neighborhood, so I didn't bother to call. I figured I'd say hi to your mother."

"The pie's for her?"

"For both of you, actually." Tyanna peered around Sheldon. "Is she here?"

Sheldon shook his head. "It's Sunday evening. She's at church."

"Oh."

"You still want to come in?"

"Sure." Tyanna spoke a little too quickly, and she prayed that had come off as casual rather than desperate.

Sheldon stood back and held the door wide for Tyanna to enter. Smiling nervously, she extended the pie. "Here you go. It's fresh."

Lowering his nose, Sheldon inhaled the enticing aroma. "Mmm." His eyes met hers. "To what do I owe the pleasure?"

"I felt like baking," she lied.

Sheldon threw his head back and laughed.

"*You* made this? Are you the same woman who used to burn cookies?"

"All right. So I didn't make it. But I didn't buy it, either. My mother made it, and I remembered how much you liked sweet-potato pie."

Her mother. The mention of her family made Sheldon's stomach lurch. "You told her you were bringing this for me?"

"Not exactly." Pride shone in Tyanna's eyes. "I just took it."

Sheldon smiled. "I knew there was a reason I liked you."

"You are such a bad influence on me," Tyanna joked.

"Do your parents know I'm back in town?"

"Yes."

"And what did they say?"

"I don't really want to talk about that."

Sheldon studied her, but her expression didn't give anything away. It didn't have to. He could imagine what had been said about him in the Calhoun household.

"What do you want to do?" he asked.

"I don't know. I was figuring maybe we could hang out. How long will your mother be at church?"

Sheldon raised an eyebrow, intrigued. Just where was she going with this? "I don't know. Another hour or so. Long enough for you?"

She seemed nervous and folded her arms under her breasts. God, what breasts. The scrap of material she wore barely covered them. She shrugged, then nervously looked away.

"Why, Miss Calhoun, whatever do you have in mind?"

"I . . ." She couldn't get her words out.

Sheldon angled his head to the side as he looked at her. "I'm not quite sure how to read you, Tyanna. Would I be accurate if I said I was getting a certain . . . *vibe* from you?"

"Yes," she answered without hesitation. Then, "I know, you'll think I'm crazy . . ."

"Actually, I'm thinking that if we're on the same page here, then an hour or two won't be nearly long enough."

She met his eyes then, a smile playing on her lips. "I can head home now."

"I'll follow you."

Tyanna didn't give herself a hard time for her decision on the drive home. What the hell. She was an adult, and if she wanted to make love to Sheldon, it certainly wasn't illegal.

*Have sex*, she corrected herself. There was a difference between making love and having sex, and what she and Sheldon were about to do was make up for a year's lost time without physical contact. At least she hoped so.

Tyanna parked in her spot, and Sheldon drove past her to pull into the visitors parking area. She got out of her car and debated walking toward him. Instead, she lingered by her car, deciding to wait for him to come to her. Yes, she wanted him, but she didn't want to appear too eager.

Tyanna walked to the front of her building to wait for Sheldon there. He got out of his Explorer and jogged all the way to her. Something about that touched Tyanna's heart—the fact that he wanted to be with her so badly that he had to run, not walk.

He placed his hand on the small of her back as he stopped beside her. Tyanna smiled up at him.

"You ready?" she asked.

"Oh, yeah."

The moment Sheldon was in the apartment behind Tyanna, he closed the door with his foot and swept her into his arms.

There was no need for small talk. No need to beat around the bush. They both wanted the same thing, and it had been one helluva long year for both of them to have gone without it.

"Come here," Sheldon whispered.

Tyanna slipped her arms around his neck, and Sheldon brought his lips down against Tyanna's.

Even he was surprised at how gentle he was, considering how fiercely he wanted her. He wanted to suck on her lips until she cried out for mercy, but instead, he softly suckled one side, then the other. With reverence, he ran his tongue along the outline of her mouth. Tyanna was like a precious jewel to be admired and respected.

Tyanna moaned softly, tightening her arms around him as she opened her mouth for him.

Sheldon slipped his tongue inside, flicked the tip over hers. Suckled the tip lightly as he ran his hands down Tyanna's body.

When his fingers reached the soft flesh of her bottom, an electric jolt shot through his body. Suddenly he wanted her naked. He needed to feel her velvet skin against his body, run his tongue along her sweet flesh. He wanted to bury his face between her thighs.

Tyanna pressed her body tighter against him, wrapping her thighs around his leg. That was all the encouragement Sheldon needed to lift the hem of her dress. A long breath whooshed out of him as his fingers trailed up her thighs, then to her behind. Damn, she was wearing thong underwear.

He needed to get this dress off. Gathering the silky material into two fists, he lifted it, but it wouldn't budge beyond her breasts.

"Zipper," Tyanna told him on a ragged breath.

Sheldon's hands fumbled with the back of the garment. He found the zipper and dragged it down. Then he nudged the material off her shoulders. The dress slipped to the floor. Tyanna stepped out of it, then looked up at Sheldon with a faint smile. Surprising him, she placed her hands on his chest and pushed him backward. His back hit the wall with a soft thud.

He raised an eyebrow as he looked down at her. "Oh, so you want it rough?"

"I just want you," she whispered, slipping her hands beneath his shirt. She pulled it over his head and dropped it to the floor. Her lips met his for a quick kiss, then her tongue was on his skin, trailing down his neck, his chest. All the way down to his abdomen.

Tyanna's hands worked the button on his jeans. She pulled the zipper down, then slipped her hands inside. With one hand, she felt the length of his erection, while she started to drag his jeans off with the other hand. Groaning his satisfaction, Sheldon tried to help her, but Tyanna smacked his hand away. She wrapped her fingers around the sides of his jeans and worked them down his thighs, her entire body sinking lower as she did.

Sheldon looked down. Clad in a black lacy bra and black thong, Tyanna was a vision right out of any guy's fantasies. Her fingers were softly stroking the backs of his thighs, while she planted feathery kisses along their fronts. And with each kiss, her lips went higher, closer and closer to his aching erection.

"Oh, man," Sheldon ground out.

She reached for his briefs and pulled them down. Then her hands were on him again, feeling the length of his hard penis, stroking him.

Shit, he was going to have an orgasm right here if she kept this up. Lowering himself, he gripped her shoulders and pulled her up. "Not so fast," he whispered in her ear.

Then he scooped her into his arms. Tyanna nuzzled her nose into his neck as he carried her to the bedroom. There, he eased her down onto the edge of her bed. Tyanna brushed her lips against his ear, then nibbled her way along his jaw to his mouth.

He kissed her urgently, their lips and tongues cemented together. Stretching his body out alongside hers, he skimmed his fingers along her smooth skin, up one thigh and over her hip, along her abdomen. He lightly fingered her navel ring. Then he was moving his hand higher, to her breast. He felt around for the bra's fastener, but it wasn't at the front.

"Take this off," he told her.

Tyanna eased up and reached for the clasp of her bra on her back. As soon as it loosened, Sheldon gathered the lacy material and pulled it off.

For a moment, all he could do was look at her. Her breasts were beautiful, firm. Slowly, he trailed a finger around her areola, and instantly the nipple puckered and hardened at his touch.

"God, I've missed this."

Tyanna felt the groan rumble in his chest the moment before his lips closed around her nipple. Her eyes fluttered shut as a jolt of pleasure shot through her body. It had been so long that she'd forgotten just how good this felt. But it was the most amazing sensation, so delicious that she could lie on her back forever as Sheldon's mouth and tongue licked and pulled and drove her wild.

She sucked in a sharp breath when his hand covered her through her panties, his mouth still at her breast. The combination of his tongue on her nipple and his fingers on her nub was making her dizzy with myriad wonderful sensations.

"I know how much you love this," Sheldon murmured. He sat up, positioning himself over her so that he could access her thong. He slipped the scrap of material over her hips. "But I know what else you like."

Tyanna gasped in pleasure as he spread her legs wide. She was as exposed as anyone could be, but even after all this time, she wasn't shy with him. And as his gaze burned her skin, she felt more alive than she'd ever remembered.

"You're just so beautiful," he said as he lowered his face between her legs. "Man, I've missed this. Missed the taste of you . . ."

Tyanna's hips lurched at the first flick of his tongue. Sheldon wrapped his arms around her legs, securing her in place. Lord help her, he was going to show no mercy to her.

A few more tongue flicks and gentle suckles and Tyanna's body exploded. Her hips rocked and she panted as the best orgasm she remembered ever having slowly subsided. But still Sheldon didn't let up, and she felt the sensations build within her again, like a coil tightening.

"Sheldon . . ." She whimpered, before the next wave of pleasure washed over her. She squeezed her legs around him, unsure how much more of this she could handle. It just felt too good.

Tyanna reached for him, and he slid his body

up hers, settling between her thighs. He looked down at her, satisfaction beaming in his eyes.

She couldn't speak. Her breaths were too frantic. So she reached for him, gently palmed his cheek, then pulled his face down onto hers for a searing kiss.

Pulling her lips away, she whispered, "I need you inside me."

Tyanna slipped her hands between their bodies, found his erection, and guided it into her. She cried out as he filled her, and Sheldon released a moan of satisfaction.

For a moment, he stayed still, and Tyanna savored the feeling of him, knowing he was doing the same with her. A whole year, yet they still felt right together, like no time had passed.

Looking deeply in her eyes, Sheldon ran his hands over her hair, then slowly began to move. He picked up the pace, pulling out, plunging deep. With each thrust, Tyanna raised her hips to meet him.

"Lock your legs around me, baby."

She did. And the sensations of their movements became more intense as he reached even deeper inside her.

Tyanna trailed her fingers along his neck and over his head, reacquainting herself with the feel of him. Though she hadn't forgotten. She had dreamed about him for months, keeping every memory of him alive.

But this was better than any dream.

Sheldon's breathing grew more ragged, matching his more intense strokes. Tyanna knew he was close, and she was close too, so she wrapped her legs tighter around him, arched into him, then suckled the side of his neck while she ran her fingers up and down the backs of his thighs.

Suddenly Sheldon moaned loudly, driving himself into her as far as he could. And as his body tensed, as he went over the edge, he took her with him.

Tyanna and Sheldon spent the rest of the night in bed. They made love, rested, made love, rested and continued that routine until the sun came up.

Now, lying naked in bed together, Tyanna couldn't help but smile. She had certainly quenched her thirst, and in grand style.

She opened her eyes and looked at Sheldon. They lay face to face. The steady flow of his breathing told her he was sleeping.

A mix of emotions flooded her this morning. Physically she was satisfied, but emotionally . . . Emotionally, she was a mess.

Sheldon was lying naked with her, as he had done so many times in the past, but this wasn't the past. Their relationship was over, and Tyanna had no clue what the future held for them.

All she knew for sure was that sex wouldn't solve anything, no matter how good it was.

Yesterday she had lied to herself. She had honestly thought that she could spend the night satisfying her body's needs and keep her heart out of it. But from the moment he had settled between her legs and looked deeply into her eyes, she had realized differently. Having sex with Sheldon was simply something she couldn't do for the sake of it. Her emotions would always be caught up in the act of their lovemaking.

That was the way it was supposed to be, but she and Sheldon didn't have an ordinary relationship. They didn't have one at all, anymore. It still irked her that in all the time they had spent together, he hadn't trusted her completely, enough to open up about the pain of losing his brother. And her heart simply couldn't accept that he'd walked away from her so easily. Initially, she could understand his fear, but why send her that letter? Why lead her to believe he was involved with someone else?

She supposed it was plausible that he was hoping she would forget him, but in Tyanna's eyes, true love wasn't supposed to be that way. True love dealt with the most difficult of struggles.

*He came back*, she could hear Wendy say, and yes, that was true. The real question was whether or not they had what it took for the long haul.

Life always presented struggles. And what would Sheldon do then? Run again? Or trust her?

Her thoughts troubling her, Tyanna climbed out of bed. She grabbed some clothes, went to the bathroom and took a long shower. When she returned to the bedroom, makeup on and dressed, Sheldon was awake and sitting up.

"Morning," she said. She sounded gruff, even though she hadn't planned it that way.

Sheldon gave her a perplexed look. "I thought I heard the shower . . . You got up and left me here?"

Tyanna sat on the edge of the bed. "I didn't want to wake you."

He stroked her exposed stomach. "I'd hoped we would shower together this morning."

Tyanna shrugged, giving a 'who cares?' attitude about the suggestion. "Next time."

There was confusion in Sheldon's eyes, and it disturbed her. Tyanna looked away as she rose from the bed.

But his arms encircled her wrist, and she looked over her shoulder at him.

"*Will* there be a next time?" he asked.

"Oh, sure."

"Sure? You make it sound like we're talking about going to a movie or something."

"What do you want me to say?" Tyanna knew she was being cold, but the way she saw it, she had no choice. She had let Sheldon back into her life, and to do that was to risk letting him back in her heart.

Sheldon frowned. "How can you do this?"

"Do what?"

He looked dumbfounded. "Act as if . . . as if last night meant absolutely nothing to you."

She chuckled softly. "Oh. Is that what you think? Of course last night meant something to me. I appreciate you coming over. It's been a long time since I've had that."

"Had that?"

"You know." But she didn't look at him. "Great sex. I guess I didn't realize how much I missed it."

Sheldon looked at her with as much surprise as if he'd woken to find a stranger in his bed.

"What?" she asked.

"You appreciate me coming over?"

"Yeah, I do."

"As if you could have just called anyone?"

"Technically—"

He sat up fully. "Forget technically. Would you have? Just called anyone to come over?"

"I didn't."

Sheldon groaned. "God, I guess I now know what it's like to feel cheap."

Tyanna once again looked away. She hadn't been prepared for this from Sheldon, and she wasn't sure how to respond. "Look," she finally said, "I'm not trying to offend you or anything. I'm just trying to keep things in perspective. You said yourself that our relationship was always about sex."

"I said that?"

"Well, it wasn't about love, now was it?"

Tyanna watched him, holding her breath as she waited for him to respond. But she soon realized that she would surely suffocate before Sheldon told her he loved her, and she released the breath of air she'd been holding.

"Just like I said," Tyanna announced, doing her best to keep her tone light. "And I'm all right with that. At first I wasn't sure what it would be like, taking that step with you again. But I think you were right. We're so great in the sack, I don't see any reason that we can't get together from time to time to scratch that itch."

"That *itch*."

"Whatever you want to call it."

Sheldon got out of bed. "Where are my clothes?"

"I picked them up from the hallway," she told him. "They're on the chair by the window."

"Thanks." His tone said he was irritated.

Tyanna watched him as he quickly dressed, then turned back to her. "I've got to go."

"Oh?"

"Yeah. Things to do. You know."

"Yeah, I guess I do. I have a few errands to—"

"I'll talk to you later," he said, cutting her off.

Tyanna stood. "Um, I can make you some breakfast."

"Naw. I'm fine."

She nodded, and the next thing she knew, Sheldon was striding through her bedroom door. She lagged behind him as he went into the hallway and put his shoes on.

He unlocked the door and then looked her way. "Later."

"Yeah."

For a good few minutes after he'd left, Tyanna didn't move. She merely stood staring at the door, as if she expected it to open.

Finally, she made her way into the living room, where she plopped herself down on her plush sofa. She went from staring at the door to staring at the ceiling.

Remembering to breathe, she slowly sucked in air, then expelled it in a frustrated rush.

She should be feeling victorious that she'd managed to play cool and nonchalant about the night she and Sheldon had spent together. Instead, all she felt was a hole the size of Texas forming in her stomach.

# Chapter 16

Sheldon pressed the heel of his hand to the horn and gave it a good, long blare. "Son of a bitch, will you move out of the way?"

The car in front of him did a jerky lane change to the left, cutting in front of an unsuspecting driver. Sheldon sped up, and as he passed the car on the way to his exit, he whipped his head to the left to get a look at the dimwit behind the wheel.

It was an elderly woman, and the look of absolute horror she leveled in his direction zapped some sense into him.

Shit, what the hell was wrong with him? This woman hadn't committed any heinous crime. In fact, she'd been doing the speed limit—in the slow lane, at that. It was he who was driving like an idiot, and quite frankly, he was only lucky that he hadn't run into a state trooper, who definitely would have given him a citation for speeding.

Sheldon slowed down as he drove along the

exit ramp. It was then that he noticed his hands were jittery. Christ, he couldn't even hold the steering wheel properly. He was damn lucky to have made it this far without an incident.

He made a concerted effort to rein in his scattered emotions as he drove the rest of the way to his mother's house. But the words *scratch that itch* wouldn't leave his mind.

*Scratch that itch.* The words burned him. Sheesh, the way Tyanna spoke, she had basically used him to get off. And it wasn't a nice feeling.

Not that Sheldon minded having sex for the sake of it, but he certainly didn't look at Tyanna as a means to simply get off. If that's all he wanted, he could masturbate in the privacy of his bedroom.

Call him a wuss, but he actually enjoyed the sharing aspect of sex, enjoyed knowing that he was giving as much as he was receiving. At least he enjoyed that with Tyanna. Sure, any vagina could make a man feel good, but he had a special connection with his ex-girlfriend's.

He had hoped that Tyanna also felt they had a unique sexual connection, but her callous attitude this morning made him think that what he had spent a year dreaming about was not so special after all.

He wasn't used to this Tyanna. Before, she had given herself to him body and soul. He had felt that way last night. But her words and attitude had shattered that illusion this morning.

Sheldon had the distinct feeling that they had taken one step forward, two steps back.

Right now, he had no clue as to where they stood. All he knew was that he couldn't obsess over this all day. Minutes later, Sheldon was thankful to be pulling into the driveway of his mother's North Miami home. What he saw made thoughts of Tyanna instantly flee his mind.

Rather, what he didn't see.

His mother was a teacher and therefore home for the summer. Every morning she either sat on the porch or worked in the garden. But this morning she wasn't outside. Was she okay? Had she had another heart attack?

Sheldon parked and went into the house. He still didn't see her. Didn't smell the scents of eggs and bacon, which often filled the air when his mother cooked for him. She had told him not to worry about her; in fact, she had urged him to get his own place—something Sheldon had planned on doing, especially now that he had found another job. But how could he live somewhere else until he knew that she was back to 100 percent?

His mother was one of the most stubborn people he knew. Despite her weak heart, she had plans to start teaching again in the fall. But what worried him was that lately she hadn't been taking her medication at the times she was supposed to. "I'm feeling much better and I can't be bothered with all the fuss," she had told him last week. Well, until the doctor told her not to, Sheldon wanted her taking her medication.

Had she not taken her medication this morning? Sheldon's concern increased as he quickly hurried through the house to her bedroom. "Ma," he called, then swung the door open.

He found her sitting on the edge of her bed with the shades drawn and no other lights on.

"Ma, what's the matter?" Sheldon flicked the light switch and stepped into the room. "Is it your heart? Do you want me to call a doctor?"

"Oh, Sheldon." Relief laced her tone. "You're home."

"Of course I'm home," he replied. "I was out last night, that's all. I guess I should have called so you wouldn't worry. . . ."

She sighed, a weary, heavy sound. Her lips went lopsided in a worried expression, and Sheldon wondered what was going on.

Millie Ford was a robust woman, with graying hair that she always wore in a bun. Though almost sixty, her dark skin was smooth and wrinkle free.

Sheldon sat on the bed next to her. "Why were you sitting here in the dark? It's your heart, isn't it? You were doing too much—"

"No, it's not my heart."

Sheldon frowned. "Then did something happen?"

"Yes," she answered softly.

"What?"

"Oh, Sheldon." She placed a gentle palm on his cheek. "I'm so worried about you."

"Nothing's gonna happen to me, Ma." He didn't need her worrying about him, not in her condition. "I'm fine."

Shaking her head, she said, "You don't understand. I got a call last night."

Sheldon's eyes narrowed. "What kind of a call?"

"Sheldon, it was a threat."

His heart started to beat faster. "What did this person say?"

"Whoever it was said to tell you that they're watching you, and they know what you did."

"They're watching me?" Sheldon asked.

"That's what he said. And . . . that you would pay. Then he hung up."

Sheldon stood, paced to the window, then turned around. "What time did the call come in?"

"A little after ten last night. This person asked for you, and when I told him you weren't home, that's when he said to tell you they're watching you and they know what you did."

"They?"

"I think he said 'they.' Yes, I'm pretty sure he did."

"Shit," Sheldon muttered.

"All night, I could hardly sleep. I was so worried."

"Oh, Ma." Sheldon went back to the bed, sat beside her, and wrapped an arm around her shoulder. "I'm sorry you had to deal with that."

She looked up at him with worried eyes. "What's going on?"

"I'm not sure."

"You have no idea?" his mother questioned.

"No," he answered. And that was the truth. The only danger to him had died with Dino.

Or so he'd thought.

There was a chance that one of Dino's associates might want to do him harm, but that was a remote chance, as far as Sheldon was concerned. He hadn't really acted on anything—just collected information. Besides, no one from that time knew he was back in town.

Except for Tyanna. And Maria.

"I'm sure it was a crank call," Sheldon told his mother.

"He referred to you by name, Sheldon."

"Maybe some old friend who's trying to get a rise out of me," he lied, knowing it sounded lame.

"I don't know." She bit down on her bottom lip, then gripped his hand. "After what happened to Dwight, I don't know what I'd do if I lost you. . . ."

"You are not going to lose me. I promise you that."

Millie rested her head against her son's chest. "I pray every day for your safety."

"I know. And God's hearing your prayers. Don't worry about me."

"You're all I have left."

Sheldon ran his hand over his mother's hair. "I know. And I'm not going anywhere. I need you to believe that." He knew Dwight's murder had brought about her heart attack, and if she made herself sick with worry, who knew what would happen to her next?

"I'll try."

Sheldon stood and pulled back the covers on the bed. "You look like you didn't get much sleep."

"I didn't."

"Did you take your pills?"

"No."

Sheldon tsked. "Ma. I'll get your pills and some water. You climb into bed. I want you to get some rest and not worry about me."

Millie swung her legs up onto the bed and pulled the covers up.

"Like I said, this is probably somebody's idea of a crazy joke," Sheldon told her. "Either way, I'm going to get to the bottom of it."

And he would.

Wendy's face broke into a smile when she heard Phil's voice on her message service. She promptly dialed his number from the phone in her office.

The receptionist at Phil's office told her that he wasn't there, so Wendy tried him on his cell.

He sounded harried when he answered. "Phil Jackson here."

"Hey, Phil. I hope I'm not catching you at a bad time."

His voice softened. "Wendy?"

"It's me."

"Hey. How are you?"

"Better than you, from the sound of it."

Phil chuckled wryly. "Yeah, I'm running all over the place today. Other than that, I'm fine."

"You working on a project today?"

"Uh-huh. We're shooting a corporate video."

"Oh. Sounds exciting."

"Not particularly. But, I can't complain. A bad day on my job is still pretty cool."

"No doubt." Wendy twirled a tendril of her curly hair. "One of these days, you're going to have to come by my place and let me make you a nice dinner. You're one of the busiest guys I know."

"You know, I just may have to take you up on that offer. I'm definitely due for a break."

"I'd say so." She paused. "Anyway, I got your message."

"Thanks for getting back to me so quickly. I've got good news for you, and I just need to firm up the details."

"Oh?"

"I've got a crew together for your video shoot. We can pull this off on Sunday if that still works for you."

"Oh, great." Wendy beamed into the phone. "Sunday is perfect."

"Cool," Phil said. "So far, the consensus is that around two will work best for them. It's me and two other guys."

"No problem."

"We'll bring two cameras to shoot the video from two different angles. That should also help time-wise."

"Whatever you say. You know what you're doing in that regard."

"It'll be good." Phil spoke with confidence. "It's fairly straightforward."

"I think so," Wendy said. "But Tyanna and I are wondering about music, which is our only complication right now. Granted, this is a demo tape, so maybe we don't have to get rights or anything. I was wondering what you think about that."

"You mean using a published song in your video?"

"Uh-huh."

"If you're not selling it, I wouldn't worry about it."

"I know you said there are generic beats available out there, if you think it's questionable."

"I don't think so. Like I said, I would worry about that only if you were producing a video that you planned to put on the market. However, if you're more comfortable with a generic beat, that's your call. You can decide what you want to do by Sunday and let us know. I can add music in the editing stage."

Wendy released a nervous breath. Sunday was

only six days away. "Phil, I am so grateful to you for doing this."

"No problem. I'm happy to volunteer my time."

A thought struck her. While Phil may help for free, he would have to pay his crew. "I know we haven't discussed pay—"

"I told the guys I was doing this as a favor."

"Still, I'd feel better if we paid them. How does a hundred bucks sound? Plus food and drinks."

"All right. I'm sure the guys will like that."

"And of course, my offer to make you dinner anytime you want it still stands. Just say when."

"Sure will."

Wendy glanced at the clock at the same moment Phil told her he would have to run.

"Okay, Phil. I'll talk to you later. Thanks again."

"No problem."

"All right, Ken," Tyanna said. She made the last of her notes on her sheet documenting his performance today. "You're done."

He clapped his hands together. "At last."

"I'm really impressed," she told him. "You have come a long way in the past few months."

Ken flashed a cheesy smile as he flexed. His skinny arms boasted muscles that hadn't been there four months earlier. The protein shakes had been working to help him build body mass.

Tyanna chuckled. "There you go. Results. It makes it all worthwhile, doesn't it?"

"It sure does."

"See you next time, Ken."

He gave her a quick nod and smile, then walked off. Tyanna was proud of him. It wasn't that easy for a man to gain weight, not fat, but with her diet counseling, Ken had been doing a great job. Slow and steady was the way to ensure lasting results.

Feeling satisfied, Tyanna sauntered over to the nearby water fountain and lowered her head to take a drink.

"This must be heaven, because you are definitely an angel."

At the sound of the deep, male voice, Tyanna whipped her head up from the drinking fountain and looked over her shoulder. Jay stood there with his arms crossed over his chest, a playful smile on his lips.

"Jay," Tyanna said simply.

He held up a hand. "Don't be offended. It's just that you are . . . so beautiful."

Tyanna could argue with him, but she knew there was no point. Jay would probably always flirt with her.

So she said, "Thank you, Jay."

Another man approached the water fountain, and Tyanna stepped away to give him access. Jay moved with her.

"I know you said you weren't interested in a relationship, and maybe I came on a little strong. But I was wondering if we could go out sometime as friends? For dinner or something. Just to hang out."

Tyanna looked up at Jay and could only shake her head with a wry expression. "You don't give up, do you?"

"I can't lie. You're a beautiful girl. Sure, I like you, but I feel kind of bad that you've been avoiding me. I just want to make amends."

Tyanna's eyes slowly roamed Jay's body. He was an attractive man, that was certain. And he was nice. Yet Tyanna had always closed her mind off to getting to know him better.

"Jay . . ." Looking over his shoulder, her heart got a sudden jolt when she saw Sheldon in the distance. He was staring at her intently, watching the interaction between her and Jay.

Tyanna's breathing became shallow. Sheldon's gaze burned her skin, and in a flash she remembered the incredible way she had spent the better part of the last evening and night.

Suddenly she felt guilty, as if even talking to Jay was some kind of betrayal of what she and Sheldon had shared.

"Tyanna?"

She wrenched her gaze back to Jay's face. "Hmm?"

"Everything okay?"

"Sure."

"Well, will you consider it? A friendly dinner

sometime?" He made a motion of drawing a cross over his heart. "I promise I'll be a gentleman."

She threw a quick glance Sheldon's way before responding. Last night had been incredible, but it had also been a mistake. It was high time she got over this foolish sexual connection she had to Sheldon. There were other decent men out there. Men who could love and respect her. Men who could be totally honest with her.

Men like Jay.

"I guess a dinner wouldn't kill anyone."

Jay's lips lifted in a charming smile. He reached for her hand and gave it a gentle squeeze. "Thanks."

"Uh, excuse me."

Both Tyanna and Jay turned at the unexpected interruption. Sheldon stood behind them, a look of irritation marring his handsome features. Jay's eyes flitted between Sheldon and Tyanna, the unspoken question readable on his face.

Sheldon did the same, looking first at Jay, then at Tyanna. He said, "Tyanna, I need to speak with you."

She pulled her hand from Jay's and placed both on her hips. "I'm not sure that's a good—"

"It's important," he interjected.

Tyanna flashed Jay an apologetic look. "I'm sorry."

"No problem. Let me know when you want to get together."

"Absolutely."

Jay gave Sheldon another assessing look, then

slowly walked away. Sheldon waited a good five seconds before tearing into her. "So he's the reason you practically kicked me out of your bed this morning?"

"What?"

"Don't give me that look. I saw how he was eyeing you up. And you didn't seem to mind one bit."

"The guy's a former client." Besides, she didn't owe Sheldon any explanations. "And I'm single, in case you've forgotten."

His eyes flashed fire. "Now you're single?"

"I have been for the past year."

Sheldon's fingers curled around Tyanna's wrist. He began walking, pulling her along with him.

"Sheldon!"

He ignored her, not stopping until he'd taken her outside the gym. The hot sun bore down on them instantly, and the humidity enveloped them like a hot, wet blanket.

Once he took her beyond the view of the glass doors, Tyanna yanked her arm away. "What the hell are you doing? You can't pull this caveman crap with me. Especially not at my workplace!"

"What's the deal with pretty boy?"

Tyanna gaped at him. "Not that I owe you any explanations, but there is no deal with him."

"And that's why he was all over you?"

"He was not!"

"It looked that way from where I was standing."

"You were standing pretty far away."

Sheldon huffed out a breath, turned, walked a few steps, then turned back to her. "I know you're *single*," he said, spitting out the word with distinct sarcasm. "But if you're going to sleep with me, I at least expect exclusivity."

Tyanna planted her hands on her hips and puffed out her chest. "Oh, really? Then I suppose we should have laid out those ground rules before we got naked, don'tcha think? Then I could have decided if that worked for me."

Why she was even leading Sheldon to believe that she had slept with another man—or men—she wasn't sure. But the flicker of pain that crossed his face pulled at her heart in a way she hadn't expected.

And she suddenly realized just how childish she had been.

Sheldon said, "I guess I'm the moron." He turned in the direction of the door.

"No, wait." When he faced her again, Tyanna blew out a frustrated breath. "Look, Sheldon." She spoke in a softer tone. "I'm being the moron. Jay and I haven't slept together. And I'm certainly not interested in sleeping with you one day and some other guy the next."

He gave a grim nod and glanced away. Tyanna frowned. She figured her words would give him some comfort, but he still seemed unhappy.

Tyanna's gaze roamed his back. His muscles

were tense, she realized. For the first time, she wondered if something other than a fit of jealousy was going on.

"Sheldon. What's wrong?"

He shrugged, but still didn't face her. "I guess I've got a lot on my mind."

"Does this have to do with Jay?"

Chuckling, he turned to face her. "Pretty boy? No."

"Then what is it?"

Sheldon watched a young couple walk past them after exiting the gym. When they were out of earshot, he said, "This isn't the time."

He started for the door, but Tyanna quickly grabbed hold of his arm. "Wait a second. You drag me out here, make a spectacle of me in the gym, and you can't even tell me what's actually bothering you?"

"Maybe later, when we can both sit down . . ."

"I have a pretty busy schedule." She flicked her wrist forward and glanced at her watch. "Starting in ten minutes."

"I can come back when you finish your shift."

"Damn it, Sheldon. This is exactly what I mean about you. You're shutting me out, and don't think I don't know it."

He looked at her for a long moment before speaking. "I'm probably making a big deal out of nothing."

Tyanna guffawed. "So much for what you said about trusting me." This time, she turned and marched toward the gym's doors. Sheldon Ford was frustrating her to no end.

Her hand was on the handle when Sheldon said, "All right."

Slowly she faced him.

"You want to know, I'll tell you. But I don't want to talk here. Can we talk in your office?"

"Sure."

"Good."

# Chapter 17

As Tyanna looked at Sheldon, her stomach took a nosedive. Something about Sheldon's expression really worried her. For the first time since she had begun to question him, she realized that perhaps something serious was going on. "You're scaring me."

Sheldon stepped behind her and opened one of the gym's double doors. "In your office."

"Right." Tyanna walked through the open door and led the way. Moments later, they were both seated at her desk. Without preamble she said, "Sheldon, what's going on?"

His Adam's apple bobbed up and down as he swallowed. "My mother got a weird call last night. When I was at your place."

"Oh?"

"Yeah, and I'm trying to figure it out. I guess that's what's got me on edge."

"What kind of call?" Tyanna asked.

"As far as I'm concerned, it doesn't make much sense. I mean, it can't. Dino is dead."

"Wait a second. The call had to do with Dino?"

"Not exactly. At least not explicitly. But Dino was the only one who wanted me dead."

Tyanna leaned her upper body across her desk. She gave Sheldon a level look. "You realize you're talking in circles? I have no clue what you're trying to say."

"Right, right. Let me start over. When I left your place this morning, I went home to find my mother pretty much hiding in her bedroom. She was definitely frightened. Now, ever since Dwight's murder, she's become much more of a worrywart, and seeing her worried has kind of set me off. I asked her what happened and she told me that she had received a phone call. What this person told her basically amounted to a threat against me."

Tyanna's eyes bulged. "What?"

"I know."

"B—but how? Why?"

"That's what I'm still trying to figure out," Sheldon explained. "I told my mother that it was a prank phone call."

"But you don't believe that."

"Whoever called mentioned me by name." Sheldon shrugged. "And now, I've been thinking. Yes, Dino is dead, but what if someone he knows wants to pick up where he left off? It's something I never considered before. I just figured, once he was out of the way, the threat was gone. But what if I'm wrong?"

Tyanna rested an elbow on the desk and planted her chin on her palm. "I don't know . . ."

"The only other person I've been in touch with is Maria, the ex-girlfriend he wanted dead."

"Do you think she—"

"No. Absolutely not. I hope I'm just overreacting, but I can't help thinking this is Dino's style. Make you sweat, then come at you full force."

"You really think so?"

"I'm not sure what to think."

Tyanna nodded slowly, trying to figure out what this all meant. She hoped and prayed the call was someone's idea of a joke. She said, "Well, I'm glad you told me."

"Tyanna Calhoun to the front desk," the loudspeakers announced.

"Shoot. That's my next client."

Sheldon pushed back his chair and stood. "No problem. Go ahead."

"What are you doing now?" Tyanna asked as she got to her feet.

"I guess I'm gonna head home. I'm worried about my mother. I didn't tell you, but while I was away, she had a heart attack."

"What?"

"Yeah. About three months ago."

"She never said anything."

"That's my mother." Sheldon shook his head ruefully.

She rounded her desk and reached for his hand. She squeezed it gently. "Is she okay?"

"For the most part, yeah. The doctor wants her to take it easy. She's the main reason I haven't looked for a new apartment yet. I want to make sure she's completely okay before I leave her alone. I feel bad enough that I wasn't around when it happened."

"I'm so sorry, Sheldon."

He shrugged. "Thanks."

Tyanna sighed softly. "I'm sorry that I have to cut this short."

"No, that's okay."

"Please call me if you learn anything new."

"I will," Sheldon assured her. "And who knows? Maybe it's nothing."

Tyanna awoke early the next day. She'd promised Wendy that she would meet her at the gym to go over their workout routine, even if it was at the ungodly hour of six A.M., when the gym opened. Wendy's shift started at seven, so that would give them an hour to rehearse the routine Wendy had devised.

Tyanna definitely wasn't a morning person, so if she was going to do this, she would need some help. Climbing out of bed, she retrieved her robe from the chair in her bedroom, then shuffled into the kitchen.

The first thing she did was pull her coffee machine out from the cupboard under the sink. As she did, her mind wandered to Sheldon. A frown pulled at her lips. She hadn't heard from him last night. Did that mean all was fine? Or had something else happened that he didn't want to share with her?

Worrying about him was something Tyanna didn't want to do, but she couldn't help it. Knowing that his story about Dino was true meant there could still be a threat to his life. Some friend or associate of Dino who knew about Sheldon and was angry with him.

Tyanna measured three heaping teaspoons of coffee into the filter. She filled the carafe with water, dumped it into the machine and turned it on. She wasn't normally up this early and didn't feel particularly hungry, but if she was going to do a workout she would need some food. A quick search of the refrigerator made it clear that the only viable option for breakfast was some toast. Well, that was something she would have to do once she finished with Wendy—head straight for the grocery store. Thank goodness she at least had some butter and a little bit of jam.

Though she didn't drink coffee daily, the aroma today had never smelled so good. Before the three cups were brewed, she pulled the carafe from the coffeemaker and stuck a cup under the steady flow. She was lucky to have a drop of milk in the fridge. Once the coffee was adequately sweetened and diluted, Tyanna took a good, long sip.

Definitely yummy! She felt her head clearing already.

She finished her toast and headed to the shower. She wasn't a happy camper this morning. She could only hope this video effort was going to pay off.

*Positive*, she told herself. *You have to think positive.*

Wendy was all smiles when Tyanna approached her in the lobby area of the gym.

"Morning, Sunshine," Wendy practically sang.

"Morning," Tyanna muttered in reply.

Wendy wrapped her arm around her shoulder and gave her a squeeze. "I hope you're wide awake and ready."

"I'm on my third cup of coffee." Tyanna lifted the Styrofoam cup filled with coffee she had purchased on the way to the gym. "I hope this does the trick."

Wendy chuckled.

"Don't you laugh at me. You're used to getting up with the birds. I'm not."

"Just remember, it will all be worth it."

"That's what I'm counting on."

"Picture the tour," Wendy went on. "You and me hitting every big city to promote the video. Signing autographs . . . After that, we'll have to move to Los Angeles. We'll be hot commodities as personal trainers, and you know personal trainers in Hollywood make big bucks."

"We can hope." Tyanna and Wendy had talked about the prospect of moving to Los Angeles, even if the video project didn't work out. People in South Florida were very concerned with their bodies and overall appearance, but that was even truer in Hollywood. If they could hook up with a few actors and musicians, or even wannabes who were willing to pay the Hollywood price for a trainer, they could do very well financially.

"Not hope," Wendy scolded Tyanna. "Make it a reality."

"You're right. Absolutely, we can do this."

Linking arms with Tyanna, Wendy led her upstairs to one of the two aerobics rooms. "I spoke with Max," Wendy said, mentioning the gym's manager. "Asked if we could borrow a couple mats and step platforms for our video. And he said no problem."

"Oh, good."

Tyanna downed the dregs of her now cold coffee and threw the cup in a nearby garbage can. By the time she turned around, Wendy was already on her butt on a mat, stretching. Tyanna shot her a mock scowl as Wendy gave her a saccharine sweet smile.

"Get over here, grumpy."

Tyanna inhaled a slow, deep breath and released it just as slowly. She was here; she may as well get in the mood to do this.

"All right." She clapped her hands together, trying to motivate herself. "I'm ready."

Tyanna moved swiftly, grabbing a mat and joining Wendy on the floor. Wendy sat with her legs spread, one arm stretched over her head as she arched over the opposite side of her body.

Tyanna mimicked Wendy's movement, stretching to one side, then the other.

"I've finalized the opening," Wendy said. "We'll start the stretches standing, work down to the ground, and from there go into low-impact aerobics with leg lifts and such before ending up on our feet again for the jazzercise and kickboxing."

The last time they had run through the routine, they had done stretches on the floor first. "Sounds good," Tyanna told her.

"Let's do it." Wendy climbed to her feet. "We may as well grab the steps as well, see where we'll position them."

They spent the next couple minutes figuring out where they would want to position the mats and the steps, taking into consideration the area surrounding Tyanna's parents' pool.

Tyanna hadn't bothered to bring any music. First of all, the gym's speakers constantly played upbeat music while it was open, so additional music would only be distracting. Besides, Tyanna figured they might be better off using computer-generated beats for their video.

"Ready?" Wendy asked.

Tyanna nodded.

"Hello, everyone. Thanks for joining us for what will be a half hour of fun and fitness." Wendy giggled. Smirking at Tyanna, she said, "I don't know."

"It sounds good," Tyanna told her.

"I'll work it all out by Sunday." She took her

place on the mat. "Today we're going to start with a warm-up. A good warm-up is essential to any exercise program. Okay, stand with your legs parted, knees slightly bent, hands on your hips. . . ."

Tyanna followed Wendy's instructions as she began various stretching exercises. Thirty-five minutes later, and covered with a sheen of sweat, they had gone through the entire routine Wendy had devised.

"Last breath in. Last breath out. Excellent." Wendy smiled so naturally and easily, it was as if she had just done a relaxing yoga exercise instead of low- and high-impact jazzercise and kickboxing. "Thanks for joining us today, and until next time, stay fit."

"Whew!" Tyanna exhaled a gush of breath and threw her body down on the mat.

"You like?"

Tyanna angled her head in Wendy's direction. "Uh-huh. That was a great workout."

"Good. I'm so glad you liked it."

"Great for toning, great cardio. Simply great."

"Thanks."

"I say we've pretty much got this down."

"I think so, too. Of course, we may or may not shoot the video in one smooth sequence, depending on the camera issues. And maybe we'll have to do it more than once. But that'll be up to Phil and the crew."

"Regardless, this is gonna be fun."

Wendy held her hands before her face in a prayerful gesture. "Oh, I hope Ronnie likes it."

"He's gotta like it," Tyanna replied, then chuckled. "We're fabulous, dahling."

"From your lips to God's ears."

By Friday of that week, Tyanna was worried. She still hadn't heard from Sheldon, and she hadn't seen him at the gym either. She knew he was working at his new job, but she couldn't help wondering if something was wrong.

Staring at the phone in her office, she wondered if she should call him. Their current relationship was up and down at best.

Maybe that's why she hadn't heard from him. Because of what she had told him during their argument over Jay—that whomever she slept with was her business.

None of that mattered now, she realized. They didn't have to be lovers or even best friends for her to call and make sure he was okay.

She grabbed the receiver and dialed his number. Mrs. Ford answered. "Hello?"

"Hello, Mrs. Ford. It's Tyanna."

"Oh," she said pleasantly. "Hello."

"How are you? Sheldon told me you had a heart attack. I didn't know. I'm sorry."

"Yes, I did. But I'm still going strong. Not going to let something like that hold me back." Millie chuckled softly. "How about you, sweetheart? How are you doing?"

"Good. Good." Tyanna fiddled with the phone cord. "Um, I'm at work right now so I don't have much time. Is Sheldon there?"

"Actually, he's not. As far as I know, he's working."

Of course. Why was she so concerned? It made sense that he was going to be busy with his new job. Still, Tyanna was disappointed.

"I can tell him you called."

"Please do. I'm at work for the entire evening."

"Okay."

But she didn't hear from him over the next several hours. She had called home several times, and there wasn't even one message from him.

Only her sister, Charlene, had called, asking how she was doing. Now that the family knew Sheldon was back in town, Tyanna was sure that's why Charlene had called, to see if she and Sheldon were once again involved in any way.

She would call Charlene tomorrow. For now, Tyanna couldn't stop thinking about Sheldon and why he wasn't getting back to her.

She wasn't sure what to make of this. Was something going on that he wasn't telling her about? The mere idea set her stomach fluttering. She remembered all the times during their relationship that she had known something was bothering him, but he had shut her out.

Wasn't that his style? Tyanna felt a flash of annoyance. As much as she hoped Sheldon had changed, he probably hadn't. This was exactly

what she didn't want to put herself through—
more days like this, where she worried and worried, while he kept her in the dark.

She didn't want to jump to negative conclu-
sions, but neither did she want to be a fool again.

It was with that thought on her mind that she
finished her shift. And it didn't bode well.

She was packing up her belongings in her office when she heard, "Boo!"

Her heart pounding with fright, Tyanna
whirled around. Jay stood behind her.

"Sorry." He flashed a sheepish smile. "I
couldn't resist."

Tyanna gave a slight nod and turned back to
her bag. "How can I help you?"

"I was hoping we could get together this weekend
for that dinner. Maybe tomorrow or on Sunday?"

Heaving her tote bag over her shoulder,
Tyanna faced him. "Sunday's definitely out of the
question."

"All right. How about tomorrow?"

"I'm working tomorrow afternoon."

"Then how about lunch?" Jay asked, not missing a beat.

Tyanna's eyes ventured to the phone, as if she
expected it to ring. Of course, it wasn't going to.

She thought of Sheldon, but a voice sounded in
her head. *Fool.* Damn him. He was making her so
confused. One minute she was wondering if they
had a chance at a relationship again. The next, she
wasn't hearing from him and she had no clue if

he was shutting her out of something important in his life.

She didn't want to deal with this again.

Hadn't she told herself that she needed to move on with her life? It was clear, now more than ever, that the only potential Sheldon had was to hurt her again. Not once since he'd been back had he said anything that would make her believe he loved her. Sure, she wanted to believe he did, but she had wanted to believe that the first time around. And she didn't want to continue a sexual relationship with him just for the sake of having great sex.

Facing Jay, she smiled. "You know, Jay, that's a great idea." At least a lunch with Jay would take her mind off Sheldon. "One o'clock? We can meet here and walk to one of the nearby restaurants."

Jay's face lit up with surprise and delight. "That'd be cool."

"Okay. See you tomorrow, then."

Tyanna watched Jay walk off. The fact that he seemed genuinely happy to be spending time with her made her heart lift a little.

Sheldon hadn't called. She doubted he was going to.

She certainly wasn't going to sit around holding her breath waiting for him.

Nope. She had made a promise to herself that she would get on with her life, and that's exactly what she was going to do.

## Chapter 18

Sheldon paced the packed waiting area in the Jackson Memorial Hospital emergency. His mind replayed the day's tragic events.

"Are you mad at me?" Matt asked.

Sheldon stopped pacing and faced Matt. The thirteen-year-old looked at him with a worried expression, his bottom lip trembling. For the first time, his voice sounded scared and childlike, unlike the tough person he always tried to be.

"Look, Matt. I'm not going to lie to you. I'm not happy about what happened today." Matt and Brian had gotten into a horrible fight at the youth center, and the police had been called. Sheldon's first trip had been to the police station with Brian, also thirteen, who was being charged with assault. After spending a couple hours trying to convince the police to go easy on the young teen, he had returned to find Matt still there—still waiting for his mother to show up and take him to the hospital. Knowing Matt needed medical attention, Sheldon had taken Matt to the hospital himself.

"I already told you," Matt said. "It was Brian's fault."

"You should have come to me before the problem got worse." According to Matt, Brian had started jeering him on the basketball court. When Matt told Brian to leave him alone, Brian attacked him—unprovoked. Of course, in Brian's version, he had blamed Matt for the fight.

Sheldon sat down beside the teen. "Matt, there are going to be a lot of times in life when people tease you, say mean things that hurt you. But as hard as it is, you're better off walking away."

"And let him get away with it?"

"No, I didn't say that. If you had come to me, I would have taken Brian aside and talked to him." During the short time Sheldon had been working with these teens, he had tried to teach them how to resolve problems without turning to physical violence. He knew it would be a long road, because for many of these kids, violence was what they saw in their homes.

Even now, after hours in emergency with Matt, his mother hadn't shown up—and this was after repeated calls to her home and workplace.

Sheldon placed an arm around Matt's shoulder, the way a parent in his life should. "What have I tried to teach you about solving problems with others?"

Matt dropped his head. "I know. But he made

me so mad, saying all that stuff about me being so weak and skinny."

A stupid argument, and now one boy was sitting in jail and another in the hospital. Sheldon asked, "What would have been better—walking away or keeping the fight going?"

"Walking away," Matt softly admitted.

"This isn't the end of the world, but you know there are consequences for your behavior. First of all, you're stuck here waiting to see a doctor to get stitches for your busted lip. But you'll also be suspended for a week. Or—"

"Oh, man."

"Or," Sheldon continued, "you'll have to do some work at the center. Dirty work. Cleaning up after everyone." It wouldn't be fun, but at least Matt wouldn't have to stay at home alone. Sheldon knew the kid enjoyed being at the youth center. "It's your choice. You don't have to tell me your decision today. But think about it."

"Okay." Matt sighed. "Where's my mother?"

"I'm sure she's gonna be here as soon as possible," Sheldon lied. He had no clue when she was going to show up. They would have to sit here until she arrived, as she was his guardian and had to okay any medical treatment.

Sheldon's heart ached for this young boy.

"You want me to call her again?" Sheldon asked. If he used the phone again, he would put in a quick call to Tyanna and let her know how his day was going.

"No." Matt squeezed Sheldon's hand. "Please stay with me."

Warmth spread through Sheldon's body. In the short time he had known Matt, the boy had started to trust him, to look up to him. Matt needed him, and Sheldon was going to be there for him.

"No problem, Matt," Sheldon told him. "I'm not going anywhere."

A huge yawn slid its way up Tyanna's throat and forced itself through her mouth. The moment her lips widened to accommodate it, she remembered where she was and who she was with, and she quickly smacked a hand over her mouth to stifle the evidence of her boredom. She failed.

However, Jay didn't seem to notice. Which was good, given the circumstances, but proof of his dim-wittedness. He just kept right on blabbing about how some exterminators duped clients by bringing in dead roaches to get their business, and how he abhorred the cheaters because they gave everyone a bad name. Apparently—or else he wouldn't be talking about it—he was one of the good ones.

Tyanna forced a smile. Had she ever been more bored in her life? She was tempted to fake choking on a sip of her water, just to have an excuse to get up and leave. Given the chance, she would—and she wouldn't return. The problem was, she still had to see Jay at Jaguar Fitness.

"People think being an exterminator is naturally a great business in South Florida, but that's not always the case," Jay told her.

"Hmm." *Spare me.* Good grief, her original instinct to keep Jay at bay had been the right one.

Tyanna feigned fascination with her straw. She jabbed at the slice of lemon at the bottom of the plastic cup, tasted the water, then poked the lemon some more.

Jay laughed. Tyanna looked up to see that he wasn't laughing at her, but at some joke he must have told. Brother. The guy was cute, but he was entirely too dull.

Thankfully, Tyanna had had a respite from his stories during the meal. She hadn't wanted to be rude by eating and running, but she had had enough of this date and simply wanted to leave.

Glancing at her watch, she said, "Oh. My, look at the time."

Jay looked at his own watch. "It's a little after two. Don't you start at three?"

"Yes, but I . . . I have to speak with Max. I told you about the fitness video Wendy and I are filming tomorrow?"

"Yeah."

Wow, he'd actually been listening to her. "Well . . . I need to firm up some details with Max. He's lending us some stuff from the gym. Plus, I have to make a couple calls. That kind of thing."

"Oh." Jay looked and sounded disappointed.

"Thanks so much for lunch," Tyanna told him. "I'm glad we're friends."

She put some emphasis on *friends*, hoping Jay would get the picture. There was no way in hell she would ever be interested in a relationship with him.

The whole purpose of this date had been to get Sheldon out of her mind and take a step toward moving on with her life. Yet it seemed she achieved exactly the opposite. If all the prospects were going to be like Jay, she may as well pull the plug on the whole dating idea.

*It's not Jay or anyone else*, a little voice told her. *You miss Sheldon.*

Maybe *that* was her problem. She did miss Sheldon, even though she shouldn't. And instead of getting him out of her mind, the urge to see him was greater than ever.

*Just to make sure he's okay*, she told herself.

"Hey, Lecia. To what do I owe this honor?" Her sister rarely called her at work.

"I realize I never asked you if I could come by tomorrow and watch the filming of the video. Charlene wants to know if she can come too."

"I don't mind. As long as everyone stays out of the crew's way, I'm sure they won't have a problem."

"Excellent. I'm interested in seeing how this whole thing comes together."

"Hmm." Tyanna briefly bit down on her bottom lip. "I'm surprised."

"Why?" Lecia asked. "You know I've always been interested in creative things."

"Yeah, well, that was a while ago. I figured now that you're a doctor . . ."

"You figured wrong," Lecia said simply. "In fact . . . I've been dabbling in some writing again."

Tyanna's eyes widened with surprise. "That *is* a shock."

"Being a doctor takes up a ton of my time, but I can't let it be my whole life. I realized recently that I still need a creative outlet."

"Good for you," Tyanna told her.

There was a moment of silence before Lecia said, "You may not know this, but I've always admired you—your free spirit and your ability to go for what you wanted, no matter what anyone else has to say about it."

Meaning their parents. "That was a stressful route as well," said Tyanna. "I think Mom and Dad just gave up on me after a while."

"I wouldn't say that. They've accepted you. You didn't give any of us a choice."

"This is true," Tyanna agreed.

"At least you'll never have any regrets about not having tried something you wanted to try. That's a big deal."

Tyanna couldn't help it—she suddenly felt overwhelmed. She couldn't remember the last time Lecia had said something this nice to her. Usually, she felt she had completely failed to live up to the Calhoun standard of excellence. And while she never would admit it to them, that knowledge often made her feel like a failure. Like someone still struggling to find her way in the world *and* make her parents happy at the same time.

"That's a really, really nice thing for you to say, Lecia. Thank you."

"I mean it." She paused. "Anyway, I'll let you go. See you tomorrow."

"Yeah, tomorrow."

"Hey, wait a second," Lecia quickly said. "About last Sunday—everyone was looking forward to Mom's sweet potato pie. But when she went to get it, it was gone."

"Oh." Tyanna cleared her throat. "Yeah."

"I thought you weren't feeling well."

"You know Mom's pie—the perfect cure for whatever ails you."

"You're too much." Tyanna could picture Lecia shaking her head with a silly smile on her lips.

"That's me," Tyanna agreed. "Anyway, I'll see you tomorrow."

"You bet."


The rest of the night was fairly uneventful. When Mrs. Bradshaw whined about not being able to do another set on the leg press, Tyanna took it in stride. She didn't bother to push the woman as she might have on another occasion. Nor did she get annoyed. Her sister's uncharacteristic praise had her in a pretty good mood. She knew Mrs. Bradshaw would complain later about how she wasn't seeing much in the way of results, how she simply couldn't stop eating sweets and fatty foods—but Tyanna would take that in stride, too. The first rule of any successful training program is that you have to want to help yourself. No one else can do it for you.

She still hadn't heard from Sheldon, and that did cause her some concern, but the fact that his mother hadn't mentioned anything weird when she'd talked to her the night before had put Tyanna's mind somewhat at ease. Still she hoped to hear from him.

However, she had other pressing issues to think about—like the video shoot tomorrow.

A sudden bout of the jitters hit her. She had done a lot of things in her life, and she'd never been this nervous. Not even when she'd gotten her first job as a bartender by fudging her resume to say she had experience.

But this . . . This was different. An entire future was riding on this.

*Which is exactly the way you shouldn't think about it*, she told herself. *Think about it as another day, a fun project you're planning for the afternoon.*

To obsess over what might or might not come out of this was bound to cause performance anxiety.

Somehow, she was able to put herself in the right frame of mind, and was much more relaxed. Of course, who knew how she was going to feel in the morning.

Tyanna was in the middle of a session with another client when a page came through, telling her that she had an important call.

"Cathy, do you mind waiting a moment?" she asked her client. Though she had told herself that she wouldn't worry about Sheldon, she knew she needed to hear his voice to take off the slight edge of anxiety she felt.

"Go ahead."

"You can do another round of weights until I get back, if you want."

Tyanna hustled to the gym's reception counter instead of her office. "Hey, Shirley. Which line?"

"Line two."

Tyanna pressed the appropriate button. "Hello?"

A small smile played on Tyanna's lips as she waited a moment, expecting to hear Sheldon's voice come on the line. Instead, she heard nothing.

"Hello?" she repeated.

"I've been watching you," a gruff voice said. "Both of you."

"Who is this?"

"Tell Sheldon that I know where he lives."

"Who *is* this?"

"He was really stupid. I followed him home from the gym and he didn't even know."

"I'm calling the police."

There was a hoarse laugh. "Go ahead. That won't stop us from finally getting to Sheldon. As soon as we're ready."

"You leave him—"

There was a soft click, then a dial tone.

Her heart beating frantically, Tyanna passed the phone back to Shirley.

Shirley looked at her with concern. "What?"

"I . . ." Tyanna waved off the question and hurried back to Cathy.

Though she hardly could concentrate. Not after a phone call like that.

There was no mistaking the threat. Sheldon was really in trouble.

God help them.

Tyanna couldn't help feeling a chill run down her spine as she stepped outside after her shift. The parking lot didn't provide nearly enough lighting for her liking.

She wished she had been able to reach Sheldon, but she didn't have a number for him where he was currently working. Part of her had hoped that he would stop by, but another part was glad he had stayed away. What if someone was out there, waiting for him to appear?

What if they had already gotten to him?

The fear was stifling, and Tyanna quickly started for her car. She didn't want to worry about anything other than the shoot tomorrow, but how could she not have concerns?

At least Wendy had already picked up the mats and step platforms, so Tyanna didn't have to worry about that now.

Making her way to the car, Tyanna remembered her impromptu self-defense lesson she'd given Sheldon the night he'd reappeared in her life. She kept her head up as she dug for her keys in her purse.

But as she neared her car, another chill swept over her and her skin broke out in goose bumps. Something made her turn around.

A scream tore from her throat.

The dark figure lunged at her, leaving her merely a fraction of a second to react. She jumped to the side and hunched her body, but she didn't move fast enough. The man's arms encircled her waist, but at least momentum was on her side. His fingers didn't quite lock, and she squirmed out of his grasp. In a quick movement she whirled around, raising her foot in a kick as she did.

Her foot landed in his gut, but it wasn't enough to knock him over, only to catch him off guard. It was the best she could do, and she turned, running to her car.

She was almost at the car door when she felt a hand clamp down roughly over her mouth. *Oh, God!* her mind screamed.

She grabbed his arm with both hands and tried to rip it from her lips. Her mouth struggled to move behind the death grip he had on her, hoping to bite him, but she couldn't move her lips enough to expose her teeth.

"Tell Sheldon his days are numbered," a raspy

voice said. Then the man let her go, shoving her forward. Her hands flew out to break her fall as she tumbled to the ground.

Tyanna's purse went one way, her tote bag the other. She quickly scrambled to her feet, but when she turned to face her attacker, he was already running away, through the dark parking lot.

A sob escaped her throat, half relieved, half frightened.

And then she started crying. Her shoulders drooped as all her strength seemed to ooze out of her.

"Sheldon," she said softly, wishing he was here right now.

Pulling herself together, Tyanna set about collecting her belongings from the asphalt.

"Sheldon . . ."

The faint sound of her voice immediately put him on guard. Gripping the receiver tighter, he sat up, sliding his feet off the edge of his bed. "Tyanna?"

"Yeah, it's me."

"What is it? What's wrong?" Was that a sniffle he heard?

"Something happened," she told him. "Something bad."

"Where are you?" he asked.

"I'm outside a McDonald's. Just sitting in my car." Another sniffle. Damn, she was crying. "I don't want to go home."

"Then come here."

"I don't know. It's late. . . ."

"Don't worry about the time. My mother's already sleeping."

"I don't want to wake her." She paused. She thought of his mother's heart condition and instantly felt bad for calling, even though she wanted to alert Sheldon to what was going on. "And I . . ."

"What?" Sheldon asked anxiously.

"I don't want to worry her. But I need to talk to you."

Sheldon had been trying to control his emotions, let Tyanna tell him what was going on at her own pace. But right about now, he thought his heart would seize from the intense worry he was feeling. So he said, "Tell me what happened, Tyanna."

"Someone came after me tonight," she answered softly.

Sheldon hesitated only a moment, Tyanna's words registering in his brain. Then he was on his feet with the cordless, searching for a shirt to put on.

"The police came to the gym. They took my statement. I'm sure the guy's long gone, but now I'm afraid to go home."

"I'll meet you there," Sheldon told her.

"At the McDonald's?"

"No, at your apartment. In the parking lot." When she didn't say anything, Sheldon added,

"You can't stay where you are all night. I'll make sure you're okay. Whatever you do, just wait for me in the parking lot. Do not go upstairs without me."

"Okay. But please, please, please—make sure no one follows you."

She sounded so frail, so vulnerable. So *scared*. And he felt helpless. He had been helpless to save Dwight, and he hoped to God there wouldn't be a repeat of that situation. He wanted to be there always to protect anyone he cared about, and that included Tyanna.

He knew Dwight's murder had been the catalyst that made him consider a career in law enforcement. He never wanted to feel helpless again, and he wanted to do a job where he could make a difference. Whether it was hunting down bad guys or stopping them before they committed their evil crimes, Sheldon wanted to be a part of the process.

But right now, Tyanna was his main priority. If only he could snap his fingers and be with her already.

"I'm on my way out right now," he told her.

"All right," Tyanna said. "I'll see you soon."

# Chapter 19

When Sheldon pulled into the parking lot of Tyanna's building and saw her standing at the rear of her car, he felt a moment of panic. Shit, he'd told her to wait for him, but he had assumed she would know better than to wait outside her car. She had practically made a target of herself.

Sheldon slammed on his brakes, burning rubber as he did. Tyanna came around to the passenger side of his car. He hit a button with his thumb, and the passenger window rolled down.

"Tyanna, what are you doing standing out here?" he asked.

She looked at him with confusion, and he knew his irritated tone had frightened her.

"I . . . I was waiting for you," she replied.

"You should have stayed in your car. If the guy who attacked you had come to your place, you would have been a walking target."

"I'm sure he didn't follow me."

"But he could have."

Tyanna slowly shook her head. "If this is why you came over, to lecture me, then you can leave right now."

Sheldon looked at her a long moment before answering. "No. Of course that's not why I came over. I'm just worried." He hit the button to unlock all the doors. "Hop in."

Tyanna opened the door to the Explorer and climbed in.

"How're you holding up?" Sheldon asked her.

"I'm still shaking a little."

She extended her hands, and Sheldon could see the slight tremble. He took her left hand into his. "I'm sorry. But you're safe now."

They fell into silence as Sheldon parked, and stayed quiet until they reached her apartment. Once inside, Sheldon wrapped his arms around her.

At first, her body shook slightly, but as he continued to hold her, she calmed. It felt good to have her in his arms like this. Felt good to know he could give her some comfort.

He kissed her temple. "Tell me what happened."

Tyanna's head bobbed up and down jerkily. "Let's sit on the sofa."

Sheldon kept his arm around her shoulders as they slowly walked into her living room. They sat together.

Angling his body toward hers, Sheldon took her hands in his. "All right. What happened?"

Tyanna glanced down, then back up at him. "This is bad, Sheldon."

His grip on her hands tightened. "What do you mean? This guy hurt you? Violated—"

"No, no. Nothing like that."

"You would tell me, right?"

Tyanna nodded. "Yes, I would."

Sheldon relaxed somewhat. "If he didn't hurt you, then it could have been worse."

"It all started with a phone call I got at the gym. I'd gotten one before, where someone hung up, and I didn't think much of it. But this one . . ." Tyanna blew out a frazzled breath. "Someone specifically told me to tell you that he's watching you, and that he's going to get you."

Sheldon's stomach filled with dread. There could be no mistaking that this was related to Dino. And he could kick himself for being so optimistic to think that because Dino was dead, the threat to his life was over. So damned naïve.

"I tried to reach you, but you were working. And you never called. . . ."

"I had a crisis with two of the teens at the youth center. One was arrested, and I went to the hospital with the other."

"That bad?" Tyanna asked.

"It got pretty ugly, but I think everything's gonna work out. Right now, I'm not worried about that. Tell me what happened."

Tyanna looked at Sheldon and gave him a brief nod before continuing. "When I was heading to my car after work, this guy came up behind me. He grabbed me. I kicked him but he clamped his hand over my mouth and scared me to death. Then he said to tell you that your days are numbered, and he threw me down."

For a full five seconds, all Sheldon could do was stare at her. His whole body froze.

Wrapping his brain around what Tyanna had just said, Sheldon rose to his feet. He knew he'd heard her, but he had to be sure. "That's what he said?"

"Yes."

"Shit." He dragged a hand over his face. "I don't understand this." Sheldon began to pace. "How the hell does anyone associated with Dino know I'm back in town?" He stopped walking, turning to face Tyanna. "And even if they did know I was back in town, why come after you? If they knew we were lovers, why didn't they come after you before? If Dino knew about you all along, he sure as hell would have gone after you before. None of this makes a lick of sense."

"I don't know, Sheldon. But obviously that call to your mother's place and the attack on me tonight proves that someone knows something." Tyanna whimpered. "The guy also said he knows where you live. That he followed you from the gym."

"Son of a bitch!"

"You said Dino was the kind of guy who liked

to make a person sweat. Do you think it's possible his goons knew where you were all along and just waited until you were back in town?"

Sheldon faced her then. Tyanna saw the frustration in his eyes. "I can't imagine that. But then, I have no clue what to think right now."

Tyanna's mind went over the incident again and again. She tried to think of any clue she had missed. "I wish I could tell what he looked like, but he was dressed in all black, and he wore a hat that came halfway over his face. I only know he's a white guy. That's all I saw."

"Facial hair?"

"Not that I could tell. And he didn't have an accent that I could identify."

Sheldon nodded, then paced over to a window. Tyanna thought he was going to look outside, but he didn't. He simply stood there, lost in thought.

And suddenly it hit her. How all this could have happened.

*Oh, no,* she thought grimly. If she was right, this was all her fault. And Sheldon wasn't going to like it. Not one bit.

Wringing her hands together, she continued to watch Sheldon. She carefully considered her words. But all that came out was, "Um . . ."

Sheldon turned around. "Did you say something?"

Tyanna's shoulders drooped as a breath of defeat oozed out of her. No matter how she worded it, Sheldon was going to be angry.

He started toward her. "What, Tyanna? What are you not telling me?"

"Just promise me you won't get mad."

Both his eyebrows shot up. "What do you mean, promise you I won't get mad?"

"Don't do . . . exactly what you're doing now. Raising your voice. Thinking the worst when I'm not even sure if . . ."

He reached for her and drew her up from her position on the sofa so that she was standing against him. He held her firmly by the shoulders. There was something in his eyes, something she could only describe as panic.

"Tyanna, you have to tell me."

"All right." He relaxed his hold on her. "I . . . I spoke to Leona, and I'm wondering—"

"Leona from Ultimate Fitness?"

Tyanna nodded.

"My God. When?"

"I don't know. A couple weeks ago. Shortly after I ran into you and you told me about Dino."

Sheldon shook his head, disappointed. "Why?"

"Don't—don't give me that. You have to know why I went to see Leona. Your story just seemed too incredible. I didn't go there to ask her outright about what you'd told me. I went figuring I'd ask some questions—ask about Dino. Of course, if I saw him alive and well, I'd know that you were lying to me."

"And he wasn't there." It was a statement.

"No. I know now that you were telling me the

truth, but at the time . . . I didn't know what to think. Anyway, when Dino wasn't there, I asked Leona where he was. As it turns out, she told me that Dino had been killed. That led to me naturally asking what happened to him, and from there it became clear that your story had to be true."

"You didn't believe me."

Tyanna shrugged, then said, "I guess not. But you knew that. It's not that I didn't want to believe you, but I also never would have figured you for the type to leave me without even saying good-bye." Tyanna sighed her frustration. "I had to know, Sheldon. I had to know for sure. If it seems like I didn't trust you, I guess I can't deny that." She paused, then added, "I'm sorry."

Sheldon turned his back on her and walked back to the window. This time he slipped a hand through the blinds and peered outside. For a long while he simply stood there. Tyanna suspected he wasn't really seeing anything.

"You must have mentioned me."

"I . . . I think so. Yeah, I did. Leona asked how I'd heard about Dino, and that's when I mentioned you. I said you were the one who told me. I told her that you had once worked at the gym. Damn, I even told her your full name, trying to see if it rang a bell. She seemed to have a vague memory of you at best."

Sheldon chuckled sarcastically. "Really?"

"Yeah. I had no clue that would cause any problem. I figured that Dino was dead. Any threat was over. What could it hurt to talk to Leona about it?"

"Did you know she was Dino's girlfriend?"

Tyanna's mouth hit the floor. "What did you say?"

Turning slowly, Sheldon faced her and nodded. "Yep. The whole time she was working at the gym."

Tyanna buried her face in her hands. She had sensed that possibility when talking to Leona about Dino's death. But in all the time she had worked at the gym, she had never known. She and Leona hadn't been close friends.

"Oh, my God. Oh, Sheldon. I'm so sorry. I never saw anything to indicate they were lovers. . . ."

"You were busy with your clients."

"True." Lord help her, she had messed up big time.

"I understand you were skeptical of my story, but to go back to the gym? The very place where the threat to my life began? This is exactly why I didn't tell you anything about Dwight, nor what my real plan was. Because I worried that you'd somehow let something slip. And I was right." He paused. "And you talk about honesty, yet you don't tell me about your chat with Leona?"

"That's not fair," Tyanna quickly countered. "Sure, maybe I should have told you about my visit with Leona. But you should have told me that Leona was Dino's girlfriend. Hell, if I'd known that, I would have known to tread lightly with her. Besides, she's not Dino. Why would she want to hurt you?"

Sheldon stared at her, and she stared right back.

"Why?" he finally asked. "Who knows why? Because of some twisted sense of loyalty? Because someone else in Dino's crew wanted me dead and the moment she learned I was back in town she told this person? Who knows, Tyanna? I don't understand how these warped minds think. All I know is that Leona has to be the missing link here. And you're the one who went to see her."

Sheldon hadn't yelled at Tyanna. Still, it was clear he was angry with her.

"I know I'm not the most credible person to speak about honesty right now," she began, "but this is my whole point about you needing to be up front with me. If I had known all the facts before, my slip-up could have been avoided. But you keep everything inside, thinking that's going to protect me—"

"I don't want to have this conversation."

"Oh, really?"

"Yeah, really."

"I said I was sorry."

Sheldon walked toward her. Stopping in front of her, he merely stared at her, then groaned. "I—I need some time to think."

"Oh, so you're going to run away again?"

"I'm not saying that."

"Then what are you going to do? Think here on my sofa? Or am I not going to hear from you for another year?"

Sheldon didn't respond right away, and Tyanna walked past him, disappointed. This was exactly why she didn't want to get involved with him again in any capacity. She knew that he could and would hurt her.

She stopped at her dining-room table and gripped the back of one of the chairs with both hands.

"Am I upset?" Sheldon asked behind her. "Yes, I'm upset, but at the situation. Things just happen sometimes, no matter what you do to try and prevent them. I need to think now, because I'm worried. Leona knows I'm back in town, and it's either her orchestrating this attempt on my life, or someone else close to Dino. Who knows? Maybe I brought heat down on Dino when I went to the cops about Dwight's death. Sometimes, they watch a person for a while before they're able to make an arrest. So maybe Dino's friends blame me for his death." It was an idea that made sense. "God, I'd hoped this would all die with the bastard."

Tyanna's body flinched at the feel of Sheldon's hands on her shoulders. She hadn't heard him approaching, hadn't sensed him. Surprisingly, his touch was soft. And it was comforting.

"This was my worst fear, Tyanna. That they would connect you to me." He rested his chin against her head. "I don't really know what to think."

Tyanna turned in his arms. "I really am sorry."

"I know you are. If someone is angry that Dino is dead and figures that in some way I brought heat down on him, then this threat is very real. Of course, people like this aren't entirely rational, anyway. They'll come up with any reason to hurt someone."

Sheldon let his statement hang in the air, and Tyanna's stomach fluttered. After a moment, she said, "There was a man working at the juice bar with Leona."

"There was?"

"Mmm hmm. Some guy I'd never seen before."

Sheldon processed the information in silence.

Tyanna asked, "You're not going to leave, are you?"

Sheldon wrapped his arms around Tyanna. "I don't really think I should leave you tonight."

It was a simple statement, not at all sexual, but Tyanna's body suddenly began to throb. "Are you tired?"

"Not really."

"Then maybe you can sit with me. We can talk? About something else," she quickly added.

Sheldon gazed down at her. "Something else on your mind?"

"Kind of. Let's sit." Taking his hand in hers, Tyanna led him to the sofa. She sat, bringing her legs up onto the sofa under her. Sheldon sat back, resting his head sideways against the headrest so that he could face her.

She sighed. "When I didn't see you around this week, I was kind of worried about you."

"You said you needed space."

"Yes, but I didn't think you'd give it to me." She smiled. "Anyway, not hearing from you . . . I guess it made me think about you more."

"Really?"

"Uh-huh. I know I've pretty much been pushing you away, but I've been thinking about you a lot," Tyanna admitted softly, her eyes locking with Sheldon's.

"You have?"

She nodded. "I've been thinking a lot about us. The way things used to be. I . . . can't seem to stop."

Sheldon's chest rose and fell as he drew in and blew out a deep breath. "What are you saying?"

"I guess I'm saying that I'm confused. About us. If what we had was real. If we can actually have a future. I loved the sex, don't get me wrong, but sometimes I wonder if that's all there is to *us*."

"Really?"

"Yes, really. Haven't you wondered the same thing?"

Sheldon couldn't dismiss her comment as being without merit. "When we dated before, my sole focus was on trying to nail Dino. You'll remember that I spent a lot of time at the gym. I'd work my shift as a personal trainer, then work with Dino at the juice bar."

"I remember."

"You think I didn't want to do fun things with

you, like go to Disney World? Or even head to the Keys to swim with the dolphins, like you always said you wanted to do."

"I don't know," Tyanna replied honestly. They had gone to dinners and movies sometimes, but mostly they had rented movies to watch at home.

"I did want those things, Tyanna. And I'm sorry that I didn't do them with you. But I was . . . I guess I was obsessed."

Tyanna didn't want her chest to fill with warmth, but it did. Just hearing that Sheldon had wanted to spend more time with her outside of the bedroom, developing a better relationship with her, made her tingle with happiness inside.

"Maybe I'm not the most romantic guy," Sheldon said. "But then, I didn't have the best example. My father was a complete ass."

"You never told me about him."

"Yeah, well, there's not much to tell. Except he beat the crap out of my mother on a regular basis. Then he died, and I have to be honest, I knew we were all better off."

"Sheldon." Tyanna sounded shocked.

"My family wasn't the Brady Bunch, like yours, Tyanna. I have no doubt that Dwight headed on the wrong path because my father was never there for him. I tried to be, but it wasn't the same. Besides, I'd moved out already, the first chance I got. I'll never forgive myself for that."

"You can't blame yourself."

"That's what my mother says. But it's pretty

hard not to. Then, I could only think about my own peace of mind, how much I couldn't stand being around my father, watching him abuse my mother. Especially because she always tolerated the abuse. Always forgave him. Always made excuses for him. It made me sick."

"I'm sorry," Tyanna said.

"It's not your fault. No need to apologize."

"When you hurt, I hurt."

"Mmm." But Sheldon's eyes took on a faraway look, and Tyanna knew he was reliving the misery of his past.

Tyanna leaned forward and softly stroked Sheldon's face. "Was that so hard?"

He jerked his eyes to hers. "What?"

"For you to share a bit of yourself with me? When we dated before, I always knew you were holding back, and I always sensed that you'd feel better if you just shared what was bothering you. But you never did."

Sheldon shrugged, his lips pulling into a tight line. "It's something I try my best to forget. I don't want to burden you with my baggage." And he'd just started to realize over the last year how much baggage he carried around. The guilt over Dwight was the worst of it. He had found some solace working with troubled teens and trying to help them get their lives together—something he hadn't been able to do for his brother.

Tyanna stroked his face again. "The fact that

you never told me anything—it made me feel like you never trusted me."

"I guess I can see that."

Tyanna sighed softly, knowing that tonight she had taken a greater step with Sheldon than she had before. He'd let her into his heart, even if just a little. She knew it wasn't easy for him—she could tell by the tenseness in his jaw—but it was a start.

"Right now, I'm worried about my mother's health," Sheldon said. "But I'd like very much for us to do fun stuff. I just don't know how much we'll be able to do before this mess with Dino's goons is straightened out."

"I don't want to live my life in fear, Sheldon."

"Neither do I."

"We have to go to the police about everything. All the threats. What we suspect."

"Yeah. We'll do that in the morning. Before you head to your parents for the video shoot. Okay?"

Tyanna nodded. "Okay."

"And maybe tomorrow night, we can head to Gameworks and play video games."

A playful gleam lit up Sheldon's eyes, and Tyanna couldn't help chuckling. "You men. You'll always remain boys at heart."

"Can you blame us?"

She shook her head. "No."

Tyanna looked into Sheldon's eyes, and something changed in that moment. It wasn't just desire she was suddenly feeling for him, but something deeper. She found herself saying, "Despite everything I've said, I know that I want you in my life—in some capacity."

Pause, then, "Is that so?" He reached out and touched her mouth daintily with his thumb, then ran his thumb along the entire surface of her full lips.

Tyanna's mouth parted slightly in soft invitation. And then as unexpected to her as it must have been to Sheldon, she took the tip of his thumb into her mouth, sucking it gently. As his eyes darkened with desire, she placed her hand on his, guiding his palm to her face.

Still holding his hand, Tyanna trailed Sheldon's fingers down her neck languidly, then lower, until he was touching the soft mounds of her breasts. A low moan escaped her. What was it about Sheldon's touch that made her body completely come alive? She wanted his hands on more of her. She lowered his hand so that it palmed the full roundness of her breast.

"Tyanna," Sheldon whispered. "I didn't think you'd want to do this again. . . ."

She didn't think so either. Not after how she'd chastised herself for falling into bed so easily with him. Hadn't she told herself that if she and Sheldon were to have any type of future, she had to get past the appeal of the sex? And she needed him to completely trust her, open up to her.

Which he had finally started to do after oh so long. It felt good to know he was taking those steps—like an aphrodisiac, making her want him fiercely.

"Just kiss me," she said.

He brought his lips to hers and captured them in a dazzling kiss, while his fingers found the taut peak of her breast and gently stroked it from outside her workout top. Tyanna moaned softly against his lips; she felt Sheldon shiver. *God, yes*, she thought. The sexual appeal was there—no doubt always would be. She could try and fight it but that was a useless proposition.

With Sheldon's free hand, he fingered her face while he kissed her. Light, skimming, electrifying touches. Dizzying sensations surged through her body. She couldn't take this teasing any longer. She wanted to be naked with Sheldon right now.

Tyanna's desire for Sheldon was actually making her light-headed. She slipped her arms around his neck. Goodness, he felt so familiar, so right. Tyanna moved backward on the sofa, pulling Sheldon on top of her. She couldn't have stopped herself if she'd tried; she wanted him so badly.

She slipped her fingers between their bodies and found the buttons to Sheldon's shirt. Sheldon eased up to give her better access, but his lips remained fastened to hers. Tyanna undid the buttons slowly, then pulled his shirt out of his pants. Hastily, she shoved the material off his shoulders. Sheldon sat up, took his shirt off, then tossed it aside.

Tyanna sucked in her breath at the sight of Sheldon's beautiful masculine body. His hairless chest allowed her an unrestricted view of his dark, flat nipples. She wanted to touch them, to taste them. The muscles in his abdomen were rippled, the result of all his physical training. And he had a slim, firm waist.

Her eyes ventured lower. His erection was straining against his pants. The sight of it made electricity course through her veins. The man was so damn desirable, she could hardly stand it.

Tyanna positioned herself so that she could take one of Sheldon's nipples into her mouth. She flicked out her tongue and ran circles around the small, taut peak. Sheldon shuddered, enjoying this sensation as much as he always had. Tyanna hadn't forgotten what pleased him, what he liked. She heard him groan with increased sexual anticipation, and she closed her mouth around the nipple. With her teeth and her tongue she teased him.

She pulled away and reached for the bottom of her shirt. With both hands, she pulled it over her head. Her breasts bounced lightly once they were free.

Sheldon took in the sight of her, his eyes fogged with desire. Completely comfortable with her nakedness, Tyanna allowed him to regard her for several seconds, watching as his face grew taut with building passion. His gaze was so hot she felt as if it literally seared her skin. She ran her tongue over her lips as she continued to grow hotter.

Sheldon reached out to touch her, but Tyanna pushed his hand away. As he gave her a confused look, Tyanna slowly pushed him away and eased herself out from under him. She stood in front of him, and he stared, mesmerized.

Tyanna pushed him backward on the sofa, then straddled him. She adjusted her body, positioning her chest at his face. She held his head in place as she rubbed her breasts over his face with aching tenderness. One breast, then the other. He tried to reach for her nipple, but she pulled it away from him with a smirk.

"Tyanna . . ."

She continued to tease him, delighting in his growls of passion.

"Tyanna, please."

Finally, she guided one nipple into his mouth.

Spasms shook her body as he suckled her, the sensation so glorious she threw her head back and whimpered. Would his touch ever fail to excite her?

Tyanna looked down at him, getting a thrill from watching his mouth on her. As he met her gaze, Sheldon let her breast slip from his mouth. Tyanna moaned softly in protest. She didn't want him to stop; she needed him desperately.

She urged her nipple toward his mouth again, but he braced his hands beneath her bottom, picked her up and stood with her in his arms.

"There should be a law against you teasing me the way you are," he rasped.

"Is that so?"

"Yes, dammit."

Ooh, she loved that she could do this to him. Make him mad with longing.

He began carrying her in the direction of her bedroom. "I'm going to have to punish you for your . . . your lack of mercy."

She locked her legs around his waist. "Oh, no."

"Someone's gotta teach you that it's not right to get a man hard and keep him waiting."

Tyanna's whole body throbbed. She couldn't wait to have Sheldon inside her, loving her the way he did best. "Is it too late to say I'm sorry?"

"Way too late."

She flicked her tongue over his ear, then whispered, "Are you gonna give it to me good?"

Sheldon lowered her onto the bed and lay on top of her. "Oh, you know it."

"Don't you dare disappoint me."

"Baby, you know I won't."

## Chapter 20

The next morning, Tyanna was out of bed by eight-thirty. While Sheldon continued to sleep, she busied herself in the kitchen making scrambled eggs and bacon. Thank goodness she'd done some grocery shopping. At least she had some food to feed Sheldon.

She brewed coffee, and for the second time in a week, the smell was heavenly. Today she definitely needed the caffeine. She had stayed up way too late with Sheldon, and she couldn't afford to be tired today.

She was taking plates from the cupboard when she heard a sound behind her. Turning, she saw Sheldon, dressed only in his jeans.

She smiled. "Morning, sleepyhead."

"Morning." He approached her at the counter and gave her a soft peck on the lips. "Something definitely smells good."

"I decided to make some breakfast." She opened a drawer and withdrew silverware. "I figured I should do what I can to replenish your energy."

He moved to the stove and lifted the cover from the pan. "This is great. You are a godsend."

"I've got some whole-wheat bread. You want some toast?"

"Why not?"

Tyanna got a loaf of bread from the fridge and brought it back to the counter. Sheldon reached into the cupboard and took out two mugs.

"You have cream?" he asked.

"In the fridge."

While Tyanna popped bread into the toaster, Sheldon went to the fridge for the cream. He filled the two mugs with coffee.

"You want sugar?" he asked.

"Two spoons, please."

As if he hadn't been gone for a year, Sheldon went right to the appropriate cupboard. It amazed her how easily they fell into the simple routine of getting breakfast on the table. She smiled. At times like this, she knew there was more to their relationship than a simple sexual attraction.

The plates of food and coffee on the table, Tyanna and Sheldon both sat. Tyanna took a sip from her mug of coffee and sighed with satisfaction.

"You needed that, hmm?" Sheldon asked.

She shot him a mock scowl. "That's your fault. I didn't expect to be up all night making hot, passionate love."

"Complaining?"

"No. But I do need to be wide awake for the video shoot."

Reaching out, Sheldon stroked her face. "You'll be great."

"I sure hope so."

Tyanna picked up a piece of crisp bacon, while Sheldon scooped up some of the scrambled eggs. For the next several minutes, they ate in silence.

As Tyanna stood to get the carafe of coffee, she asked, "Do you want to stay here, or go with me to my parents' place?"

Sheldon's lips slanted downward in a wry scowl. "Go to your parents'?"

"Yeah." She stood and refilled both their mugs. "You can watch the filming of the video."

"You're serious, aren't you?"

"Yes."

"I doubt your parents would be happy to see me."

Shrugging, Tyanna sat once again. She couldn't argue with that, but she also didn't particularly care. If Sheldon was going to be in her life in any capacity—and it seemed that he was—then her parents would simply have to accept that.

"If you want to come, come. Don't worry about them."

"Naw. I'm gonna head home after we see the police. Make sure my mother is okay."

They finished eating and Tyanna cleared their breakfast plates. Sheldon joined her at the sink, washing the few items they'd used. As he reached past her to put the last glass in the dish rack, he surprised Tyanna with a soft kiss on the lips.

Then he smiled at her, a warm, sweet smile, and Tyanna knew the kiss was all he wanted. It wasn't going to lead to a wild and passionate coupling—which was good in the sense that they didn't have time for it right now. But it was also good because it gave Tyanna a certain comfort level with him she hadn't had before.

"You want to get in a shower with me?" Sheldon asked. "I promise I won't make you late."

Looking up at him, she giggled. "Should I trust you?"

"Absolutely, baby."

Minutes later, they were naked in the shower. Sheldon lathered up the sponge with soap and washed every part of her body. As he washed her backside, Tyanna braced her hands against the slick ceramic-tile wall. Her body was taut as she waited for his fingers to explore her curves and crevices. . . .

But he didn't. He was a perfect gentleman, simply doing the job he had promised to do.

Tyanna frowned at him as he passed her the sponge.

"What?" he asked, but his tone said he knew exactly why she was frowning.

"Nothing." She poured a liberal amount of liquid soap onto the sponge and rubbed it in with her fingers. But it was her hand she used when she reached between his legs to wash him there.

Slowly, she ran her soap-slicked hand over him, stroking him to arousal.

"That's not fair." His breath was hot against her ear.

"No?"

"No. You're the one who said you had to get ready for your project."

She wrapped one arm around his neck as water sluiced over her back. "Yes, but I can spare a little time. What about you? Want a quickie in the shower?"

"You don't give a guy an easy choice."

She giggled as he spun her around. This time, his fingers roamed her body with a purpose very different from the one they'd had minutes before.


Sheldon rested his hand on the small of Tyanna's back as they walked toward the front door of the Aventura Police Department closest to her apartment.

At the door, Tyanna halted.

Sheldon asked, "You okay?"

She inhaled deeply and looked up at him. "Yes."

Sheldon gave Tyanna a quick kiss on the cheek, then opened the door. He followed Tyanna inside.

A wall and glass partition separated the front of the police station from the back, keeping civilians in the waiting area. A policewoman sat behind the glass. She watched Sheldon as he made his way toward her.

He spoke through the small hole in the partition. "Hi. My friend and I would like to speak with a detective."

"What's the problem?" the female cop asked.

"My friend was attacked last night. She already reported the incident, but there's much more to the story. Someone is trying to kill us, and it has to do with a previous murder."

"All right. Have a seat for a moment. I'll have someone come out and speak with you."

It took only a few minutes for a detective to come out and meet them. Sheldon and Tyanna stood to greet the man. He extended a hand, shaking first Sheldon's, then Tyanna's hand.

"I'm Detective Martin. How can I help you?"

"My friend and I have a problem," Sheldon answered without preamble. He filled Detective Martin in on the entire situation, starting with Dwight's murder, Sheldon's attempt to get information on Dino Benedetto, and the fact that someone now was threatening Sheldon's life and the lives of those he cared about. "Last night, Tyanna was attacked outside her workplace, Jaguar Fitness," Sheldon went on.

"I'm sure you'll find the information on file," Tyanna said. "I spoke with an Officer Daly."

Detective Martin nodded. "You think the two incidents are related."

"I'm sure of it," Sheldon answered.

"I heard about Dino Benedetto's death," the detective said. "I know the guy was bad news."

"It's obviously someone close to him who's after us now," Sheldon said. "The one known link is his former girlfriend, Leona. But there could be someone else. A family member, maybe."

"If we're talking Dino Benedetto and the illegal operation you told me about, then I'm sure Miami-Dade handled this. They handle the more serious cases within Dade County."

"So we should talk to the Miami-Dade police?" Tyanna asked.

"No, that's not necessary. You live in Aventura, and that's where last night's crime took place. I'll consult with Miami-Dade, however, and see what kind of info they have on Dino's associates and family in the area."

"What about arresting Leona?" Tyanna asked.

"I can't simply arrest her," Detective Martin answered. "Not without talking to her first. I'll see what she says and go from there." He paused. "Now, what I'll need from both of you are sworn statements to the facts you've told me. I'll get you the forms."

Detective Martin went to get the forms, then left Tyanna and Sheldon alone to write their statements. They finished before he returned, so Sheldon asked the cop at the main desk to call him back to the front.

"Thanks," the detective said as he took the sworn statements from Sheldon and Tyanna. "That'll be all for now. Of course, if anything else happens, please call me."

"Is that it?" Sheldon asked, somewhat surprised.

"For now. We'll let you know if we find any hard evidence."

Sheldon wanted to ask the detective more questions, like when he might possibly hear from him, but he already knew what the man would say. He also knew how hard it had been to find hard evidence on Dino, so he didn't feel very hopeful right now.

"All right," Sheldon said. He placed an arm across Tyanna's shoulders. "We'll wait to hear from you."

"Take care," Detective Martin said.

Sheldon and Tyanna made their way outside. On the sidewalk, Sheldon glanced at Tyanna. "You've been pretty quiet."

"Just thinking about everything," she said.

"I know you're worried, but it's in their hands now." Sheldon and Tyanna walked to their cars, which were parked beside one another.

"I hope they put the fear of God into Leona and she tells them who she's associating with." In the meantime, Sheldon would call Maria and see if he could learn anything from her.

"I hope this is enough to scare them into stopping this bull," Tyanna commented.

Sheldon stood with her while she dug her keys out of her purse. She unlocked and opened her car door.

Sheldon took her hands in his. "Have a great

day," he told her. "I hope the shoot goes extremely well."

"Thanks. What are you going to do?"

He paused a long moment before answering. "I would have told you before . . . But, I guess I wanted to know that I stand a chance in hell."

Tyanna perched her hands on her hips. "Is this something bad?" She kept her tone light, but already that feeling of disappointment that came from knowing Sheldon didn't always include her in his life began to creep through her.

"It's nothing bad. I . . . I went to a bunch of the police departments in the area." When she didn't reply, he added, "For application forms."

A slow smile spread across her face. "You want to be a cop?"

He nodded.

"Wow. When did that happen?"

"Somewhere along the line when I wanted to make Dino pay for what he did to my brother." He paused. "Besides, I have to find something to do with this life of mine other than fitness. Something that will impress your parents."

He flashed a sweet smile, and Tyanna couldn't help wondering what had gotten into him. Was he really hoping to impress her parents? She didn't care if he worked as a personal trainer for the rest of his days, as long as he was happy. And it was a job he did well.

As if in answer to her question, he said, "I guess I'm feeling like you. I want a more challenging career. Not that I don't like being a trainer, but I can't see myself doing that in ten years. I really love working with the kids, but I figure there's a need for more sensitive cops out there to deal with them. Especially after how they handled Brian yesterday." He shrugged. "That's what's been going through my mind."

Tyanna pressed a hand to Sheldon's belly. "I think that's great."

"We'll see how it goes," he said matter-of-factly. "Anyway, don't you have to be going?"

"Yeah. Please call me on my cell if anything happens, okay?"

"Sure."

A cool breeze came off the ocean, mussing Tyanna's hair. Sheldon brushed the tendrils away from her face.

His touch was gentle yet stimulating. Tyanna looked into his eyes. Did she see something there she hadn't before? She wasn't sure, but it stole her breath.

Just as gently as Sheldon had touched her, he lowered his face to hers and kissed her lips. Moaning softly, Tyanna slipped her arms around his neck. He was offering her sweet and sensitive and her body wanted hot and wild. She flicked her tongue over Sheldon's and kissed him with building urgency.

A raw, wild sound rumbled in Sheldon's chest, and he pulled away. Their lips made a soft suctioning sound.

"If you don't get in that car in the next thirty seconds, you're not going to make it to your parents' place."

"I know, I know."

He stepped away from her, and she sulked playfully. "Call me when you're finished," he said. "I'll come back and meet you. To make sure you're okay, of course."

"Already preparing for your civic duty?"

"You know it." He winked. "And like I said, if you're up to it, we can do something. Gameworks. Whatever."

Tyanna smiled up at him. "All right. I'll see you later."

As Tyanna drove to Wendy's place, she couldn't stop thinking of Sheldon. Her mind wandered from the danger they faced to the night they had shared together. And whenever she thought of the latter, she couldn't keep a silly smile from forming on her face.

The attack last night had been terrifying, but her time spent with Sheldon had been exhilarating—like in the beginning, when she had started to fall in love with him. She had seen a glimpse of the vulnerable Sheldon again, the one she had always sensed whenever he shared with her some of his life's pain. And again this morning, when he had opened up and told her about his dream to become a police officer. She knew he was making a concerted effort to share more with her. Maybe he was simply one of those guys for whom it was pretty hard to open up.

Tyanna knew she was walking right back into dangerous territory with her former beau. If she fell for him again, it would be as intense as the first time. Maybe even more so.

So if he hurt her . . .

Tyanna pushed that thought out of her mind. There was no point jumping the gun. The first priority was to figure out how to deal with the current threat.

Wendy was standing outside the gate of her apartment complex when Tyanna pulled up. She even had the steps and mats beside her, which was quite the feat considering the distance from her unit to the gate.

Slowing down, Tyanna turned the corner into the area in front of the gate and pulled up before Wendy. She hit the power button to open the passenger side door, then also hit the trunk lever.

All smiles, Wendy opened the door. "Morning, Sunshine."

"Hey, Wendy." Tyanna got out of the car and walked around to the grassy area where Wendy had all the items. "How'd you get all this stuff out here?"

"There was a shopping cart around, so I used it. I figured I may as well; makes things a little quicker. I know you're not always the most . . . punctual."

"Ouch." But she couldn't deny the truth of that

statement. Even this morning, she was running ten minutes late. And she had no one to blame but herself for initiating the shower scene with Sheldon.

Not that she was complaining. . . .

The sound of a snapping finger made Tyanna flinch. "Earth to Tyanna."

"Sorry. I zoned out."

"This is not the time, Sunshine. We've got to get this show on the road!" Wendy giggled.

Pushing thoughts of this morning out of her mind, Tyanna grabbed a mat, tucked it under her arm, then headed to the back of her car. She lifted the door to the trunk and placed the mat inside.

Together, she and Wendy filled the trunk with the items. Moments later, they were seated in the car.

"So, you ready?" Wendy asked.

"Absolutely."

"I'm so excited. I keep thinking I'm going to forget the whole routine, or just plain freeze as soon as the cameras start rolling."

"That's totally natural. But you know you'll be nothing short of amazing."

"I sure hope so."

"You will be."

Tyanna turned the car around and got onto the road.

Wendy said, "We'll both be great. I spoke with Phil this morning, and he seems pretty positive. Everything's on schedule."

Tyanna merely nodded.

"Hey." Wendy's voice held a note of concern. "I know you're not an early bird, but this isn't that early. Is everything okay?"

Tyanna replied, "Actually, there's something I have to tell you."

Wendy looked at her. "What?"

"I had a scare at the gym last night."

"What happened?"

Tyanna filled her friend in on the attack, then the fact that Sheldon had come over to be with her. "I've been so up and down where Sheldon is concerned, but his presence last night was pretty comforting. Though, he was mad at me when he first came over."

Wendy's eyes registered surprise. "Mad at you? Why, did he think you'd put yourself at risk?"

"No, not that." The road ahead of her was clear, and Tyanna glanced at Wendy. "It seems I'm the one to blame for this new threat."

"But how could that be?" Wendy protested, automatically defending her friend.

"Remember I told you I went to Ultimate Fitness to find out if Dino was really dead?"

"Yeah."

"Well, turns out Leona was Dino's girlfriend. I had no clue. I thought she'd just worked at the juice bar. And I told her that Sheldon was back in town."

"Oh, hon."

"It makes complete sense that she would be angry with Sheldon, for the same reason Dino was." Tyanna sighed. "The question now is, How angry is she? Enough to simply try and scare Sheldon? Scare me?"

Reaching across the seat, Wendy rubbed Tyanna's forearm. "I'm so sorry."

"We're hoping the police can get through to her."

"Let's hope," Wendy agreed. "Otherwise, you let me know if you need me, and I'll go pay Leona a visit myself."

Tyanna knew her friend was kidding, but that was an idea she'd thought of after she and Sheldon had gone their separate ways. Maybe if the police failed to get through to Leona, she would try to appeal to her. "I was thinking of that."

"Hold up," Wendy said.

"I'm not saying I will, but if the police can't get through to her . . . I mean, I knew her. Maybe if I talk to her, it will make a difference."

"I doubt it."

"I doubt it too. But I feel bad. I have to do something."

"If you decide to go see Leona, I'll go with you if you want."

Tyanna angled her face in Wendy's direction and smiled at her. "You're such a great friend."

"You know I'll always be there for you."

Tyanna squeezed her hand. "I know."

\*   \*   \*

A round of applause erupted as Tyanna and Wendy finished the rehearsal of their routine. Blushing, Tyanna looked up at her family—her mother, sisters and niece. Even Michelle was clapping.

"You guys," Tyanna said, shaking her head. But she was smiling.

"You've sold me," Charlene said. "And Michelle too, apparently."

"Honestly," Lecia began. "That was great."

Taking Wendy's hand in hers, Tyanna pulled her to her feet and led them both in a bow. "Thank you, thank you."

Giggling, Tyanna looked across the patio to see her father appear at the patio doors. He said, "Looks like the crew has arrived."

Tyanna squeezed Wendy's hand. "This is it."

Together, they headed into the house to greet Phil and the crew. He was accompanied by two other men.

"Hey, Phil." Wendy hurried to him, tipping on her toes to give him a warm hug.

"Hey, sweetie." Phil kissed her on the cheek. "Hello, Tyanna."

"Hi."

"This is Monty. Rafael."

Everyone said their hellos. The men had an enormous amount of stuff, more than Tyanna had anticipated. Black boxes filled the foyer.

"Let me show you where we're going to set things up," Tyanna said. She and Wendy led the men outside and showed them the area where they'd set up the mats and platforms. Then they sat at the patio table and watched while the crew did their work.

It took a good half hour for them to set up the camera and lights in what they felt were the perfect positions. Tyanna wandered around them for a short time, taking in the whole process, but for the most part, she sat at the patio table with her sisters. Wendy, however, seemed almost like a puppy dog, following Phil around pretty much everywhere. And when she had to stand back, she stood nearby.

Tyanna watched Phil and Wendy with increasing curiosity. What was going on there? Whatever it was was very interesting. Very interesting indeed.


A little over three hours later, Phil announced, "That's a wrap, everyone."

Grinning from ear to ear, Tyanna turned to Wendy. The two embraced each other with enthusiasm.

"We did it!" Wendy exclaimed.

From what Tyanna could tell, the shoot had gone smoothly. More than smoothly, judging by the satisfied expression on Phil's face.

They'd done the routine three complete times with short breaks in between. Phil experimented with different camera angles, different views. Once, he used the pool as a backdrop. Twice, he used the vast backyard and canal as the backdrop, but from slightly different positions.

The whole process had fascinated Tyanna. While one camera had been set up on a fixed tripod, Monty walked around them with a camera on his shoulder. Monty's handheld camera allowed him to film them at more flexible angles while the fixed camera got them from one position. Phil assured them it would all work out beautifully in the editing process.

The hardest part had been to perform as if they weren't being taped. Tyanna supposed it was a little easier for Wendy, because she spoke directly to the fixed camera as if it was a live audience.

"That was pretty neat." Tyanna looked around to see Lecia and Charlene standing behind her. "I had no clue it took so much work to tape a video."

"And this was fairly simple, in terms of shooting," Phil told them. "If it was indoors, we'd need more lighting, filters. All kinds of stuff. Sound is a bigger issue when taping outside, but you were all great spectators. Very cooperative."

"What about music?" Lecia asked. "I thought you would have something funky playing."

"Actually, music is something we'll add in postproduction," Phil explained.

"Wendy and I were worried about copyright issues," Tyanna told Lecia.

"And given the dialogue in the video, adding music later is actually much better," Phil continued. "That way, we can control the sound, make sure the levels are right so the dialogue isn't drowned out."

"Well, I'm definitely impressed," Charlene told everyone. "With the taping *and* the performance. If Ronnie Vaughn doesn't like it, then the guy's a moron." She smiled sweetly.

"I agree," Phil said. "Everything went as well as it could have." He glanced at his watch. "We're gonna start to clear our stuff out of here."

As the crew went about dismantling the lights, boom and camera, Wendy asked Phil, "How long do you think the editing stage will take?"

"I'll watch the footage tonight. Get an idea of how it all looks on video. I'll get a better idea then."

"I'd like to watch it with you," Wendy told him. She looked at Tyanna, then back at Phil. "Both of us."

"Whenever it's convenient for you," Tyanna added.

"And I'd love to start choosing music," Wendy continued.

"Sure. That's doable."

Wendy smiled brightly at him. "Great."

"I need some water," Tyanna announced. "I'm gonna head back to the table."

"I'll meet you over there in a few," Wendy told her.

Tyanna walked back to the patio table with her sisters. On her way there, she threw a surreptitious glance over her shoulder to watch Wendy and Phil.

Wendy was smiling like an idiot at the man, nodding her head in agreement to something he was saying.

There was definitely something there.

Tyanna waited until the camera crew had left before approaching Wendy.

"So," Tyanna began, linking arms with Wendy. "What was *that* exchange about?"

Wendy angled her head to face Tyanna. "What exchange?"

"I saw how long you hugged Phil good-bye. Looked to me like you didn't want to let him go."

Wendy's lips spread in a slow grin. "It was obvious?"

"Uh-huh."

Wendy took a step backward and crossed her arms over her torso. Tyanna got the impression she was wishing that Phil's arms were wrapped around her, rather than her own.

"I've got a crush on him," Wendy admitted.

"No way. Phil?"

"Yes, way."

"When did this happen?"

"I think I've had a crush on him for a long time but didn't realize it. The problem is, Phil is so hard to read. Sometimes he'll flirt with me and I'll think he likes me, but other times he's strictly business."

"He didn't seem strictly business today."

"Nope." Wendy was smiling like a fool. "He was pretty flirtatious today." Suddenly she frowned. "The problem is, I don't know what to make of it. I mean, is he just being nice . . . ?"

"You're gorgeous. How could he not like you?"

"It's kind of embarrassing to say this," Wendy began in a hushed tone. "But the last time I saw him I deliberately dressed kind of hoochie mama."

Tyanna laughed. "You didn't."

"Not totally hoochie mama. But it was definitely provocative, right down to the high-heeled sandals. I was alone with him in his office and doing everything but coming right out and saying 'I want you.' "

"And?"

Wendy's expression soured. "And he seemed as impressed as if I had shown up in a cloth sack."

"Oooh. That's not good."

"Yeah, so I don't really know what to think."

"Maybe he's turned gay," Tyanna offered, then chuckled.

"Oh, God. I hope not."

"I doubt it. He'll come around."

Wendy was back to smiling. "That's what I'm counting on."

# Chapter 21

"Hey, there." Tyanna beamed at Wendy. She had just arrived at work to start her shift and was surprised to see Wendy still there, on the gym floor.

Wendy placed her free weight on the floor beside the bench where she was sitting. "Hi."

"Did you hang out so we could chat?" Tyanna asked.

"Actually, I did."

"Cool. What's going on? You heard from Phil?"

Wendy frowned. "Actually, I haven't. That's what I'm worried about. He said he'd let us watch the video footage, and that was last week. And I'd like to get this thing rolling as soon as possible."

Tyanna understood Wendy's anxiousness over the project. She felt it, too. "Phil *is* busy. And he did this for us as a favor."

"I know. But it's Monday. A full week since we did the shoot. Don't you think we should have heard from him by now?"

Tyanna shrugged. "That's not really long, considering his schedule."

"Not really," Wendy acquiesced, "but . . ."

"But that's not it," Tyanna finished for her.

Wendy finally stood. "No. One minute the man is hot where I'm concerned, the next cold. I'd been hoping to hear from him sooner than this. And I've called a couple times. I just wish I knew if he's interested."

Tyanna looked at her friend, saw how miserable she seemed. And she felt helpless. She truly didn't know what to say. Relationships were complex at best—she knew that firsthand. Thankfully, she and Sheldon had been getting along. Over the past week, they had continued to see each other, continued to make love in the easy way that they always did. But the question of what lay in their future still plagued her whenever he left her bed. It was something she was trying not to think about now.

Tyanna ran a hand over Wendy's arm. "Give him some time. If you want, I can call him about the video—"

"No." Wendy shook her head. "I'll call him. It's not like I don't have a reason to. And if I don't reach him on the phone, I'll simply go see him in person."

"Are you sure you want to do that?"

Wendy nodded. "One way or another, I need to know if there's anything going on between us. Seeing him is probably the only way I'll get an answer."

\*   \*   \*

There was no time like the present.

Wendy's talk with Tyanna had spurred her into action, and when she left the gym, she decided to head straight to Phil's South Beach office and surprise him.

The video was an excuse to see him, for which she was grateful. Though they had been friends for years, she didn't want to keep pestering him without a reason.

Some days, she felt like a complete idiot for continuing to pursue him. Other days, she felt all he needed was some time. She knew that his past relationship had made him wary, but she had always been there for him as a friend. Slow and easy was the way to get to his heart.

Hopefully, today she'd get *some* indication of whether or not he was actually interested in her.

Wendy was dressed in gym wear—a tank top and formfitting shorts, and a pair of Nikes. Not her first choice, but she still looked decent. Besides, she wanted to catch Phil before he left for the day, which meant she couldn't chance heading home to change.

Now on Washington, Wendy parallel parked at a meter, then made her way across the street to Phil's office door. She didn't allow herself a moment's hesitation. She simply opened the door and stepped inside.

The pretty receptionist looked up at her instantly. "Hello. Can I help you?"

"Um," Wendy began, shifting from one foot to the other. "I'm here to see Phil. He's in the back, right?"

The receptionist opened her ledger. "You have an appointment?"

"I'll just go on back."

Not giving the woman a chance to say anything else, Wendy simply strode to the back of the office.

But she stopped abruptly when she didn't see Phil in the immediate area. Darn. Her hands went to her hips. Was he not here? She glanced around, seeing the door off to the right.

The editing room.

She walked in that direction. The door was closed, but she thought she could hear sounds inside. She rapped on it lightly.

"Come in," Phil called a moment later.

Wendy paused, drew in a calming breath, then opened the door, a smile already pasted on her face. Inside the room sat Phil and another man.

Phil looked at her in surprise. Was that a hint of a smile she saw lifting the corners of his lips? It grew, leaving no doubt. "Wendy."

His smile set her stomach fluttering. "Hi," she said softly. "I was in the area. . . ."

Phil pushed his chair back and stood. "John, you continue without me."

"I don't want to bother you if you're busy," Wendy told him.

Phil stepped out of the room, closing the

door behind him. "No. I'm actually glad you stopped by."

"Really?" More fluttering.

"Mmm hmm. I've got a surprise for you."

Wendy's eyes lit up. "What kind of surprise?"

Phil walked toward his desk and Wendy followed him. There, he opened a drawer and took out a black video cassette holder. He passed it to her.

Wendy looked at the case, then up at him. "What—"

"It's your workout video. Complete with music, a title, and credits."

A startled laugh spilled from her lips. "Oh, my God. You mean it's finished?"

"Yep."

"But I thought . . . You said you were going to let me watch the footage with you."

"I've still got all the footage. If you want a copy, let me know. I just figured I'd surprise you with a finished copy you can send to Ronnie Vaughn."

"I'm definitely surprised."

"I know you were probably wondering what was going on with me, but that's why I didn't call you back. I wanted the video done before we spoke again." He paused. "I only hope you like what I've done."

Wendy threw her arms around Phil's neck and hugged him. His body felt warm and strong against hers. "I'm sure I'll love it. Thanks so much. And this was faster than I expected."

"I had some time on my hands," Phil explained as they pulled apart. "I figured I'd work on it. Once I did, I couldn't stop."

"I can't wait to watch it. Thank you again." She smiled up at him, suddenly unsure of what to say. She wasn't quite ready to leave. "Um, do you have any time tonight? I'd love to take you to dinner and show you my appreciation." When Phil hesitated, Wendy said, "Don't say no. After all you've done, I owe you that much. And you deserve a break."

He slowly nodded. "You know, I think I could use a decent dinner tonight."

Wendy's heart lifted. "I can make you a home-cooked meal."

"Tonight's probably not the best night for that. I'm gonna be here pretty late."

"Oh."

"But if you want to meet me back here around nine, we can head somewhere on Ocean Drive for a bite. If you don't mind heading back this way."

Wendy waved off his last statement. "I don't mind at all. That way, I can watch the video, then let you know what I think."

"All right, then. Nine o'clock."

Wendy grinned. "You got it."

The moment Tyanna's break started, she headed to the phone. She'd gotten a message from Wendy and wanted to call her back.

Wendy picked up after the first ring, saying, "Hey, Tyanna."

"I'm gonna block this number the next time I call you," Tyanna joked.

"I knew it would be you."

Wendy sounded a little harried, like she'd done a sprint to get to the phone. "Did I catch you at a bad time?"

"Kind of. I'm almost out the door." Pause. "To have dinner with Phil."

"Dinner," Tyanna said in a sing-song voice. "That's an improvement compared to earlier today."

"Yeah." Wendy had a smile in her voice. "I went by to see him. Which is actually why I called. He finished our video for us."

"What do you mean, finished?"

"Completed it. And I would have waited to watch it with you, but you know me. I'm too impatient. I have to tell you, Tyanna—I am *so* pleased. The video looks amazing."

"It's ready to go out to Ronnie?"

"It's ready to be marketed across the country."

Tyanna gnawed on her bottom lip, a nervous bubble growing in her stomach. "I want to see it."

"I'll bring it to the gym tomorrow. You won't be disappointed." She paused. "I hate to cut you off, but I've got to run."

Tyanna shook her head slowly, a smile playing on her lips. "Go have fun."

"I'm gonna try."

"I'm sure."

"I'll fill you in on all the details later."

"You better."

Wendy hung up, and Tyanna chuckled softly. Sometimes, her friend was a trip. But if anyone deserved to find Mr. Right, it was Wendy. She idolized her parents' relationship, and ambitious as she was, her biggest dream was to find a man with whom she could settle down and have a houseful of children.

"I'm rooting for you, Wendy," Tyanna said softly. "I hope Phil knows exactly what a prize you are."

A few hours later, Tyanna was working with a client when she was surprised to find Sheldon on the gym floor. Her heart fluttered, then her lips curved into a slow grin.

Sheldon wasn't looking her way, and she wondered how long he had been here. His back was to her as he worked the bench press.

Tyanna crossed her arms over her chest as she watched him. He really did have the most incredible physique. His upper body was well shaped and strong, and his arms were the kind a woman wanted to wrap herself in. It was no wonder Shirley was infatuated with Sheldon. But to his credit, he hadn't encouraged her flirting with him since the first time Tyanna had found them chatting at the reception desk.

And perhaps because Tyanna had been abrupt

with him during their date, Jay hadn't bothered her lately. A friendly hi and bye when he saw her, and that was it. Which suited her fine.

But then, maybe Jay had seen her and Sheldon hanging out and put two and two together.

"What next?"

Tyanna was startled by the sound of her client's voice. She looked down at Misty, who sat at the leg press. "Um . . . the leg extension."

"Oh," Misty whined. "I hate that."

"You want great legs, don't you?"

"Yeah."

"You know what they say. No pain, no gain."

"I'm sure you didn't have to work this hard for yours."

"Actually, I did. I've been at it for years, though. That makes the difference."

Misty frowned, but walked to the next leg machine nonetheless. Though Tyanna followed her, her eyes were on Sheldon. He stood, stretched his magnificent body, then turned and looked in her direction.

Their gazes met, and it was a moment of magic. Goodness, what was it about the man?

Sheldon smiled at her. Tyanna smiled back. Again, Misty's voice tore her attention away.

"Sorry?" Tyanna said.

"I asked how much weight I should use."

"Go ahead and add an extra five or ten pounds. Whatever you feel comfortable with. The key is to gradually increase the weights."

"Maybe I should just consider liposuction."

"Very funny." Tyanna stood with her hands on her hips, much like a parent would do to give a young child the image of authority. Most of her clients appreciated that it took hard work to get the results they wanted. A couple, however, complained every step of the way.

Misty adjusted the weight, then got on the machine. As she did, Tyanna's eyes ventured across the gym once more—but to her dismay, she no longer saw Sheldon. Where had he gone?

A couple seconds later, she jumped when she felt hands encircle her waist. She quickly looked over her shoulder.

"Sheldon!" she said in a startled whisper.

Still holding her, Sheldon's mouth moved to her ear. He nibbled on the lobe.

Tyanna instantly reacted, pulling herself out of his arms. She glanced around as she did. Misty had seen them, as had everyone else in the near vicinity.

Taking several steps away from the machine, Tyanna looked into Sheldon's eyes. Her own narrowed in question. "What's gotten into you?" Sheldon wasn't one to show any public affection. At least that's what she'd been used to when she worked at Ultimate Fitness. So she wasn't sure what to make of him now.

"You look scrumptious," he replied.

Though she gave him a look of shock, her heart pounded at his words. "I'm working," she whispered when he took a step closer to her. She glanced at Misty, sure her client would be irritated. Instead, she was smiling from ear to ear.

"You don't want me to eat you?"

Tyanna's eyes nearly popped out of her head—as a jolt of electricity shot through her. "I am not even going to go there."

"Maybe later," he suggested. "You know I don't disappoint."

Lord help her, she was getting aroused right in the middle of the gym. Her face and neck grew flushed.

"Will the real Sheldon Ford please stand up?"

He shrugged nonchalantly. "You always complained that I was never openly affectionate with you in public. Remember that one fight we had, where you accused me of being embarrassed to show people that I cared about you?"

"And you said it simply wasn't in your nature," Tyanna responded, almost wishing he'd return to his old self.

"People can change."

Tyanna eyed him warily. "You *are* in a mood."

"A good one. There haven't been any more threats. I guess I'm starting to relax a little. Cautious optimism. Also, my first interview for the police force went well."

"Oh, Sheldon. That's wonderful."

"Yeah, I'm feeling pretty good about it. So, in light of all my good news, I say we celebrate tonight."

"Celebrate?" Tyanna raised a curious eyebrow.

"Yeah."

"I can only imagine what you have in mind."

A mischievous smile played on Sheldon's lips. "You know damn well what I have in mind."

He reached for her, but Tyanna stepped away from him, flashing him a mock scowl.

"All right," he gave in. "I'll let you get back to work. But maybe you want to join me in the pool later? Or the steam room?"

An image of the two of them, nearly naked and wet, filled her mind. "Maybe."

"You have your swimsuit?"

"Yes."

"When are you finished?"

"Another hour."

Sheldon winked. "See you in the steam room."

Tyanna didn't respond. Instead, she walked the few steps back to Misty. But she knew she'd be in the steam room, just as Sheldon wished. And she knew that he knew it, too.

"I'm sorry," Tyanna said to Misty. "I shouldn't have—"

"No, don't apologize. If I had a guy as hot as that all over me, I can tell you I'd definitely be ignoring everyone else."

Tyanna could no longer keep a smile from creeping onto her face. She stole a glance at Sheldon and found him looking at her.

He was hot, and he was irresistible.

A dangerous combination.

*     *     *

Tyanna's heart started beating out of control when she went to the changing room to shower and get into her bathing suit. She'd seen in Sheldon's eyes something mischievous and daring when he'd flirted with her—and she could only imagine what might happen between them in a darkened steam room with no one else around.

It hadn't been a fantasy of hers to make love in a steam room until the first time Sheldon had surprised her there weeks earlier. Now, she secretly wondered if her fantasy would come true.

Dressed in her provocative black bikini, her skin damp from her shower, Tyanna paused outside the steam room, butterflies tickling her stomach. Closing her eyes, she inhaled deeply, then pulled the door open.

But when she stepped into the steam-filled room, she knew her fantasy would have to wait. Sheldon wasn't alone. Another gym patron, a woman Tyanna had seen a couple times, sat inside.

Feeling a measure of disappointment, Tyanna met Sheldon's gaze. From the far end of the room, he flashed her a soft smile. Tyanna walked only a few steps to her right, taking a seat several feet away from Sheldon, playing as if she didn't know him. Even with an audience, she didn't trust herself so near to him. Definitely not a good thing. And considering Sheldon had shown her a different side tonight as well—a flirtatious side she hadn't seen in public before—she couldn't be sure what *he* was capable of.

Besides, she decided as she got comfortable on the second ledge, this way it was more fun. Stealing glances across the dark and steamy room. Knowing they were so close to each other but couldn't touch.

The heat and steam enveloped her, and Tyanna rested her head back on the ceramic-tile wall. The more relaxed one was, the longer they could stay in this heat. Already she felt her pores opening up, her sweat glands working. She loved the eucalyptus; it was good for her skin.

A couple minutes later, sensing Sheldon's eyes on her, she opened hers. As she'd known, he was staring at her. Though it was hard to see his eyes with clarity, she felt them with ease. And she knew he was dying to be closer to her.

A smirk pulled at the corner of her mouth. An idea hit her, the idea to tease the hell out of him. Lifting her legs up, Tyanna lay back along the ledge. She bent one leg at the knee and seductively angled it over the other. It was a pose designed to make Sheldon even hotter than he already was.

She glanced his way. One look at Sheldon told her she was getting to him. Good. He deserved it for having practically attacked her in front of Misty and everyone else in the gym.

Oh, yeah. Payback was fun. As Tyanna watched Sheldon squirm, she took the game of her seduction one step further. Easing one shoulder up at a time, she slipped the straps of her bikini off her shoulders. Because the other person in the steam room was a woman, she had no problem bringing her bikini top down to a level she wouldn't have dared to do in front of another man, even though she was still covered.

She closed her eyes and didn't open them until she heard footsteps. The other woman was on her feet, making her way to the door.

The moment she disappeared, Sheldon was on his feet. Tyanna's breath snagged at the sight of his beautiful, nearly naked body moving swiftly toward her.

"Damn, woman," he ground out when he reached her side. "Are you trying to drive me nuts?"

"Just getting comfortable."

"Comfortable my ass. Is this how you always undress in this steam room, regardless of who's in here?"

"You mean like this?" She slowly peeled the bikini top off her breasts.

He was silent for a moment as his eyes took in the sight of her nakedness. "I knew it," he told her. "You're trying to torture me."

"I thought you'd enjoy it," Tyanna replied coyly.

"Hell, yeah." He threw a quick look over his shoulder to make sure they were still alone. "But I want more."

"Oh?" Tyanna was proud of how cool she'd sounded.

Sheldon ran a finger down her abdomen. "My first choice was to go into the pool with you. But I figured what I wanted to do with you was too risky for the pool. Considering that anyone can see in there through the windows from the gym floor." His fingers skimmed the side of her breast. "But here, it's dark. . . ."

It actually felt like her heart stumbled. Sheldon *did* want to make love in here. "It's also hot."

"Don't I know it."

He placed his hand over her breast. As Tyanna's eyes fluttered shut, her nipple hardened against his palm. She wanted his hands all over her, but this was so risky, regardless of the late hour. Someone else could walk in here without warning.

His lips brushed hers, and Tyanna's eyelids instantly opened. "Sheldon . . ."

As she opened her mouth, his tongue made its way inside. Hot steam and the flavor of eucalyptus mingled with his tongue. His fingers pulled at her hardened nipple, sending waves of pleasure through her.

Tyanna was aware of the danger, but suddenly she didn't care. She felt electrified, as Sheldon's touch always made her feel. There was no way she would ever tire of him. Whatever the spark was between them, it was one Tyanna doubted could be snuffed out.

Sheldon kneaded her other nipple into a tight ball while his tongue tangled with hers. The combined heat of the steam room and the heat of Sheldon's touch was making her light-headed.

He pulled his lips from hers, asking, "You know what I'd like to do to you in here?"

"No."

"Everything." He lowered his head to her nipple, and to Tyanna's surprise, his tongue was even hotter than the steam. She watched as he pulled at her nipple with his teeth, laved it with his tongue. All the while she wondered if the heat and pleasure would make her pass out.

"I can never get enough of you." He brought his lips back to hers at the same moment the door squeaked open. Tyanna's body jerked in surprise, and in a swift movement, Sheldon adjusted her bikini top, covering her.

A man came in and wandered to the far corner of the steam room. Sheldon's back now faced Tyanna, and he pretended he had simply been standing and stretching. Tyanna watched him as she regained her composure. He glanced over his shoulder at her, and she bit down hard on her bottom lip to keep from cracking up.

He gave her a quick smile, then sauntered out of the steam room. Tyanna counted to thirty, slowly sat up, then made for the door.

She and Sheldon would continue this at her place, where there would be no interruptions.

## Chapter 22

The next morning, Tyanna got up before the sun, unable to sleep. She and Sheldon had forgone food in the interest of satisfying their carnal hunger, and now she needed a different form of nourishment.

She carefully sat up, making sure not to wake Sheldon. Her feet hit a mound of clothing as she swung them to the floor. His T-shirt and jeans were beside the bed, as were her clothes. The two of them rarely took it slow and easy; when it came to sex, they were always hot and hungry for each other.

With the help of the night-light in the hallway, Tyanna found Sheldon's shirt and slipped into it. At the bedroom door, she stole a quick glance at Sheldon. A smile touched her lips at the sight of his sleeping form in her darkened room.

Tyanna quietly walked out of the bedroom. She was entirely too comfortable with him in her bed. Which made her wonder what would happen if things didn't work out for them. As of now, they were simply going with the flow. There had been no talk of a future. No talk of love.

She had no doubt that Sheldon was hanging around in her life as much to make sure she was safe as to satisfy his lust. But when the threat was over, where did that leave them?

Guarding your heart was a tough task, that much she knew. And in part because she didn't know the status of her relationship with Sheldon this time around, Tyanna hadn't told her family that they were seeing each other again. It didn't feel right, and she knew her family would have a million questions, just as they had the day she'd told them Sheldon had returned to town. And other than one time, she and Sheldon hadn't even discussed her family.

That was something that gave her cause to wonder about what Sheldon wanted. If he wanted long term with her, wouldn't he have asked her already whether or not she'd told her family that they were once again involved? Her family's approval of him had been an issue between them in the past, one Sheldon had often pressed.

Tyanna didn't want to think about any of this anymore, so she made her way to the kitchen. Opening the fridge, she inspected the contents. Milk, orange juice, some eggs, bread and jelly. Enough for breakfast.

She reached for the orange juice and took a long swig straight from the carton. Her mother would be appalled, but hey, she lived alone.

She returned the juice to the shelf in the fridge, then stood staring, wondering what she should eat. Cereal, she finally decided. That would be the easiest and quickest thing at this hour.

Hearing footsteps, she turned.

Rubbing his eyes, Sheldon shuffled into the kitchen, topless and wearing his black boxers. Tyanna shook her head as she shot him a mock scowl.

Why was it that Sheldon never stayed asleep anytime she got up to prepare breakfast?

"What are you doing up?" Tyanna asked.

"I missed you," he replied.

"Why do I think you just happen to be hungry? You always seem to wake up whenever I get food."

He slipped his arms around her waist from behind and nuzzled his nose against her soft neck. "I'm hungry for you."

"Still?"

"Baby, I'm always hungry for you."

Tyanna playfully elbowed him in the rib. "My stomach needs nourishment."

"Hey," Sheldon began, taking his hands off her, "so does mine."

"Then grab a bowl. I'm only having cereal."

"Cereal is fine."

While Sheldon went to the cupboard and got out two bowls, Tyanna opened the pantry. She stared at the two choices, then asked, "Lucky Charms or Bran Flakes?"

"*Lucky Charms?*"

Tyanna cut her eyes at him. "Don't give me stress. A girl's got to have one vice."

"It's just weird. Both choices are at opposite ends of the spectrum."

"So?" Tyanna challenged. She would never tell him that after he'd left her, she had started eating her favorite childhood cereal again for comfort. That and chocolate.

Sheldon shrugged. "It's just that I never would have thought . . . you're so health conscious."

"Anything in moderation."

Sheldon's eyes met hers. "Even me?"

Tyanna hesitated. "Yes. Even you. Now what do you want?"

"Lucky Charms."

"Really?" Tyanna could only shake her head. "And you give *me* the third degree!"

Tyanna took the box of cereal to the kitchen table, then went to the fridge. Sheldon got spoons, brought them to the table, then sat.

The jug of milk in hand, Tyanna made her way to the table. Before she could sit, Sheldon grabbed her, pulling her onto his lap. The skin of her bottom grazed the hair on his thighs.

Tyanna giggled. "Sheldon," she protested. "I need to eat."

"Don't worry. I'm going to feed you."

Sheldon filled one of the bowls with cereal and milk. He dipped the spoon into the bowl, taking up some of the Lucky Charms. He carefully lifted the spoon to Tyanna's mouth. He fed her, then fed himself, then fed her again. They continued that routine until the bowl was empty.

"I don't know about you, but I'm still hungry," Tyanna announced.

Sheldon tightened his hand around her waist. Her butt moved over him, and she could feel the length of him against her, growing hot and strong.

Tyanna's breathing grew shallow at the same moment her stomach grumbled. "What did I tell you?" she asked.

"All right," Sheldon said. "Let's finish eating before anything else."

"Before we go back to bed. To sleep," Tyanna stressed.

Sheldon looked into her eyes. "Why am I getting a distinct 'you're tired of sex' vibe?"

Tyanna lifted the box of cereal and filled another bowl. "I didn't say I was tired of sex. . . ."

"But?"

"But." She paused. "But maybe we should see how long we can actually last without sex. And a great way to start would be by me getting off your lap."

With Sheldon's hold on her slackened, Tyanna got up and moved to the adjacent chair. "There. Don't you feel better already?" she asked.

Sheldon looked at her with narrowed eyes. "No sex."

No sex. Could she do it? She didn't know. But not for the first time, she wondered if sex was all there was to her relationship with Sheldon. For whatever reason, he always turned her on in a most primal way, which could be why it was so hard to get him out of her system.

"Yeah. No sex. Now let's see how long it takes you to hit the door."

Now Sheldon frowned. "What are you trying to say?" he asked. "You think I can't lie in bed with you and keep my hands off you?"

"Sometimes I wonder," Tyanna replied. She poured milk into her bowl of Lucky Charms.

"Like you do a good job of keeping your hands to yourself."

"Touché." She dipped her spoon into the bowl, then paused. "But honestly, I guess I'd like to know we're more to each other than just sexual partners."

"Let's go to bed." Sheldon pushed his chair back and stood.

"Whoa—"

"To sleep," Sheldon stressed. "I'm gonna show you that as much as I may want to make love to you, we can have intimate moments that don't involve sex."

Maybe she was developing a multiple personality, because she didn't like the fact that Sheldon had agreed so easily to her "no sex" request. But she said, "All right. Just as soon as I have another bowl."

They both ate more cereal, and when they were

finished, Sheldon took Tyanna's hand and led her back to the bedroom. Clearly, he wanted to show her that there was more to their relationship than the physical. Exactly what did that mean?

For once, she just wished the man would come out and tell her that he loved her. Or that he simply enjoyed spending time with her but didn't care about her enough to marry her one day. Then she'd know.

Goodness, here she was, thinking about marriage once again. When did that happen?

No, that wasn't right. As she climbed into bed and Sheldon pulled the covers over her, Tyanna acknowledged that the better question was, How had she ever let go of the fantasy that they could have a life together? Because as much as she tried to deny it to herself, she was still in love with Sheldon. He had to know how she felt about him, despite everything she'd said to the contrary.

Sheldon got into bed next to her and lay alongside her, his front pressed against her back. Slipping his arm around her waist, he reached for her hand.

Tyanna closed her eyes as Sheldon linked fingers with hers. This was nice. Comfortable and cozy.

Silence filled the room for a long while, but though Tyanna was tired, she couldn't sleep. Sheldon was the only man who had the power to crush her heart. She hadn't expected to be back to this point—with him in her life, in her bed.

She was contemplating a move to Los Angeles if her fitness video venture was successful. What would happen then?

She said, "Our video is finished. Postproduction and all."

"That was quick," Sheldon replied.

"Yeah. Apparently Phil decided to work on it right away and get it done. It's ready to be sent to Ronnie Vaughn. I get to see it a little later today."

"That's great." Sheldon sounded tired.

"Wendy's seen it, and she thinks Ronnie will be impressed."

"I'm sure he will be."

"And . . ." Tyanna hesitated, not sure how to say her next words. "Wendy and I were thinking that if everything goes as we planned, we might move to L.A."

"Move?" Sheldon asked. "Permanently?"

"It's something Wendy and I were considering," Tyanna explained. "There's big money in the fitness business out there. . . . Plus, if Ronnie Vaughn does one of our videos, we think it would make sense. We might do a whole series. I don't know. . . ."

"But if you move to L.A.," he began, his voice sleepy, "how are we going to build a future together?"

For a full five seconds, Tyanna didn't breathe. She waited for Sheldon to go on. When he didn't, she said, "A future together?"

"Mmm hmm," he replied softly.

This was the first time Sheldon had ever mentioned such a thing, and a weird mix of emotions swirled inside Tyanna. She felt a rush of joy tinged with a bit of fear. A life with Sheldon. Did she dare hope?

She had given up on any dreams of marriage and a family. And during this time she and Sheldon had been spending together, she had deliberately tried to push thoughts of a future out of her mind. Oh, it had become painfully clear that she still loved him, but she had tried simply to enjoy their time together, no strings attached.

She snuggled closer to him, wiggling her bottom against his groin. No doubt about it, she could handle this—waking up next to Sheldon every day.

"Sheldon?"

But he didn't answer. Tyanna could hear the steady sound of his breathing.

*How are we going to build a future together?*

She smiled. That, in a nutshell, was the closest Sheldon had ever come to telling her that he loved her.

And for right now, it felt good.

Closing her eyes, she savored the moment, content to fall asleep in the arms of the man she knew she still loved.

When Wendy rolled over, one foot tangled in the sheets while the other one went over the side of the bed. Her eyes popped open. She was instantly aware that she wasn't in familiar surroundings.

It took another moment for her to remember—
she was in Phil's bed.

*Phil's bed.* The realization made her warm
inside.

But where was Phil?

Slowly she sat up. The room spun, but still she
didn't lie back. She had no clue what time it was,
only that she had to work today.

Glancing down, she saw that she wasn't wearing what she'd had on last night. She was in an
oversized white T-shirt, which had to be Phil's.

She didn't remember changing. Had Phil
changed her clothes for her? A moment of panic
hit her at the same time she felt the throbbing in
her head.

Good Lord, just how much of a fool had she
made of herself last night? Slowly but surely, a
couple details were coming back to her. She'd
had a couple of those Call-a-Cab drinks at a bar,
where they'd gone after dinner. The drink's
name had intrigued her, and man, they hadn't
been kidding about it. If she hadn't been with
Phil, she had no clue how she would have made
it home.

But she hadn't made it home—she'd made it
back to Phil's place. Had they finally made love?
God, how awful would that be if they'd made
love and she didn't even remember it!

Wendy slipped the covers off and climbed out
of bed. Man, she needed some aspirin and she
needed it badly. Steadying herself, she glanced

around the room. It was then that she noticed her black dress was draped over a chair in one corner of the room.

But there was no sign of Phil's clothes.

Wendy opened the bedroom door and went out into the hallway. Hearing no sound, she padded quietly toward the living room. It was early, not too long after sunrise, she was sure, so she couldn't imagine Phil having gotten up already if they'd been sleeping together.

She found him snuggled under a blanket on his plush beige sofa. His tall body was cramped into the too-small space, one foot hanging over the side. He lay on his back, and the way his neck was angled over the armrest must have hurt.

"Phil." When he didn't respond, Wendy moved to the side of the sofa and sat on the floor near his head. She rubbed his arm. "Phil."

Phil's eyes flew open. He seemed as startled as she had been when she'd woken up and found herself in his bed.

"Hi," she said, offering him a smile.

"I didn't think you'd be up already."

"I made an ass of myself, didn't I?"

"No, not an ass."

"Just an idiot," Wendy offered.

"You were pretty drunk. You've got to have a killer hangover."

"I do. And I'm hoping you have some aspirin."

"In the bathroom cabinet above the sink."

Wendy's eyes ventured from Phil's face to the

length of his body. He wore a T-shirt, and she could see the outline of his white briefs beneath the thin sheet. It didn't look as though they'd been intimate, but she had to ask. Had to be sure.

"Did we . . . ?"

"No," Phil answered quickly. "Nothing happened. You know I'd never take advantage of you."

Wendy felt a mix of disappointment and relief. "Of course." She got to her feet. "What time is it?"

Phil looked behind her to where the entertainment center was set up. "Seven twenty-four."

"Oh, shit! I'm supposed to be at work." She'd never missed a day's work without calling in. "I've got to get out of here."

But as she started to hustle off, the floor swayed beneath her and her head pounded something awful. Phil was on his feet in a flash, gathering her in his arms.

"Easy," he said.

"I don't feel so good."

"You're in no shape to go anywhere."

"But my job—"

"Call them. Tell them you're sick."

Wendy managed a weak nod. "You're right. I can't go in like this."

"You can have my bed all day if you need it."

"Why don't you join me?" she asked. Realizing how he would construe her words, Wendy quickly added, "The sofa's too small for you. I feel guilty for keeping you from getting a good night's sleep."

Phil met her eyes, then glanced away. "I don't think that's a good idea."

And with those words, Wendy felt like the world's biggest loser. She'd been chasing a dream with Phil, a dream based on her own foolish notions. The man was her friend, nothing else.

If she didn't desperately need sleep to cure her awful headache, she would run from his apartment and not look back.

Instead, she tried to play it cool. "I only meant that we could share the bed so you wouldn't be uncomfortable. But you're right. That's a bad idea. However, I insist you take the bed and I take the sofa. It's only fair."

"No. You go on back to the bed," Phil told her, his tone insistent.

Wendy didn't want to argue. She wanted to disappear into a black hole. "All right. If you insist. But first, can I use your phone?"

"Absolutely. There's one in the bedroom."

Wendy nodded briefly, then practically ran back to the bedroom. Inside the room, she closed the door behind her, then rested her body against it. She inhaled a series of jerky breaths, none of which made her feel any better.

She was a fool. She would call work and tell them she couldn't make it in today, get some sleep, then get the hell out of here.

And forget about Phil once and for all.

＊　　＊　　＊

Tyanna wrapped a terry-cloth robe around her body as she hurried to the door. She had hoped whoever it was would go away, but the frantic knocking hadn't stopped.

She frowned when she looked through the peephole and saw Wendy. Opening the door in a rush, she said, "Wendy, what's wrong?"

"I feel like a big idiot," Wendy replied glumly. "I—" Her eyes darted beyond Tyanna's shoulder, and she promptly shut her mouth.

Tyanna turned and looked behind her to see Sheldon standing there. She turned back to Wendy. "Wendy, you don't look good at all. Come in."

"No. I didn't mean to bother you. I just wanted to drop this off." She dug a video out of her purse and passed it to Tyanna. "Since I'm not going to see you at work today."

"If you two need to talk . . ." Sheldon said.

"No." Wendy waved off the suggestion. "I'm fine, really. Hi, Sheldon. Bye, Sheldon." She forced a smile, then pivoted on her heel and disappeared down the hall.

"Wendy." Tyanna stepped into the hallway, watching as Wendy darted to the stairs. Wendy clearly wasn't going to stop. To Sheldon she said, "I wonder what the heck that was about."

"You want to go after her?"

Tyanna shook her head. "I'll never catch her. I'll just call her on her cell, find out why she's not at work. I hope she's okay."

"You want to watch the video?" Sheldon asked.

"Oh. Yeah." Tyanna closed the door. "May as well."

She walked to her bedroom, and Sheldon followed her. There she turned on the TV, put the cassette into her VCR, and hit PLAY. Then she joined Sheldon on the bed to watch it.

The music and credits started, and Sheldon clapped, embarrassing her. And when she saw her image the first time, she giggled. She looked different on videotape—at least different from what she'd expected. It took a moment to get used to, but once she did, she almost forgot that she was watching herself and Wendy, that's how absorbed in the video she got. The background looked amazing. All the cuts from one angle to another were smooth. The video was, as Wendy had said, totally professional. Her friend was right. It was ready to be marketed.

"That looks pretty damn great," Sheldon announced.

Tyanna turned to him, a smile dancing on her lips. "It does, doesn't it?"

"Hell, yeah. You're gonna knock this Ronnie guy's socks off."

Squealing, Tyanna threw her arms around Sheldon and hugged him. "Oh, Sheldon. If he likes it, this will be a dream come true."

Sheldon planted a soft kiss on her lips. "Congratulations, sweetheart."

"Well, he still has to review it."

"And he'll no doubt love it."

Tyanna's eyes were filled with happiness as she looked into Sheldon's. "I'm so excited. This is what I've wanted for a long, long time. If we can really do this, I may finally have a career that I love. My father should finally be happy."

"I'm proud of you," Sheldon told her. But he suddenly felt a weird sensation, like his stomach was falling. If this fitness guru loved the video, Tyanna might move away. He wasn't quite ready to deal with that possibility.

"Ronnie Vaughn is such a success. To have a fitness video released under his name . . . This could not only be a dream come true, but also a financial success."

"I'm sure it will be."

She gave him an odd look. "You okay?"

"Sure." What was he supposed to say to her? Don't go to L.A.? He had no right to stand between her and her dreams.

Extending a hand, Sheldon trailed a finger softly down the length of her spine from the top of her neck to the small of her back. She moaned softly and arched into him. A simple movement, but with Tyanna, even simple was seductive.

"I know what you're trying to do," she practically purred.

"No sex, remember?"

"Well, that was earlier. . . ."

Sheldon kissed the tip of her nose. "Nope. You said you wanted to see if there was more to our relationship than the physical, so at least for the rest of the day it's hands off."

"Oh." She sounded disappointed.

Sheldon got off the bed. "I've got to head home, anyway. Check on my mother. Deliver another application to the Broward County Sheriff's headquarters and then, off to work."

"You've got a full day."

"Yep. But I should be at the gym later tonight."

Tyanna stood to join him. She slipped her arms around his neck. "You want to get a shower?"

"I'll get one when I get home."

"All right. . . ."

Sheldon kissed Tyanna's forehead, then lightly brushed his lips over hers. "I . . . I'll miss you today."

Tyanna stroked his cheek. "I'll miss you, too."

*Chapter 23*

*I love you.*

Three simple words. Were they really so hard to say? Sheldon had wanted to, he really had, but even as they were on the tip of his tongue, he'd opted for the safe "I'll miss you" instead.

What was it that held him back?

He knew what—the memory of his father. Dear old Dad, who said those words all the time, whenever he wanted something.

All his life, Sheldon had tried to believe he wasn't like his father, but maybe they were more alike than he wanted to admit—because it was Tyanna's talk of possibly moving away that had inspired him to tell her he loved her. Did he want to say the words in order to make her stay, or did he really love her?

He didn't want to lose her.

But he didn't want to hold her back either, especially not with three words that could easily make a prisoner of her like they had of his mother—a mother who needed him around right now.

Sheldon sighed as he drove. He was probably being too hard on himself. He knew his mother wouldn't agree with his errant thoughts, and maybe his mother was right. Because telling Tyanna that he loved her wouldn't be about controlling her or keeping her around. It would be because that's what he felt in his heart.

He would never try to control her. If she wanted to move to Los Angeles to pursue her dream, he wouldn't stand in her way—no matter how much he would miss her. The way he felt about her, he wanted her around always—but he also wanted what would make her happy.

If that didn't include him . . .

The thought made him sad, even as the realization hit him that this was what love was all about. For so long, he hadn't been sure what love was. But now he knew that love was wanting what was best for the other person, no matter what you wanted for yourself.

"You're nothing like your old man," he said, smiling at the words. "Nothing like him at all."

Sheldon saw the plume of smoke long before he turned the corner onto his street. But when he realized that the fire was burning at the end of the crescent, where his mother's house was, his pulse started to race.

Fire trucks lined the street and firefighters were out en masse, hoses spewing water at the fire.

As he drove closer, a uniformed officer ran

toward his car, arms waving, imploring him to stop.

Sheldon did, then wound down his window.

"You can't go any farther," the cop told him.

"But I live on this street."

"Sorry. You're gonna have to park around the corner until the fire's out and the firefighters are gone."

Sheldon heard the man, but he wasn't paying much attention. He was looking beyond all the commotion to the heart of the flames. His eyes narrowed on the house that was a blazing inferno.

And his heart nearly split in two.

He jammed the car into park, jumped out of the car and started to run. He heard, "Sir!" behind him, but he didn't stop.

By the time he'd forced himself through the crowd of neighborhood residents to the front of his mother's house, he felt arms around him, trying to hold him back. He struggled to get free.

"Sir, you can't go in there."

"My mother," Sheldon rasped.

He pulled an arm free and tried to lunge forward, but the arms around him tightened their grasp on him.

"Sir, there is no way you can go into that house!"

"My mother. Do you know if she's in there?" he practically shouted. There was no reason she shouldn't be.

Someone grabbed him from behind and jerked

him around. A pair of blue eyes pierced his. "We can't let you go in there. You go in there, you die."

The words were like a stab in the heart. "But my mother . . ."

"Sir, we're doing the best we can. I know it's hard, but I must ask you to remain with these officers while I find out who they might have brought out."

"Alive?" He wailed, tears running down his face. Two pairs of arms held him back while he struggled in anguish.

The blue eyes shifted uneasily. And Sheldon knew. Oh God, he knew.

"Ma!" He tried again to free himself, but the officers continued to grip his upper body in an unbreakable grasp.

Sheldon wrenched his head around to see over his shoulder, taking in the devastating view of the raging flames. If his mother was in there . . .

Overwhelmed, Sheldon leaned against the blue-eyed man's shoulder and began to sob.

It seemed his heart didn't beat at all as he sat and watched the firefighters battle the blaze. Merely an hour later, his mother's house was completely destroyed.

But he didn't care about that. Well, he cared, but that's not what mattered most. Material things, for the most part, could be replaced. But he could never replace his mother.

No one had seen her, and Sheldon was doing

everything in his power to remain hopeful. Until the last ember died and a thorough search of the house had been done, he wasn't going anywhere.

Neighbors crowded the streets, everyone watching the action. Mrs. Lundy, their neighbor to the right, had offered him solace in her home, but Sheldon had declined. The only place he wanted to be was directly across the street, observing everything.

Feeling a gentle hand on his shoulder, Sheldon looked up. It was Brenda, another neighbor. "Any word?" she asked.

Speech was too much to manage right now, considering the lump of fear lodged in his throat, so Sheldon shook his head.

"Can I get you anything?"

Again, he shook his head. Then he turned his gaze back to the house.

He heard soft footfalls and knew Brenda was walking away. It's not that he meant to be rude, but he wanted to be alone with his thoughts right now.

If his mother was dead . . .

An official investigation of the fire would follow, but Sheldon didn't need to hear any report to tell him this was arson.

His mother was careful. She never left a kettle on a hot stove, never left a candle burning too long. There was no way anything she did had caused this fire.

Someone had torched the house.

The same person who had attacked Tyanna in the parking lot of Jaguar Fitness. The same person who had called his mother's house leaving a warning for him.

Right now, Sheldon wanted to shoot himself. He never should have come back to town. By doing so, he had done the very thing he had never wanted to do: put those he loved at risk.

He had been sure that the threat to his life had died with Dino, but that had been a grave error in judgment. He had failed to consider the network of Dino's associates, people who still held a grudge even though Dino had been killed.

And on the drive from Tyanna's he had convinced himself that he was nothing like his father, but he was wrong. He'd come back to town for his mother and for Tyanna—selfishly. If he truly cared about their safety, he would have stayed away. Doing so would deny himself his heart's desire, but at least his mother and Tyanna would be safe.

That was the most important thing.

Sheldon's thoughts were interrupted by the sound of a car skidding to a stop. He jerked his head up to see the passenger door of a Ford Focus fly open.

His mother emerged, running toward the house.

Sheldon's heart actually soared in that moment, a feeling of relief so sweet it made him feel he could actually fly.

In a flash he was on his feet, charging across the street to his mother. "Ma! Ma!"

She whipped her head in his direction, and he saw on her face the same expression of horror he knew he'd worn the moment he had realized it was their house on fire.

He ran to her and swept her into his arms. "Oh, Ma. I was so worried about you!"

"Sheldon, what in God's name—?"

"I don't know. I came home and found the house on fire. No one could tell me if you were in there...." He gripped her tighter. "God, I was so scared...."

His mother pulled back and looked up at him. "I was at a church meeting. You weren't in there when this started?"

"No."

"Oh, thank the Lord." She glanced at the house, then back at him. Her face crumbled. "My house. Sheldon, it's gone. Everything . . ."

"I know." Sheldon ran a hand over her hair. "I know, Ma. And it's not going to be easy to rebuild. But at least we still have each other. At the end of the day, that's all that matters."

She didn't respond, simply hugged him tighter and began to cry.

"How did this happen?" she sobbed. "Why?"

"I don't know, Ma." He couldn't tell her what he suspected, that the fire had been meant for him. Whichever of Dino's goon friends had set it, they didn't care who they hurt. They were simply out for blood—anyone's blood.

"But don't you worry about that now," he went on. "Let the firemen do their work, investigate the cause of the fire. Then we'll worry about it. For now, we have to decide where we want to go. Mrs. Lundy has offered to take us in."

His mother nodded, but she had a distant look in her eyes.

Sheldon turned her in his arms, leading her slowly toward their neighbor's place. "Come on, Ma. Let's go inside and have a seat."

Hours later, Sheldon was hunched in a phone booth, listening to the ringing on the other end of the line. After what seemed like forever, someone picked up at Jaguar Fitness.

"Tyanna Calhoun, please."

"I believe she's with a client right now."

"Tell her it's urgent."

"Who's calling?"

"This is her boyfriend, Sheldon Ford."

*Her boyfriend* . . . The words had come naturally, rolling off his tongue. And they suddenly made it all the more difficult to give her the news.

If he told her about the fire, she would freak. She would worry about him, and she didn't need that right now. Not when she was excited about her fitness video and the prospects that lay ahead.

Damn. How could he tell her about the fire? He knew what she would say, that he wasn't trusting her with what was going on in his life, but this wasn't about trust. This was about protecting her.

"Sheldon?"

Her soft voice startled him. He could hear a smile in her tone, and his heart cracked. "Hi," he said.

"What is it?" she asked, picking up on his mood. "What's wrong?"

"Um . . . nothing."

"Sheldon . . ."

"Ever since I left your place, I've been thinking," he managed to croak.

"About me?" she asked happily.

"Yeah, you could say that." He paused. "I was thinking about the fitness video and your plan to move to Los Angeles."

"I didn't say I *was* moving."

"But you said you wanted to. The business is better there."

"That's a while off," Tyanna told him. "And who knows what Wendy and I will do?"

"Well, I think you should go."

There was a pause. "You mean, move there?"

"Yeah. This is your dream. And I don't want to stand in your way. Not that I would, considering you told me you didn't see a future for us anyway."

"Hold up, Sheldon. What on earth are you talking about?"

"Your future."

"Just ten hours or so ago, you mentioned wanting a future with me."

"I was premature in saying that."

The silence nearly tore him up. He knew

Tyanna was confused and hurting, but this was the best thing. He had no other choice if he wanted to keep her safe. And who knew how long this threat to his life would exist, or if he'd escape alive this time? It wasn't fair to plan a future with her. Not under these circumstances. And as far as he was concerned, Los Angeles was one of the safest places she could be right now.

"What's going on, Sheldon? The truth."

"I already told you."

"I think you've told me a load of bull."

"All I want is for you to go for your dream one hundred and fifty percent. And if that means heading to L.A. to deliver the video to Ronnie Vaughn personally, that's what you should do."

"What aren't you telling me?" Her voice was softer now, tinged with sadness.

"I'm gonna be busy getting my career started up. You're gonna be busy with yours. And I think . . . that's just the way it has to be."

Before Tyanna could say another word, Sheldon hung up. Some would call it the coward's way out, but the way he figured it, he didn't have a choice.

He hadn't protected Dwight, and now his brother was dead. Today he'd come damn close to losing his mother. He wasn't going to sit around and watch as someone else he loved was hurt.

With any luck, he could see this situation resolved once and for all. But in the meantime,

Tyanna would be upset with him for pushing her away. This was for her own good—but she didn't understand and never would. He held no illusions that when this was resolved, he could ask her to take him back again without getting a slap in the face.

Sheldon gritted his teeth as he stepped out of the phone booth. Knowing what he had to do didn't make the situation any easier. Pushing Tyanna away hurt him more than it had the first time. It hurt enough that he felt he was losing a piece of himself.

But he'd be damned if he put his wants and needs before what was best for her. He wasn't going to be like his father.

He was going to protect Tyanna and his mother, no matter the cost.

For the rest of her evening at work, Tyanna did her best to fight her foul mood. Many times, she found herself on the verge of tears, but she'd be damned if she let them fall.

She had no clue what was going on, but she didn't believe a word Sheldon had said to her about giving her space to pursue her career. That was a load of hogwash if she ever heard it, but that knowledge didn't make things any easier.

Something was going on. But what?

As she sat at her desk picking at a fruit salad, she realized that it didn't matter. What mattered was that she had asked Sheldon—practically begged him—not to shut her out, no matter how bad any given situation might be. She thought she'd gotten through to him, but clearly she hadn't.

Even now, he still didn't trust her. And if he didn't trust her, they could never have a future, regardless of how much she loved him.

And to think that just today, she had thought that he had been on the verge of telling her that he loved her. *What a freakin' joke.* Whatever his issues were, she just hadn't been able to crack the shell around his heart.

Once again Tyanna's eyes misted with tears. Angry, she brushed them away. She didn't want to cry over him. Not when she had known better than to fall for him again.

She could be mad at him, but the truth was, she should only be mad at herself.

Despite knowing better, she hadn't acted better. And once again, she was left with a broken heart.

"Hey, Wendy," Tyanna said a short while later. She hadn't spoken to her friend since Wendy had left her apartment in a rush, and now Tyanna desperately needed to hear her voice. "I hope it's not too late to call."

"No. I wasn't sleeping."

*Sheldon's a big jerk*, she wanted to blurt out, but she knew the tears would follow. So she said, "I watched the video."

"Isn't it great?" But Wendy didn't sound that enthusiastic.

"Yeah, it's fabulous. You know, I never told you before, but thanks for coming up with this idea. And thanks for everything else. If it wasn't for your connection to the friend who knows Ronnie Vaughn, we wouldn't be where we are right now. Then, your connection to Phil, who was able to do this for us."

"Hmm," was Wendy's reply.

"Wendy, what's up? I know something's wrong. Is it serious?"

"I'm just a moron."

"This is about Phil, isn't it?"

"Uh-huh. First Phil, then something else. I'm not sure I want to talk about it right now."

"Believe me, hon. I know how you feel. I'm having that kind of day myself. Makes me want to head straight to L.A. and deliver the fitness video to Ronnie Vaughn in person."

"You know, that sounds like a good idea. I need a couple days to myself. I told Max I'm not heading in tomorrow."

"You're not?"

"Nope."

Tyanna paused. "Look, sweetie. I hate to hear you sounding so down. Do you mind if I come over tonight? We can hang out for a while. Chat. I'll even pick up some of that double-fudge ice cream you love so much."

"Oh, that was a low blow." But for the first time

since they'd started talking, Tyanna heard a smile in Wendy's voice.

"There's no point in you moping around your place and me moping around mine when we can mope together. What do you say?"

Wendy giggled. "All right, hon. Just keep in mind I won't be great company."

"Nothing your best friend and some double-fudge ice cream can't fix. I'm gonna try to leave here early, depending on if my last appointment shows or not."

"See you when you get here, then."

"Later."

Wendy dug her spoon into her container of ice cream, scooping out a healthy portion. She filled her mouth with the double fudge, then closed her eyes in delight.

"This is amazing," she managed around her mouthful. "I feel better already. Thank you."

"No problem," Tyanna told her.

Tyanna and Wendy were sitting cross-legged on the floor in Wendy's living room, hunched over the coffee table and their respective containers of ice cream. Tyanna didn't care for double fudge at all. Her comfort flavor was butter pecan. And she planned to eat every last drop from the one-liter carton. She was constantly in the gym, so she wasn't worried about calories.

The movie *Thelma and Louise* was playing on Wendy's VCR. Tyanna had picked it up on the way over, because it was their favorite movie. Considering this was going to be a girls' night, this flick was completely appropriate.

"You see?" Wendy said, pointing her spoon at the television. "That's where they go wrong. Letting that man into their lives." Brad Pitt's character was doing his striptease. "Though he *is* too cute. But like they say, you have to watch out for the cute ones."

"And the ones who are good in bed. Look at how easily he seduces her." Tyanna shook her head.

"Score one for the men. Again. Why do they always seem to have the upper hand?"

"Because we let them have it," Tyanna responded. "We hand them our hearts on a silver platter."

"*Pfft.*" Wendy scowled. "Sex. Relationships. It's all overrated."

"Ain't that the truth."

Both Tyanna and Wendy dug into their ice cream. Despite their words, Tyanna knew they were both full of it. They were two women who had the same hopes and dreams as most other women. But they were hurting, and needed to pretend that men didn't matter in their lives.

Tyanna turned to her friend. "What did Phil do?"

A frown marred Wendy's pretty face. "It's more a question of what he didn't do."

"I thought things were going well."

"So did I. And I don't really think I was reading him completely wrong. I mean, you saw him at your parents' place. Did he look like he wasn't interested?"

"I thought he was."

Wendy stabbed her spoon into her ice cream. "You also said he could have turned gay."

"I did, but I was only kidding."

"I know . . . but maybe you hit the nail on the head. Maybe after his last girlfriend, Phil decided he can't be bothered with women." Wendy ate more ice cream. "I woke up in his bed early this morning."

Tyanna's mouth nearly hit the floor. "But you just said—"

"*I* woke up in his bed, drunk as a skunk. *He* was sleeping on the sofa. He assured me that he would never take advantage of me. How sweet of him!"

Tyanna chuckled. "Well, that is admirable."

"I know. But he couldn't even look at me when I was talking to him. I think I must have thrown myself at him in a drunken stupor, but he doesn't want to tell me about it. And he certainly doesn't want anything to do with me."

"Hey, if Phil isn't interested, that's *his* loss." Tyanna tried to sound upbeat. "You're such a beautiful woman. Such a beautiful person."

"And you're a biased friend."

"Maybe, but I wouldn't lie about that. Ever."

"I love you for that."

"It's the truth."

Wendy smiled briefly, but her glum expression

quickly returned. "At least this way, I know to give up on my silly dreams where he's concerned. And if I did hit on him like some lovesick teenager, I can blame it on being drunk."

"Yeah, I guess that's a plus."

"And I didn't sleep with him."

"Even better."

"There are other men out there. Men who will appreciate me."

"Of course there are."

Yet despite her words, Wendy looked at Tyanna and burst into tears.

"Hey." Tyanna reached for her friend and wrapped an arm around her. "I didn't realize you had it for Phil this bad."

Wendy sniffled. "It's not Phil. I got a call from my mother this evening."

Tyanna's stomach suddenly lurched. For Wendy to be this upset, it had to be something serious. "How bad is it?"

"My father is moving out."

"Oh, my God."

Wendy chuckled, but the sound held no mirth. "Uh-huh. Seems he up and lost his mind. Told her he's not sure if he ever loved her. Something about how he married her just because of me."

"Oh, no."

Wendy pulled back and looked at Tyanna from tear-filled eyes. "Yeah, that didn't make me feel very good, let me tell you."

"That was a horrible thing for your father to

say. And considering your parents had two more children and have been together for twenty-six plus-years, I think it's a line of bull."

Tyanna reached for a Kleenex from the table and passed it to Wendy. Wendy wiped her eyes. "My mother is crushed. My sister says she's worried that Mama's gonna end up in the hospital. She won't eat, she stays in her room all day and cries." Wendy blew her nose. "I'm just so glad my brother and sister are there for her. I'll have to make the trip up to Orlando in a few days."

"I'm really sorry, Wendy." Tyanna hated to see her normally happy, bubbly friend cry.

"I feel so silly, crying over this at my age. People separate and get divorced all the time."

"You have every right to be upset."

"If you'd seen my parents together—they were always the perfect couple. I can't believe my father would do this to her. Maybe if I'd been there . . ."

"Sweetie." Tyanna rubbed Wendy's back. "I know it hurts, but there was nothing you could do. None of this is your fault."

Wendy's guilt-filled expression said she believed otherwise. "I hated when my parents left South Florida for Orlando when I was sixteen. For one, I was no longer close to you, my best friend. I moved back here the day I turned eighteen, and I know that broke my mother's heart. But I also left her with my younger brother and sister to take care of." Wendy shrugged. "I don't know. Maybe there was extra stress because I was no longer around. . . ."

Tyanna put her arm around Wendy's shoulders. "That was eight years ago, sweetie."

Wendy sniffled. "I know. It doesn't make sense. I guess I'm just in shock. My whole life—I've always dreamed of having a relationship like my parents'. And now I learn that my father is saying he probably never loved my mother? Everything I believed was a lie. I wish he'd just gone out and had an affair."

"Maybe that's what this is about."

"I wouldn't be surprised. Nothing about relationships surprises me anymore." Wendy released an angst-filled sigh. "Today has been a day of tough lessons. You always told me I was too much of a romantic. I think you were right."

Tyanna didn't know what to say. If this had happened to her parents, she would be completely devastated. A breakup was a shock for any child, no matter how old you were. She knew it wouldn't help to give Wendy meaningless words that would never ease what she was going through.

"Have you talked to your father?"

"Nope. And right now, I don't want to."

Tyanna ate another spoonful of ice cream. "Well, I hope this is just one of those life-crisis moments for your father. Maybe he's just going through something and it will all work out."

"I hope so, but I'm not counting on it."

They fell into silence, eating their ice cream and watching the movie. Finally, Wendy spoke. "What about you, Tyanna? If you're picking up *Thelma and Louise*, then I know you're having man troubles, too. But I just saw Sheldon at your place this morning, so I thought all was well on that front."

The ice cream in Tyanna's mouth suddenly soured. "Guess he fooled us both."

"What happened?"

"Hell if I know. One minute, he was telling me he wanted to build a life with me, the next he was calling me at work, practically begging me to move to L.A. to pursue my dream and leave him behind."

"That makes no sense."

"Tell me about it."

Wendy gripped Tyanna's hand and gave it a squeeze. "Something must be going on. How could he be in your bed this morning, yet breaking up with you hours later?"

Tyanna felt the hot sting of tears. She did her best to hold them back. "I asked myself that same question a little over a year ago, remember? I didn't believe Sheldon could cut me out of his life and not look back. But he did, which is why I knew better this time. Knew better, but didn't do better."

"I'm sorry."

"Me too."

"Both of us dealing with heartache at the same time? Must be something in the water today," Wendy said sarcastically.

"Who knows? Stranger things have happened."

"Did you consider calling him back?" Wendy asked. "If nothing else, he owes you an explanation. Not some lame brush-off."

"I thought about it. And like you said, I'm sure there's something else going on. But you know what? He's doing exactly what he did the last time. Not trusting me with whatever is happening. He'd rather have me suffer. And I just can't deal with that. Not anymore."

Tyanna finished off the last of her butter pecan ice cream, then sat back against the sofa and placed a hand on her belly. She'd stuffed herself, and in the end, she didn't feel much better.

Wendy finished off her double fudge and leaned back beside Tyanna. "This sucks. No offense, Tyanna. The ice cream was great, but my life right now . . . Sometimes, I just want to get away from it all."

"That's it!" Tyanna exclaimed, looking at Wendy. "What a great idea."

Yes, that's exactly what she needed. She wasn't ready to head off on a cruise ship for six months, but a day's drive somewhere nice would hopefully boost her spirits. Wendy's, too. "And I'll go with you. We'll be Thelma and Louise on our own adventure!"

"One that doesn't end in tragedy," Wendy added wryly. "I'm not quite ready to sacrifice it all over a man."

Tyanna angled her body sideways, resting her

head against Wendy's. Her friend sounded better already. "That's the spirit."

Wendy asked, "You really want to go somewhere?"

"Yes," Tyanna replied with enthusiasm. "Why don't we drive down to Key West? Or Key Largo? We can spend the night, then get you back bright and early for your next day's shift at the gym."

"That does sound great."

"Okay. Then it's set. I'll go home, get some stuff together. I'll pick you up in the morning."

"All right."

Wendy's lips curled in the faintest hint of a smile, but Tyanna could tell even that was forced.

Tyanna stood and placed her hands on her hips. "No more feeling guilty." She took Wendy by the hand and pulled her up from the floor. "You are going to get some sleep. Because you have to be up bright and early for our trip to Key West. Got it?"

Wendy managed a smile. "Yes, ma'am."

"Good." Tyanna hugged her tightly. "I love you, sweetie."

"I know. I love you, too."

"And we're gonna get through this. Me and you. Both of us are gonna be just fine."

# Chapter 24

For the fifth time, Sheldon called Tyanna. For the fifth time, he hung up when her answering machine picked up.

He ground out a frustrated breath, wondering where she was. Maybe she just wasn't taking any calls.

He'd considered calling her at work, had started to in fact, then decided against it. Even now, he wasn't sure what he'd say to her if he got her on the line.

Mostly, he wanted to know she was okay. Not that she'd tell him. At least if she hung up on him, he would know she was angry, and angry was good.

Angry would mean she was putting him behind her.

Hell, maybe he needed to leave well enough alone. Hadn't he hurt her enough? His voice was the last thing she would want to hear, considering everything.

Swallowing the lump in his throat, Sheldon made his way from the row of pay phones back to the long line where his mother was standing. They were at Miami International Airport, and his mother was waiting to get her boarding pass. Last night at Mrs. Lundy's, Sheldon had told his mother all the details of what was going on. Then, he had tried to convince her to head to Brooklyn to stay with her sister for a while.

"I can't have you around here if someone is trying to kill me, Ma. This was too close."

"Then come with me," she had said. "I'm going to be a nervous wreck in New York without you. I don't want to lose the only son I have left."

"You are not going to lose me," Sheldon assured her. "I'm going to deal with this once and for all. Someone has to stay to deal with the insurance company anyway. Then you can come back here and we can get a new place. I'm not going to let these people ruin our lives any more than they already have."

Sheldon walked with his mother through the line. She didn't have any luggage other than a small carry-on her neighbor had given her; everything they'd owned had been lost in the fire. Millie wore a haggard expression.

"Did you reach Tyanna?" she asked.

Sheldon ran a hand over the back of his neck. "No."

"Don't make the same mistake you made last time, Sheldon. Leaving her the way you did before. She deserves better than that. You both do."

"Ma—"

"No, hear me out. You didn't ask my input the last time. You just took off, assuming that was best."

"I had to protect you and Tyanna."

"A lot of good that did."

Ouch. His stomach dropped at his mother's words.

She reached out and gently touched his face. "I don't mean that the way it may have come across. I'm not blaming you, by any means. I am only trying to say that sometimes, despite our best intentions, things don't go the way we want them to. You left, thinking you were doing the best thing. You broke Tyanna's heart in the process, yet the danger isn't gone. How different would it have been if you hadn't shut her out?"

"I didn't want to take that chance."

"Fine, you didn't before. But now you know the answer. She may be in danger anyway, so you two are unfortunately in this together. And to push her away again—you will lose her forever."

"I'm prepared for that."

"Are you? I've seen how much happier you've been in these past weeks. And now, you're walking around like your head is stuck in a toilet. Is it worth it? Are these pathetic souls who are trying to ruin your life worth giving up Tyanna?"

Sheldon hadn't quite thought of it that way before. "I don't know, Ma."

"Tyanna adores you. And I adore her. It's time

we all move past the pain that's held us back and embrace a positive future. And that includes you letting go of whatever issues you have where your father is concerned."

Sheldon opened his mouth, then promptly shut it. He and his mother had never discussed his father like this before.

"You don't think I know why you run from relationships? But you couldn't run from Tyanna, could you? Then you got scared and used the first excuse you could to get her out of your life, under the pretense that it was the best thing for her."

"It wasn't a pretense."

"It was, even though you were too foolish to know it. You are nothing like your father. And I'm sorry if my perceived weakness in staying with him affected your outlook on relationships. I always knew when he was at fault, when he did me wrong. But he needed me." She held up a hand when Sheldon started to speak. "I know what you're going to say. But I stand by my decision. Maybe now I'd do things differently. I don't know. The point is, my relationship with your father should have no bearing on your relationship with Tyanna."

Sheldon was surprised at the lump of emotion that formed in his chest, making it hard to breathe.

"If you're going to stay here and resolve this whole mess," Millie went on, "then for God's sake, don't let Tyanna out of your life once again. I will never speak to you again if you do."

"Ma!"

"I'm serious," she told him, giving him a stern look.

They were now at the counter. His mother provided the appropriate identification to get her boarding pass. Minutes later, she was set to go to the gate.

Sheldon walked her to the farthest point he could. Her eyes filling with tears, Millie drew him into a hug. She hugged him as though she weren't coming back for a long time. "Be careful, son."

"I will be."

"And remember what I said."

"I will."

"I love you."

"I love you too, Ma."

Another quick squeeze, and she was on her way. As Sheldon brushed away his unexpected tears, he vowed to make Dino's hooligans pay for what they had done to his life, to those he cared about.

Yeah, he was going to end this. Or he was going to die trying.

Tyanna and Wendy barely made it back from their trip to Key West in time to get Wendy to work on schedule. Tyanna dropped her off at the gym minutes to seven, then headed home to get a bit more sleep before she'd have to get up for work herself.

Crawling out of bed at three-thirty in the morning for the three-hour drive back to Miami hadn't been fun, but Tyanna was glad she and Wendy had taken the trip. She didn't even mind having splurged on a hotel room for only five hours of sleep. Sitting on the beach and drinking a couple piña coladas had done them a world of good. So did the bit of flirting they'd engaged in with some of the gorgeous men at the restaurant where they'd had dinner the night before. It was all in good fun, of course, and there hadn't been a thought of taking it further. But it was exactly what both Tyanna and Wendy needed at the time.

Thankfully, the weather had cooperated for their short stay, giving them plenty of sunshine. By the time they'd left, Wendy was smiling and laughing with sincerity.

Now at home, Tyanna opened her apartment door and stepped inside. Though she knew it was foolish, the first thing she did was head to the answering machine.

Not one message. Her heart sank.

But what had she expected? That Sheldon would have called and told her what a big idiot he was? She shook her head with chagrin. She was such an idiot, hanging onto the past.

While it sucked having her heart broken again, at least Sheldon had given her the courtesy of a phone call when he ended things this time. That was an improvement, rather than cutting her off cold turkey.

Yet if it was an improvement, why did she feel as lousy as the first time?

A long sigh oozing out of her, Tyanna opened her bedroom door. She felt more than lousy and knew exactly why. Because she had kept that small bubble of hope alive inside her heart. The hope that after how Sheldon had shared himself with her once again, there was more to their relationship than the physical. But knowing that Sheldon hadn't even tried to reach her while she'd been away was the pin that popped that bubble.

Tyanna undressed and climbed into bed. Her heart lodged in her throat as she pulled the sheet over her. Sheldon's scent was everywhere.

How could she sleep in this bed, where she had once again given Sheldon her body, heart, and her soul?

*Ring, ring, go away. Come again another day. . . .*

The phone! Opening her eyes, Tyanna rolled over in bed, reaching for the receiver.

She brought it to her ear and said groggily, "Hello?"

Two beats passed, then, "Hi."

Every nerve in Tyanna's body screamed with awareness, a reaction she didn't like at all. She felt a mixture of relief and anger.

She cleared her throat and sat up. "Sheldon."

He was silent again, and Tyanna wondered if he'd called simply to have her talk. She was about to tell him that she didn't have time for this when he spoke.

"How are you?" he asked.

If he meant, "Are you wallowing in misery?" Tyanna would never give him the satisfaction. "I'm fine."

"Good." Pause. "That's good. Um, I tried reaching you yesterday."

So, he had called. Why hadn't he left a message? "I was out of town," she told him. "Had a great time."

"Then you're doing okay."

"Why wouldn't I be?"

A few thoughts came to mind, thoughts that didn't make it to his lips. Sheldon's tongue suddenly felt like sandpaper. He could hardly form a decent thought, much less speak. But what was he supposed to say to her now that she had practically told him she didn't miss him in the least?

*For God's sake, don't let Tyanna out of your life once again. I will never speak to you again if you do. . . .*

Damn, what was wrong with him? Hadn't he called to tell Tyanna how he felt and what was going on? So why weren't the words coming to him?

It was easier said than done. He didn't want to make the wrong decision. There was still a part of him that feared telling her, because he figured she'd run right out and try to do something about it. Just the way she had quickly gone to the gym and spoken with Leona when he'd come back to town and told her about Dino. Tyanna had a feisty side when ready, and if she felt protective—or guilty—he had no clue what she would do.

"Sorry, Ma," he muttered.

"What did you say?"

"Nothing."

*Nothing.* Well, wasn't that special. Tyanna wished Sheldon were here so she could smash the receiver she held over his head. The man was more than aggravating. She knew him well enough—at least she thought she did—to know that he hadn't called simply to see if she was okay.

She asked, "Are you finally going to tell me what's going on?"

"I . . . well . . . nothing." He groaned. Man, did he ever sound like an idiot. "Okay. Maybe I'm preoccupied with something."

"Wow. I'm surprised you admitted that."

"Come on, Tyanna. You should know that with whatever I'm doing, I'm keeping you my number-one priority."

"Really? And exactly how should I know that? Just a couple days ago, you told me to move to Los Angeles and forget about you."

"I told you not to let me stand in the way of your dreams."

Tyanna grunted her frustration. "I heard you fine and dandy two days ago, thank you very much. So if you have nothing else to say—"

"Just," he interjected, then paused. "Just give me some time."

"Time?" she asked, appalled. "You know, I wanted to believe that after everything you said to me when you came back into my life that you would be able to reach deep inside yourself and learn how to trust me, but I was wrong. So if you want time, I'll give you time. How about the rest of your life?"

And then she slammed down the receiver. What she really wanted was to hurl the phone across the room. But of course that wouldn't solve a thing.

Tyanna let out a long, angry groan as she dropped backward on her pillows. She pulled the covers over her once more.

*Forget Sheldon. Forget ever expecting him to respect and trust you the way you need him to. Forget all the silly dreams you once again started to have.*

Forget it all.

Action. Sheldon had to put everything else out of his mind and take action.

He had known better than to expect Tyanna to be happy to hear from him, and now he had to put the disappointment of their phone call behind him. The sooner he resolved this whole mess, the better.

He picked up the phone and called Maria.

Relief washed over him when she answered. "Hey, Maria. It's Sheldon."

"Hi, Sheldon." She sounded pleasantly surprised. "How are you?"

"Not too good, actually."

"What's wrong?"

For the next several minutes, Sheldon explained the recent events.

"Dear God," Maria said. "Burned your mother's house down?"

"With no regard for anyone else. Sure, they want me, but what if the neighbors' houses had caught fire? I have no clue if the person who started the fire knew no one was home, or if he just didn't care. My mother could have been killed." And if she had been killed, Sheldon would never forgive himself.

"I thought for sure this was all over," Maria commented sadly.

"So did I." Sheldon paused. "I need to find out a couple of things. First of all, I need to identify the guy working at the juice bar with Leona. Tyanna says he looks just like Dino— young guy though, early twenties. Wears glasses, maybe."

"Mmm. Could be Tony Benedetto," Maria answered. "Dino's cousin."

"The one from New York?"

"Right."

"All right. So Dino's family still owns the juice bar. That may explain some things. What do you know about this cousin?"

"Whatever Dino did, Tony did. That boy aimed

to please, which suited Dino well. In fact, Tony did a lot of Dino's dirty work in the operation—picking up the steroids, roughing up the competition. That sort of thing. He didn't start working at the juice bar until Dino's death, from what I understand. I'd met him before, of course, and didn't like him one bit. If you've got problems now, I would bet money that Tony is involved."

Sheldon would bet money on it too. He made a mental note of the name. "All right. My next issue. And I know you're trying to put the whole Dino situation behind you, so I hate to even ask. But I'm hoping you'll be willing to corroborate my story for me."

"Sheldon, you don't even have to ask. If that's what it takes to put an end to this whole sorry mess, you know you can count on me."

"What else do you know about Tony?"

"He's older than he looks, about five years younger than Dino, I think. A little shorter, but you can see the family resemblance easily. From what I remember, he was always trying to impress Dino, always trying to be a big-shot Benedetto. Made me sick. Who knows? Maybe he feels he has to take over where Dino left off."

"Hmm. That could be." Which meant things could go either way. If Tony was just a wannabe, perhaps he could be scared straight. But if he felt a sense of power now that Dino was dead, he would be a formidable threat to deal with.

"I guess that's all," Sheldon said. "Thanks, Maria. I appreciate your help."

"Hey, no problem. Let me know if you need me to talk to the cops."

"Will do."

Hopefully, the police wouldn't need to talk to her again—she'd been through enough already. But Sheldon was happy to know he had Maria on his side.

When Tyanna walked into the gym, Shirley instantly beamed at her from the reception desk. "Hey there, stranger," she said.

Tyanna wasn't in the mood to chat, but it wouldn't be fair to take that out on Shirley. "Hi, Shirley."

"How was your day off?"

"Good, actually," Tyanna replied truthfully. "I went down to Key West. It was a nice change of pace."

"Key West." Shirley rested her chin on both palms. "My favorite spot."

"I'll bet." No doubt Shirley went down to Key West for all the popular events. Including Fantasy Fest over Halloween, which was an outrageous show of costumes made of as little material as possible. Wherever there was a party, you could find Shirley.

"Any messages for me?" Tyanna asked.

"Not that I know of."

"All right." Tyanna turned to head off.

"Yo, wait a second," Shirley said, stopping Tyanna in her tracks. "There's something I want to show you."

"What?"

"Something I saw in the paper yesterday."

"*You* read the paper?" Tyanna joked. At least she was starting to feel better. "I didn't think you had any interest in anything other than fashion magazines. And men."

"Shut up." Shirley cut her eyes at her as she reached for a rolled-up newspaper beneath the counter. She unrolled the paper, then opened it to the second page. "Here," she said, lying the paper on the counter in front of Tyanna. She pointed to the photo. "Isn't this that hottie you're always hanging with here?"

Tyanna's eyes went to the article. A large color picture was immediately beneath the headline: NORTH MIAMI HOME BURNS TO THE GROUND.

Her heart spasmed as her eyes focused on the picture. A crowd of onlookers stood to one side outside the burning house, but it was one figure in particular that caught her eye. One person the photograph seemed to focus on.

Sheldon.

He looked distraught as he watched flames lick at the home he shared with his mother.

Tyanna knew the house well, even though it was barely recognizable in the photo.

"Isn't that him?"

Shirley's voice drew Tyanna from the horror of

the moment. "Yes." She cleared her throat. "Yes, that looks like him."

"Holy . . . I thought so." Shirley shook her head. "What a sad story. He and his mother lost everything."

"When?" Tyanna managed the hoarse word out of a throat clogged with emotion.

"This is yesterday's paper," Shirley said. "You must have been out of town when it happened. They featured this on the news."

"Can I take this?" Tyanna was already closing the paper.

"Yeah. I saved it for you."

"Thanks." Tyanna scooped up the paper and practically sprinted to her office. There, she opened up the newspaper once more and spread it on her desk.

So this was what Sheldon was dealing with. Tyanna couldn't stop her heart from aching. And she couldn't help feeling guilty for the way she had gotten angry with him on the phone hours earlier.

Lord have mercy. Was his mother okay? How were they holding up? Who was looking after them?

Why hadn't he told her?

Did he think she couldn't be compassionate enough, or did he think this was too much for her to deal with? No, for him to have pushed her away, there had to be more to this devastating story.

Even as Tyanna scanned the article and read that arson was suspected, she already knew that had to be the case. And she didn't have to wonder who was behind this vicious attack on Sheldon: one of Dino's friends. Maybe the very person who had pulled the trigger and ended Dwight's life.

She released a shaky breath. Knowing that people this evil actually existed in the world caused a chill to snake down her spine. At least the article hadn't reported any casualties. Apparently, Sheldon and his mother hadn't been home at the time. That was a blessing.

Tyanna sat back in her chair, her mind racing. The fire must have happened after Sheldon left her place that last morning. Which would explain his phone call to her hours later, encouraging her to head to Los Angeles to "pursue her dream."

Sheldon had to be out of his mind with worry. But what was he going to do? The article said there were no suspects—yet.

Tyanna wanted to talk to Sheldon, to know how he was coping, where he was staying. But he didn't have a cell phone, and because she'd hung up on him, she didn't have a way to reach him.

Damn.

As much as she hated some of his decisions, she knew why he hadn't told her. Once again, he was trying to protect her.

She was a silly fool, but her heart actually melted at the thought. A small smile crept onto her face. One minute, she was yelling at him for not having included her in what was going on. The next, she was appreciating his testosterone-driven gesture.

It was hard to stay mad at him—at least right now, under these circumstances. In the way that she understood everything about Sheldon, Tyanna understood the guilt he felt over losing his brother, and that he must feel even worse, now that the threat to his life had come right to his home. He was no doubt beating himself up over the fact that his mother lost everything—almost including her life. Not to mention the fact that Tyanna herself had been attacked outside the gym.

In Sheldon's masculine way, he probably felt this was too much for her to handle and wouldn't fill her in until it was resolved.

But Sheldon, after all this time, didn't understand her. At least not fully. Because if he did, he would know that she wasn't the type of woman to sit idly by and wait for a man to take care of things.

Besides, she was already involved. These jerks knew where she worked, and if they had burned down his house in order to get to him, what might they do to her?

"It's your own fault," she mumbled. None of this would be happening if she hadn't gone to see

Leona in the first place. She had to take her share of the blame. And blame or no blame, she wasn't going to sit around, waiting to find out what they would do next.

Perhaps she was wrong about Sheldon. Maybe he understood her all too well.

# Chapter 25

Wendy sensed Phil before she saw him. And when she turned and saw that she was right—that he was there beside her—her heart went berserk.

He flashed her a soft smile. The memory of their last time together soured Wendy's excitement, and she quickly looked away.

"Hey," he said, his deep voice washing over her.

Wendy swallowed uncomfortably. To her client, she said, "That was a great session, Lynn. You can hang out and do some more cardio if you want, or you can head to the showers. Regardless, I'll see you next Monday."

"Thanks."

Wendy smiled and gave Lynn an encouraging squeeze on the shoulder. Then, reluctantly, she turned back to Phil. "How can I help you, Phil?"

"Wow." His eyes bulged. "That's not a very friendly greeting."

"Sorry. I'm a little preoccupied." Not half an hour ago, she had spoken with Tyanna about what was going on with Sheldon, and had learned that Tyanna was heading to her old workplace to put the fear of God in Leona. "And I'm surprised to see you here." She fought a frown. "Did you come by to tell me what a fool I made of myself the last time you saw me?"

"No." He sounded truthful. "Why would you think that?"

Wendy waved off the question. "It must be something pressing for you to come by my workplace."

"Where have you been?" Phil asked. "You just disappeared."

Wendy chuckled mirthlessly. "You were trying to reach me?"

"Actually, I was."

Wendy started walking to the path at the side of the gym floor, and Phil did the same. "Oh, you wanted to give me the complete video footage, right?"

"Well, I did want to talk to you about the video, but that's not why I was trying to reach you."

Wendy paused, giving him a curious look. For the first time, she noticed the concern in his eyes. "You were . . . You were actually worried about me?"

"Yeah, I was worried. I called your place a few times. The gym. I couldn't find you anywhere."

Goodness, he was actually telling the truth. "If

you weren't trying to reach me about the video, then why were you calling?"

Phil looked around, then back at her. "Maybe we can talk in private?"

Wendy felt a fluttering in her stomach. What was going on? But she managed a cool, "Sure. Let's head outside."

Several seconds later, they were standing near the front sidewalk. The sky was overcast, promising rain.

Wendy looked up at Phil, waiting for him to talk. He blew out a breath, then said, "I think . . . I think I gave you the wrong impression the last time we were together."

God, not this. Wendy's stomach plunged to her feet. "Phil, this really isn't necessary."

"Yes, it is. And I'm pretty sure I hurt you."

Wendy covered her face. She didn't want to talk about this.

"But not in the way you obviously think."

She lowered her hands and met his eyes. "However I'm feeling, it isn't your fault. I'm only sorry I let things get as far as they did, and I hope to God I didn't offend you."

Phil shook his head. "You haven't offended me."

"Phil, you don't have to spare my feelings. I know that's what you've been doing—"

"You think so?" he asked, cutting her off.

"I really just want to forget—"

Gripping her shoulders in his hands, he drew her to him and silenced her with a kiss. It was so unexpected that Wendy's back went ramrod straight.

Moments later, Phil pulled away. Before he could speak, Wendy did. "What was that?"

"Long overdue." Confusion passed over his face. "Either that or a mistake."

Wendy simply stared at him. "I don't . . . I don't get it."

"The way you've been acting around me recently . . . I kinda thought . . . I guess I assumed . . ." He blew out a frustrated breath. "Look, I'm sorry."

"For God's sake, don't apologize." He'd finally kissed her, really kissed her, and Wendy wanted to know why. "I'm just trying to figure out why you . . . kissed me." And oh, she wished she'd kissed him back, not reacted like a deer caught in the headlights. "Because you sure as hell haven't been interested in any of *my* advances."

"That's where you're wrong. I *was* interested. *Am* interested. But I made myself hold back."

Wendy continued to stare at him, her eyes narrow slits. "Made yourself? It certainly didn't seem like you were having a tough time of it."

Phil's eyes flashed disbelief. "Do you actually think you're easy to resist?"

"You made it seem easy." She shrugged nonchalantly. "Someone even suggested you might be gay."

Phil threw his head back and laughed at that. "Oh, come on. You know me better than that."

"I didn't know what to think. Except that one way or another, you weren't interested."

Phil reached for her face and gently cupped her cheek. It was now drizzling, but Wendy didn't care. With Phil touching her, she felt warm all over.

"You know how hard a time I had with Laura. And what I regretted most about that was the fact that our relationship had started off as a great friendship, but I lost that friendship once we crossed the line to being lovers." He trailed a finger over her mouth. "I let that regret come between what I was starting to feel for you. I forced myself to put aside any thoughts that you and I could have a relationship. When you were near me . . . it was torture not touching you. I could barely look at you, I wanted you so badly. Then you'd hug me, and I'd want to let go of all my reservations. If you only knew how many cold showers I took after spending time with you."

Wendy finally laughed. "Really?"

"Really."

Sighing happily, she angled her face into Phil's hand. She kissed the palm.

"When I look at you, I see so many different qualities than what I saw in Laura. Better qualities."

"Laura was quite a number."

"I know. You called it, but I couldn't see it. And when I look back, I can see how selfish she was. But I didn't at the time. I know you're not anything like her."

Phil trailed his fingers down her neck, and Wendy closed her eyes, savoring the glorious touch.

"After you left my place I felt really bad. I knew I'd been giving you mixed messages. The look of hurt and embarrassment in your eyes made me do a lot of thinking. And . . . and I guess I'm kind of thinking that if we got involved and it didn't work out, that wouldn't mean we'd lose the friendship. Not if we were both mature enough."

Wendy stepped toward him, slipping her arms around his neck. This was where she wanted to be for the rest of her life.

She looked into his eyes. "Worst-case scenario? I agree. I wouldn't want to lose the friendship, either. And I'm with you—I think we're mature enough that we wouldn't let that happen." Wendy pressed her body closer against his. "But that's not something we have to worry about today . . . is it?"

Phil slowly shook his head. A smile pulled at the corners of his mouth. "No. Today, I think we should worry about making up for lost time. How's that for a plan?"

"Sounds good to me," Wendy replied, standing up on her tiptoe. But before he kissed her again, she giggled and said, "Wait."

Phil's eyes narrowed. "What?"

"You said you wanted to talk to me about the video."

"Oh, that's right."

"Well?"

"Have you sent it to Ronnie Vaughn yet?"

"Not yet."

"Good."

"Why?"

"Well, I was thinking . . . maybe you shouldn't send it to him."

Wendy's eyes narrowed. "Come again?"

"I'm a producer, with a legitimate production company. I've got a bit of experience in the areas of marketing and distribution. So I was thinking . . . Maybe I could market the video, under your *own* label—yours and Tyanna's—which, ultimately, will give you both more control. It might be harder to get the project off the ground, but nothing worth having is ever easy."

Wendy smirked at him. "Ain't that the truth."

"So, you'll consider it?"

"Absolutely. I think it's a great idea." She paused. "Now, where were we?"

Phil's eyes danced with his evident emotions for her, warming Wendy's heart. Then he lowered his mouth to meet hers, and this time Wendy wasn't stiff at all. She practically melted in his arms, finally knowing that Phil indeed was as attracted to her as she was to him.

Leona's eyes grew wide with alarm when she saw Tyanna walk up to the juice bar. She tried to mask her surprise with a smile, but failed miserably.

"Tyanna. H—hi."

"You can spare the pleasantries, Leona."

Leona flashed her a shocked look. "Excuse me?"

"I know what you've been up to. Ever since I came to see you weeks ago, my life has been filled with more drama than I care for. You know exactly what I'm talking about, so I won't spell out the details."

Leona glanced nervously at the handful of patrons at the juice bar. She forced a chuckle. "I have no clue what you're talking about."

"Really? So you have no idea who attacked me where I work—not too long after I talked to you about Sheldon. You have no idea who burned my boyfriend's house to the ground just days ago? And let me guess, you have no idea who put two bullets in the back of his brother's head?"

A startled gasp erupted from the patrons. Leona narrowed her eyes at Tyanna in warning. "You should watch what you say, what you accuse people of—"

"Are you going to deny knowledge of what I've said?"

"Will you . . ." Leona unclenched her teeth. "Just wait a second. I'll come around and talk to you."

The man Tyanna had seen behind the juice bar the last time strolled in from the back office. Arms crossed over his chest, he eyed her with the coldest expression she had ever seen.

Yet she didn't flinch.

"You don't scare me," she told the man as Leona came around the end of the bar toward her. "But you should be afraid. The police know about you." Her gaze wandered between Leona to Cold Eyes. "Who knows? Maybe you got sloppy and left some clue at the scene of the fire." She gave a confident smile. "People like you always get what you deserve one day."

Leona's eyes made a frantic movement between the man and Tyanna. "You—you're way off base."

"Am I? We'll see about that, won't we?"

"Why don't we go somewhere to talk? Somewhere private."

"With you? I don't think so. Just remember what I said. You've screwed with me and Sheldon for the last time."

Then, her heart pounding, Tyanna turned and marched out of the gym. She hoped to hell that her bluff worked. And if her bluff failed, then she hoped that the fact there had been an audience would deter Leona and Cold Eyes from doing more to hurt her or Sheldon.

It was raining softly outside, and Tyanna kept up a steady pace to her car. She'd had to park out of the way, around the far corner of the building, the only place she had found a spot. On her way, she whispered a silent prayer that this would be the last time she or Sheldon ever had to deal with anyone associated with Dino.

She was at her car door when she felt the blinding blow. Then her knees gave way and her world turned to darkness.

Sheldon's uneasy feeling started around noon and got increasingly more intense. He wasn't sure exactly what bothered him, only that something felt wrong.

Of course, it could be the unsettling conversation he'd had with Tyanna the day before. He couldn't get it out of his mind, and it left him wondering if he'd lost her forever. Or it could be the frustrating "We'll let our know if we find any hard evidence" comment he'd received from the detective at the police station when he'd gone in to talk about the threats to his life. Sure, the detective had started a file, but Sheldon doubted he'd do anything other than sit on it before there was "hard evidence."

If he ever made it onto the force, he swore he would show more compassion than Detective Martin had.

Sheldon drove around, aimless, not sure what he should do. He knew what his heart wanted—what his mother wanted. And after about half an hour of going back and forth over the issue, he finally made a decision.

Tyanna wouldn't like him showing up at the gym, but he had to make sure she was okay. As he was heading northbound on his I-don't-know-where-the-heck-I'm-going drive, Sheldon took the first exit, then whipped around to head south on I-95 toward Jaguar Fitness.

The rain had picked up substantially since the time of Sheldon's last visit to the police station, and already parts of the highway were pooling with water. Not exactly the best day to go for a leisurely drive, especially one that put him farther from the place he needed to be right now.

"Damn you, Ford. You're always making the wrong decisions."

There was nothing he could do but drive at a safe speed to the gym. Because of the weather and where he had started from, it took Sheldon another thirty-five minutes to arrive at Jaguar Fitness.

Shirley greeted him with a huge smile the moment he walked in the door. "Hey, stranger."

"Hi." Sheldon surveyed the gym floor.

"I read about the fire! My God, what a horrible thing for you to go through."

His eyes jerked to Shirley's. "You read about it?"

She frowned softly. "You and Tyanna. Yes, I read about it. Do I really look like the type to not care about the news?"

"Tyanna?" he asked, ignoring everything else Shirley had said.

"Yeah, she made some sarcastic remark when I showed her the article. As if all I read are fashion magazines. Which is so untrue."

"You showed her the article about the fire?"

Shirley shook her head at him. "I'm not talking about *Cosmo*'s hot dating tips. Of course the article about the fire."

That weird feeling, the one that said something was wrong, hit him stronger than ever. Again, he surveyed the gym floor. "Where is Tyanna?"

"Beats me. She stopped by earlier to see Wendy, then said she was going to head to her old gym. But that was at least a few hours ago."

Sheldon's head started to swim. "Her old gym?"

"That's what she said. But I expected her back here by now."

Her old gym. Shit!

Sheldon spun around on his heel and ran through the door.

## Chapter 26

Despite the road conditions, Sheldon drove like a man possessed. He had to get to Ultimate Fitness and he had to get there yesterday.

Damn Tyanna. She just couldn't leave well enough alone. The first thing she had done when he'd told her the story about Dino was head to Ultimate Fitness to check it out. It didn't take a genius to figure out why she had decided to visit her old workplace, after learning about the fire.

This was exactly what he had feared. That Tyanna would get some crazy idea in her head to try and take care of this situation. This wasn't an episode of *Miami Vice*, where all had to end well. She didn't know what these people were capable of.

Dwight hadn't known either.

Sheldon should have sat her down and drummed the seriousness of the situation into her head. But would that have kept the free-spirited Tyanna standing on the sidelines, cheering him on?

Not likely.

None of that mattered now. He had to get to Ultimate Fitness.

He only hoped it wasn't too late.

Tyanna awoke to a throbbing headache. Immediately, she realized she was in a warm, pitch-black space.

Her hands were tied together behind her back. Her feet were also bound, her legs bent at the knee. But worse was the piece of material stuffed in her mouth. There was a foul taste in her throat, and she could only imagine where the cloth had been.

Good Lord, what had happened to her?

Her breaths now coming in a frantic, uneven rhythm, she scrambled to put the pieces together. The last thing she remembered was heading to her car after leaving Ultimate Fitness. She had made it to her car door. . . .

Then nothing.

Someone had hit her over the head and knocked her out cold!

Tyanna tried to move her legs, but couldn't fully extend them. She quickly realized she was in a confined space. A confined space with an odd odor.

Grease, maybe?

She wriggled from her side onto her stomach.

Her face brushed the floor. A carpeted floor. Squirming some more, her arm came up against a wall. Metal.

Oh, God. Her heart went into overdrive. The greasy smell. The confined space.

She was in a car trunk!

Panic washed over her. For several seconds, Tyanna pulled desperately at her wrists, hoping to free them, but she was secured with some type of tape, and it was impossible to get free. Then she lay still, trying to figure out what to do.

She felt an overwhelming sense of defeat.

*Not impossible,* she told herself several seconds later. *Just difficult. But you will get through this. You have to.*

She twisted and squirmed until she was on her stomach, hoping to kick her feet, but then her full body weight crushed her hands. She quickly shifted herself onto her side once more.

A sob crawled up her throat, but it didn't have anywhere to go. God help her, if she started to cough, she could suffocate.

*Slowly,* she told herself. *Breathe slowly and concentrate.*

She drew in a hot, strained breath through her nose, then did her best to let it out in a steady stream. How much longer could she breathe in here?

The faces of her family members passed through her mind. If she were to die like this, how would they ever get over it? Lecia, Charlene . . .

They would be devastated. And little Michelle. Would Tyanna live to see her niece grow up?

The thought made her throat fill with emotion, which only made it harder to breathe. She had to stop thinking like this. She could not—would not—die in there.

She started to kick out sideways with her feet.

Sheldon stormed into Ultimate Fitness, knowing the expression on his face was lethal. He looked to the left, shooting his deadly gaze in Leona's direction.

Seeing him, her face crumbled. Clearly afraid of what he might do, she took a few steps backward.

"Hey, buddy."

Sheldon whipped his head to his immediate right when he felt the slap on his shoulder. Pete, the gym's manager, grinned at him. "You look like you're ready to rip someone apart."

"Pete. You're just the man I need to see."

"Oh? What's up?"

Sheldon glanced at Leona, who eyed him warily, then back at Pete. "I wish this was a social call, but it's not. Something major's going on. I don't know how much you're aware of, but if you know and you don't tell what you know, you could very well face charges."

"Whoa. Wait a second." Pete held up his hands. "If you're talking anything illegal, I have no clue what you mean."

"Sorry. Let me fill you in on what's happening." Sheldon walked Pete a few steps away, to a spot where they wouldn't be overheard. Then he explained everything that was going on, starting with Dino and the illegal steroids he had sold from the gym.

"I swear, man," Pete said when Sheldon was done, "I had no clue."

Sheldon couldn't be sure. He had always thought that Dino was cutting Pete in, considering he was the gym's manager. Still, he could be wrong. "If that's the case, then you won't mind helping me.

"I'll do whatever I can to help you find Tyanna. She's a doll."

*More than a doll*, Sheldon thought. Emotion clogged in his throat as he once again contemplated the seriousness of the situation.

He said, "I'm gonna speak with Leona. See what she says. You . . . Considering Tyanna's car is parked outside but there's no sign of her, maybe you need to call the police."

"Sure thing."

Pete headed to the main reception desk, while Sheldon marched to the juice bar. The expression on Leona's face said she wanted to flee, but Sheldon had a feeling that she knew better. She stood rooted to the spot, fear dancing in her eyes.

"Leona." Sheldon's voice was commanding, even if his stomach was filled with butterflies. Two young men sitting at the juice bar got to their feet and walked away.

"This can be ugly," Sheldon began, "or it can be easy. Your choice."

"I—I," she stuttered.

"I know Tyanna was here. Her car's still outside. And I doubt she went for a walk in this weather." He glanced around. "Where's Tony?"

"I wanted nothing to do with this," Leona said in her own defense.

"Then I suggest you help this come to an end. Because I swear, if anything has happened to Tyanna, there will be hell to pay."

Leona's bottom lip quivered. She knew Sheldon was deadly serious.

"Where did Tony take her? And I suggest you start talking, because the police will be here soon."

A pained expression crossed Leona's face. "I . . . I think to the house."

"What house?"

"Our house."

"You two are living together?" Sheldon shook his head. "Forget it. I don't care. Just tell me where the house is."

"In the Grove. Not too far."

"What's the address and how do I get there?"

Leona gave Sheldon the information.

"What's he going to do with her?"

"He wants to get to you. Tony's got some crazy idea that he needs to live out Dino's agenda. I didn't mean for it to get this far. If I knew it would, I never would have told him you were back in town. But Tony's crazy. Whatever he wants, he gets."

Crazy . . . Crazy enough to kill to keep Dino happy? Sheldon had to know. "Is he the one who killed my brother?"

Leona's eyes watered. She nodded. "Yes. All Dino had to do was ask, and he was all too willing to obey."

Sheldon felt the sting of tears, but he fought them. They wouldn't bring his brother back, and he had to be strong right now. Tyanna needed him.

"I'm so sorry. . . ." Leona moaned.

"Yeah, well, you'll be even sorrier if you don't help Tyanna now. I'm sure your cooperation will make the difference between a bit of jail time or many, many years in prison."

"I want to help."

"Good. Get your stuff together. We're going for a ride."

But Leona didn't get to go for that ride. Well, not with Sheldon, anyway. Seconds before Sheldon and Leona were about to leave the gym, the police arrived. After hearing her story—she rambled on and on about her part in it—they immediately arrested her and put her in handcuffs.

*The only ride she would be taking now was in the back of a cruiser*, Sheldon said to himself.

"Can you tell me your version of what happened?" one of the two cops asked him, once the other one had taken Leona out of the gym.

"Right now?"

"Yeah."

"My girlfriend is missing!"

"Officer Colburn has already put a call into dispatch, and they're contacting the Coconut Grove and Miami-Dade police, advising them of the situation."

"You mean you two aren't going after this guy?"

"The house is in Coconut Grove, and this is Coral Gables. But don't worry, there'll be cops there in a matter of moments."

Sheldon stared at the man in disbelief. "I . . ."

"What happened?"

"No offense, but I can't go into all this right now," Sheldon told the man, surprised he would even think otherwise. "I—I want to be at that police station when they find my girl," he lied.

The officer nodded. He dug into his pocket and retrieved a business card. "Hey, I understand. But please call me as soon as possible. We can set up a time for you to come into the station and give that statement."

"Sure." Sheldon took the card, then rushed out of the gym and to his Explorer.

Unlike most of the streets in South Florida, which were numbered, the ones in Coconut Grove had names. Sheldon only hoped he'd make it to the house without any complications.

*Please, God. Let Tyanna be okay. Let the police get to her in time.*

*   *   *

Despite the rain, Sheldon made it to the Coconut Grove home as fast as he would have had the roads been dry. As he turned onto the lush, tree-lined street, he saw that police had surrounded a house. Several cops were in the street with their guns drawn, taking cover behind their police vehicles.

Sheldon slammed on the brakes when he neared a cruiser that was blocking his route. Something was wrong. These cops looked like they were ready to take down a small army—which was not the scene he'd expected.

He jammed the car into park and jumped out. Two cops were instantly in his path.

"You can't go past here," one of them said.

"But my girlfriend . . ."

"You can't go past here," the cop repeated. "We've got a dangerous situation we're trying to get under control."

Helpless, Sheldon looked down the street to where the majority of cops were, weapons drawn. Damn, this had to be bad. "How bad is it?"

"There's a man with a gun in one of the houses. He's not surrendering, and we have word that he may have a hostage."

Shit. Tony wasn't going down without a fight. What was wrong with the man? Did he feel that since Dino had died in a police shoot-out that he had to do the same thing?

Sheldon ran a hand over his head in frustration. "My girlfriend was kidnapped by the guy with the gun. I need to know if she's okay."

"I wish I had more information for you. I'm just making sure the scene's secure."

"Can you ask somebody?" Sheldon asked impatiently.

"Sir, there's a SWAT team getting control of the situation right now. All we can do is stand back and wait, for the moment. I have to detain you here."

Damn! Sheldon spun around, clenching his fists. What the hell was he supposed to do now?

He just wanted to know that Tyanna was okay.

He turned. It was then that he saw the ambulance. His heart plummeted to his stomach. How had he not noticed it before?

"Why's the ambulance here?" he asked, frantic, wondering if someone was hurt.

"Standard procedure—"

"POLICE! DROP YOUR WEAPON AND COME OUT WITH YOUR HANDS ABOVE YOUR HEAD!"

At the sound of the command over the loudspeaker, Sheldon whipped his head in the direction of the house.

"I SAID, DROP YOUR WEAPON. COME OUT SLOWLY, WITH YOUR HANDS—"

There was immediate silence as the front door opened slightly, then two quick popping sounds pierced the air. It sounded like firecrackers, but it took Sheldon only half a second to realize it was gunfire.

Every cop instantly reacted, returning several rounds of gunfire in the direction of the front door. It all happened so fast, the scene surreal.

The shooting stopped, and Sheldon kept his eyes glued to the front door. He watched in horror as someone stumbled forward, then fell to the ground.

Tony.

A sea of uniforms converged on the fallen man. Some charged the steps and ran into the house.

But where was Tyanna?

While the two cops who'd stopped him were watching the unfolding chaotic scene, Sheldon used the opportunity to take off.

He ran full speed toward the house, his stomach sinking every step of the way. There was no sign of Tyanna. If Tony had had her in the house, wouldn't she have come out already?

Of course she would have. Unless the unthinkable had happened.

"Please, God."

"Sir." Another cop grabbed hold of his arm as he was about to charge up the steps. "You are interfering with a crime scene."

"Then arrest me," Sheldon snapped. "My girlfriend is somewhere in that house!"

The cop met his eyes with a hard stare. His hand went to the spot on his belt where he kept his handcuffs. "Sir, you need to calm down."

Sheldon knew the man was serious. He drew in a deep breath and let it out slowly. "I'm sorry. My girlfriend was kidnapped by the guy you just shot. I have no clue where she is. . . ."

"We have officers checking the house. If she's inside, they'll find her."

Sheldon closed his eyes, frustrated. His hands were tied. He could attempt to run in the house and look for Tyanna himself, but he wouldn't make it far with all the cops around.

All he could do was stand and wait.

After a few minutes, one of the officers emerged from the house and announced, "It's clear in here."

"Clear?" Fear gripped his heart. God, had Tony taken Tyanna somewhere else? Dumped her body before he'd come to this house?

He glanced around in frustration, thinking—thinking and looking for another spot where Tyanna might be. That's when his eyes were drawn to the late-model Lexus parked under the carport.

"The car!" Sheldon exclaimed. Then he sprinted toward it.

# Chapter 27

She was dead.

Sheldon's insides felt like they had been ripped out by a pair of cold, steel hands. He stood and watched, feeling empty yet full of rage and despair at the same time.

He had failed, just like he had failed to save his brother.

The cops and paramedics wouldn't let him near her as they worked at cutting away her binds and removing the gag. Sheldon stood as close as he could, watching with a leaden heart. He wanted to hope, but he had seen Tyanna's body as she was pulled from the trunk. It was limp. And with that huge gag stuffed in her mouth, it was completely plausible that she might have suffocated. Either that or suffered heatstroke.

His mind was plagued with all the things he could have done differently. If he hadn't returned to Miami, none of this would be happening right now.

He wouldn't have lost his house.

*Tyanna* . . .

Emotion threatened to overwhelm him, and Sheldon bit down hard on his bottom lip.

"We've got a pulse!" one of the paramedics shouted.

*A pulse.* Sheldon's heart jumped with hope.

There was a buzz of excitement. Sheldon edged closer, watching as the paramedics lifted Tyanna's body onto a gurney, which they quickly pushed to the ambulance. An oxygen mask covered Tyanna's face, and though she was still unconscious, it seemed as though she was making small movements.

*Thank you, God.*

"I want to ride with her," Sheldon announced.

"Who are you?" one of them asked.

"Her fiancé," he replied.

The man gave him a nod, and Sheldon climbed aboard. He gave a fleeting thought to the fate of his car. It might be towed by the time he came back for it, but he didn't care. Tyanna was his first priority.

He settled himself beside her and took her hand in his. "I love you, Tyanna. Don't leave me. Not yet."

*I love you, Tyanna.*

The words penetrated her psyche, illuminating a light of hope in the dark corners of her mind.

*I love you.* . . .

It was Sheldon's voice.

Where was she?

Tyanna struggled to open her eyes, but couldn't. Instinctively, she knew that she wasn't in that horrible, dark place anymore.

"Don't leave me, Tyanna. You hear? I need you in my life. Even if I've been a moron by not making that clear to you."

Tyanna tried to respond, but it was such a struggle.

"It's okay. You just lie back. I'm here with you. And I'm not going anywhere."

She felt warmth surrounding her hand. Sheldon was touching her. Squeezing her. Her heart filled with warmth.

"It's all over now. Leona's going to jail. Tony's dead. He won't hurt you again. No one will hurt you."

The words were like a jolt of energy, giving her strength. Tyanna put every effort into squeezing Sheldon's hand in return.

"Tyanna?" She heard the excitement in his voice. "Tyanna, can you hear me?"

She squeezed his hand again.

Laughter. Sheldon's laughter. Whatever she was doing was working.

She felt his lips brush her hand. "I love you, Tyanna. Did you hear me? I love you."

It took her greatest effort, but she finally opened her eyes. After a moment of blurriness, her gaze focused on Sheldon's face.

"I heard you," she said, her voice hoarse but audible. "Finally."

Sheldon rewarded her with a huge grin. Then he leaned over her and gave her a soft kiss on her lips.

"I love you, Tyanna. I always have. Always will."

Two weeks later, Tyanna had put the frightening event of the kidnapping behind her. The doctors had awarded her with a clean bill of health after one day in the hospital, and she had been elated to go home.

With Sheldon.

He was now living with her. The two had fallen into cohabitation quite easily. She didn't wake up and wish he wasn't in her bed, she didn't secretly wish he'd leave after a few hours.

It just felt right.

Any objections her parents had over their renewed relationship had quickly fizzled when they learned of all Sheldon had done to save her life. Quite frankly, they knew that had it not been for Sheldon, Tyanna might not be with them any longer.

"You ready?" Sheldon asked.

Tyanna zipped up her suitcase. "Yes," she replied. "But I wish I knew where you were taking me."

"If you knew, it wouldn't be a surprise."

"Surprises are overrated."

Sheldon sat on the bed and frowned at her. "Would you rather not go?"

Tyanna glared at him playfully. "Not on your life."

They had already spent a couple peaceful days in Naples, which had been wonderful both for rest and relaxation, and for some intimate moments together. Since the attack on her life, things between them had been completely different. For one, Sheldon constantly told her that he loved her. He openly shared his feelings with her. And while they still spent passionate times together at home, they did a lot of things outside of the home. Like walks on the beach in the morning, or trips to Gameworks to play video games. It was fun for Tyanna to watch Sheldon be toally carefree as he got excited over various games. He was finally putting his brother's death behind him and moving on. Of course, he would never forget Dwight, but at least now there was some real closure. His mother was still in New York, having decided not to return to teaching this year in lieu of continuing to take it easy. Thankfully, she was doing well.

"All I want to know," Tyanna began, "is why we're leaving from my parents' place to go wherever you're taking me. Why not leave in the morning?"

Sheldon got to his feet. "Because."

Groaning, Tyanna lifted her suitcase from the bed. "Fine."

Sheldon chuckled softly. "We'd better get going. Everyone's no doubt waiting for us." He gestured to her large suitcase. "I told you we were only going away for three days. I don't know why you need all this stuff."

"Considering I don't know *where* we're going, I have to be prepared."

"At least your family can't blame me for us being late."

This evening, Sheldon, Tyanna, her sisters, Wendy and Phil were gathering at her parents' place for a celebratory dinner. Not only did they have Tyanna's life to celebrate, but they also had Tyanna and Wendy's video venture. Phil had convinced them to let him market the video under their new label, The Soul Sisters Workout Series. Tyanna couldn't be more excited.

"All right," Sheldon said. "Let's go."

Sheldon brought the larger suitcase downstairs, while Tyanna carried the smaller one. They placed the luggage into the Explorer, then made their way north to Fort Lauderdale.

At her parents' house, Tyanna's mother opened the door. She greeted them both with a warm smile. "Tyanna. Sheldon. Come in."

When they both stepped into the foyer, Roberta hugged them each in turn.

"Sorry we're late," Sheldon said. "But you know your daughter."

Roberta laughed. "Oh yes. I certainly do."

"Is everyone here?" Tyanna asked.

"Yep," her mother replied. "They're all out back."

Tyanna and Sheldon followed Roberta to the backyard. Everyone greeted each other with a hug.

"Your ribs smell divine, Daddy," Tyanna said as she sat at the table.

"You know I never disappoint," Byron told her.

Tyanna smiled at Wendy and Phil. They sat opposite her, Wendy resting her head on Phil's shoulder. Seeing them happy and cozy brought warmth to her heart. Finally, all their lives seemed to be on the right track.

"Now that everyone's here," Charlene began, "shall I pour us all some wine?"

Lecia held up he glass. "Please."

Charlene made her way around the table, filling everyone's glass with red wine. Tyanna looked over her shoulder at Sheldon, who was standing with her father. The two were chatting about something. It was a sight she wouldn't have seen a year earlier, and her eyes suddenly watered. She was thrilled to know that her family was finally accepting Sheldon.

"Byron, Sheldon." Roberta rose from her seat and beckoned them to the table. "Come on over here. I'd like to make a toast."

Byron and Sheldon made their way to their seats and everyone turned their attention to Roberta. Her face lit up with a graceful smile as she looked at Tyanna and Sheldon, then at Wendy and Phil. "I would like to make a toast to new ventures. I am absolutely certain that your video will be a hit. But I'd also like to toast another type of venture—one more precious. Love."

Everyone raised their glass. "To love."

"I love you," Sheldon told Tyanna after everyone had drunk to the toast.

"My, you just can't seem to stop saying that now."

"I know what I had, and I know what I almost lost. I'm gonna say it until you're sick of hearing it."

Tyanna had waiting long enough to hear Sheldon tell her those three little words that meant so much. "Oh, I'll never be sick of hearing it."

Sheldon brushed his lips over hers. "I didn't think so. I love you."

"Oh, baby. I love you, too."

Pushing back his chair, Sheldon stood. Tyanna looked up at him, surprised. He said, "Excuse me, everyone. Since we're toasting love, I'd like to say something." He reached into a pocket on his slacks. "Actually, there's something I'd like to do."

As Sheldon got down onto one knee, Tyanna felt light-headed. She knew what he had to be doing, but she could hardly believe it.

Sheldon produced a stunning diamond ring. It wasn't in a box, which was how he had been able to hide it from her. "Tyanna, you know how much you mean to me. With you, my life is finally complete. And I want . . ." He paused, took her hand. "I want to be with you forever. So, will you—"

"Yes!" Tyanna shouted and threw herself into Sheldon's arms.

A cheer erupted around them, followed by applause. Tyanna kissed Sheldon, not wanting to let him go. This moment was perfect. And so much more special because she was surrounded by her family and dearest friends.

Sheldon pulled back and slipped the ring onto her finger. Tyanna splayed her fingers, staring in awe at the beautiful ring. "Oh, sweetheart. I love it."

"We're going to have a great life together."

As Tyanna returned to her seat, she saw Wendy wipe her eyes. All her family was grinning.

"Congratulations, sweetheart," Roberta said.

"Thank you, Mommy."

Michelle, in her highchair, started to fuss. Charlene pushed her chair back, but Tyanna said, "No. Let me."

Tyanna wiped at her own tears as she walked the few steps to Michelle's highchair. She lifted her niece into her arms. "Hey, sweetie. What's the matter? You feeling left out?" Michelle flashed a wide grin. "There you go. All you wanted was to be held, hmm?"

"Newly engaged," Lecia began, "but looks like she's ready to be a mom."

Tyanna whipped her head in Lecia's direction. "Uh, I don't think so." She took her seat beside Sheldon, still holding Michelle. "I mean, one day, yes. But let me plan the wedding first."

Michelle laughed, as though she knew otherwise.

"She really is adorable," Sheldon pointed out.

"Absolutely," Tyanna replied, as if that was a given. "She's got Calhoun blood flowing in her, doesn't she?"

"We'll make beautiful babies," Sheldon said softly. "We both know that life is short. Maybe we shouldn't wait."

"Da!" Michelle exclaimed, startling everyone.

"She heard you," Charlene said. "Quite clearly, she approves."

"Is that so?" Sheldon asked, taking Michelle's small hand in his. "You want a little cousin?"

"Da!" Michelle said again, this time slapping the table's edge as if to emphasize her point.

Then everybody laughed.

Let the incomparable
# KAYLA PERRIN
tell you all about *love*!

**"A writer that everyone should watch."**
*New York Times* bestselling author Eric Jerome Dickey

## Tell Me You Love Me
0-06-050350-5 • $6.50 US • $8.99 Can
Once burned, twice shy . . .
and ready to love like never before!

*And Don't Miss*

### SAY YOU NEED ME
0-380-81379-3 • $6.50 US • $8.99 Can

### IF YOU WANT ME
0-380-81378-5 • $6.50 US • $8.99 Can

**Soulful love with a new attitude
from HarperTorch.**